Farrec
MALANNA
Kati
CALLARDA
Farrec

Levua
ATNIONA

Lilia of the Valley

Lilia of the Valley

THE CALLARDAN CROWN
BOOK ONE

KAILIE WARD

CHRIS WARD

PHOENIX RISING ENTERTAINMENT LLC

Phoenix Rising Entertainment LLC

Paperback ISBN: 979-8-9901049-0-7

Ebook ISBN: 979-8-9901049-1-4

Book Cover by Laolan

Visit www.kailieward.com

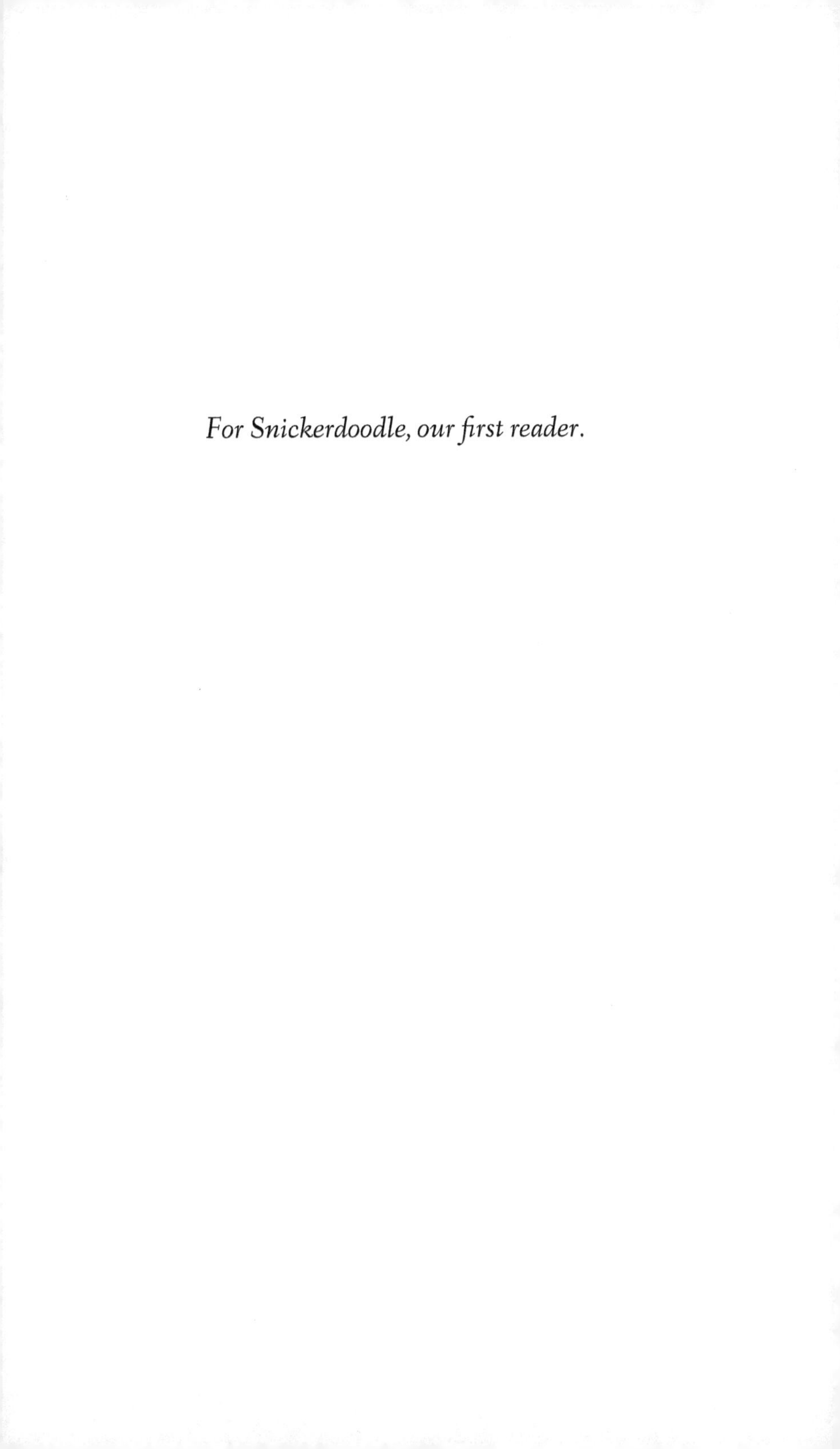

For Snickerdoodle, our first reader.

Prologue

If the princess dies, it will be my fault for not being able to run fast enough, far enough. No! She cannot die! Should the worst happen, she may be our last hope.

Fear being the only thing keeping Marcus moving, he staggered, his aching legs crying for a respite.

He had been on the run for seven days, most of that through the blasted woodlands. The first couple of days he had traveled northeast, away from the conflict in Katiera, the capital of Katniona, as he tried to decide what to do with his precious bundle.

Who did he trust with one of the king's greatest treasures? More to the point, one of the *queen's* greatest treasures? It had to be someone the queen trusted, of that he was certain. No one else would do. It also had to be someone he knew.

Brianna, he had finally settled on. She was the queen's friend of a good many years, and the sister of one of his best friends since childhood. He had known her for most of her life. If ever there was a good, honest woman, it was her.

Grateful for a direction, Marcus then headed east, towards Levua, a coastal town. Now that he was heading somewhere, he only stopped when he could go no longer.

His thoughts now free from figuring out where to take the precious bundle, his mind wandered to the situation that had forced him to flee the castle. War with Malanna had erupted quickly, and the army of Katniona hadn't been able to muster sufficient defenses. The battle had quickly reached the capital, with the battle lines drawing ever closer to the castle. The king was injured and had decided to send his children into hiding. The three princes had been sent to their allies in the south. Deciding it best to separate at least one of them, the king had decided to send his daughter elsewhere.

"Take her, Marcus."

"Your Majesty...no. You are injured. You should take her."

"I cannot, I will not abandon my people!"

"I don't know that I'm up for this! Surely a trained knight would be better!"

"I have no extra men to send with her."

"And I'm dispensable."

"Never, my friend. Now, go. I know she will be safe with you."

"Your Majesty...I-I will protect her with my life."

"I know."

The precious bundle he carried in his arms had long since left them numb, the pain forgotten hours ago, if not days. Though he took care of himself well, as a scribe his arms were never trained to carry such a load for so long, nor his legs to carry him so far. Yet he didn't dare put his bundle down unless he absolutely had to—which appeared to be now, as it began to make noises and squirm.

He made a sharp left off the trail, and prayed they hadn't been heard. Once secreted in a grove a good distance from the path, he set the bundle down. His arms thanked him by flaring to life, the searing pain reminding him of just what he had put them through. His legs also thanked him by buckling.

With trembling fingers, he unwrapped the blanket. The year-old babe inside had hazel eyes and beautiful, golden hair that hung to her shoulders. She began to make noises that indicated she was getting hungry.

Marcus set down the pack, which seemed to grow heavier by the mile. He opened it, shoving his sweaty brown hair out of the way when it fell in front of his eyes. His flight from the castle had been frantic, and he now searched the pack for what little food he had been able to secure to sustain the child. Knowing how important this child was, he'd eaten only what he could scavenge on the road, saving all of the better food for the babe.

He dug out a water skin and a bit of stale bread. *Thank goodness she rarely cries.* When Marcus returned his attention to the bundle, he froze; the blanket was empty. His pulse quickened. He stood and quickly scanned the grove. He saw her and sighed in relief, his pulse slowing. The sigh was quickly followed by a gasp when he saw what she was doing.

She had crawled over to examine a beautiful, but very poisonous, flower.

He hurried to her side and knelt next to her. She'd not actually touched the flower, yet, and it was only poisonous if ingested. "Now, Princess," he tried for a calm voice, but he was certain he failed, "It is a very bad thing to wander off." His hands trembled, still exhausted, as he bent to stop her.

Rather than looking chagrined, the baby pointed to the flower and said, "Mawcus! Smell!"

Marcus's eyes flew wide open and he forgot what he was doing. Never before had she called him by his name, nor had he yet heard her utter such an intelligent request. Where had this come from?

Accustomed as he was to doing the royal family's will, Marcus did as the tiny princess commanded. He smiled as he took in the familiar scent of the lily of the valley. He had always loved the smell, in part because it reminded him of his mother. The woman had always kept some in a little bowl in their home when he was growing up.

"They are beautiful, just like you," he said with a smile.

She didn't seem to hear him, for she remained focused on the flower. Before he could stop her, she tugged on it until it came loose. She rolled onto her back from the loss of resistance to her tug and laughed. As it always did, her laugh made him smile.

Wait, I shouldn't let her play with this! It's poisonous!

"Princesses are not supposed to play in the flowers," he said as he gently took away the flower. He then picked her up and carried her over to the stream that was running along one edge of the grove, holding her hands to keep them away from her mouth.

In his rushed packing, he had grabbed a chunk of soap. While at the time he hadn't thought of much reason to do so, he was suddenly grateful he had tossed it in the bag rather than tossing it aside.

He scrubbed her tiny hands as best he could, as any residue from the flower left on them could be dangerous. He then dried her hands with his handkerchief and returned her to her blanket. A thought struck him as he sat, and he frowned. "I suppose you won't be a princess for the present, which means we need a new name for you, Kalysta."

He pulled her onto his lap even as she tried to crawl back over to where her flower had fallen. "You seem quite taken with these flowers," he observed. After a moment of thinking, he said, "I hereby name you Lilia, after the *lilium convallium*." He sighed as he set her back on the blanket. "Come, Lilia. You must eat something."

Marcus held out the bread he had retrieved from his bag earlier to the little girl. She grabbed it with eager little fingers and stuffed it into her mouth. Then she looked up at him. Something about her gaze touched him.

He didn't think her old enough to know what was happening, but her hazel eyes told him that she wasn't frustrated for not being with her parents, nor for the time spent wrapped in the bundle as he ran. Her eyes held patience, as if she truly did understand the circumstances and had accepted it. Her eyes also held amusement. She obviously found joy in the little things in life, which he knew would help her adapt to her new situation.

He mourned for what she would no longer have, for the important people she may have recently lost. He was, however, grateful that she was, at least for now, alive. As she finished her morsel he said, "Come now, Princess, er, Lilia. Back into your blanket."

The little girl laid back, pulling the blanket as best she could around her as she did so. Marcus finished the bundling, stood, and picked her up. His limbs, especially his arms, protested vehemently at the now familiar weight, but he ignored them. They had only an hour or two left of daylight, and he hoped to reach their destination, and depart again by sunset.

He was no woodsman, but he made his way back to the road in as silent a manner as he could. He was about to step out of the cover of the trees when he heard the sound of metal on metal. He quickly backed up into the shadows and froze as the sound repeated, closer. It was still a couple of minutes until the source came into sight. Two Malannan knights ambled past on horseback. The sound he had heard was their armor clinking as they moved. His heart started racing. His breathing grew shallow

"I highly doubt the scribe brought the princess this way," one of them said in their native tongue. Marcus also served as an interpreter at times, languages being one of the many things he had studied. "Not only was there no word of them in the towns we passed through," the knight continued, "but there isn't anything further east from that last village, we've reached the coast. I say we give up and head back, we've done our due diligence. Surely someone else has found her in another direction."

The words would have relieved him, but the bundle in his arms started to protest his stillness. "Shh…" he whispered into the blanket.

"You are probably right," his companion replied, reining in at just the point where Marcus would have returned to the path. He withdrew his water skin as his companion drew rein next to him. "Let's hope so," he said after a swig, "or else we'll be in deep trouble with Her Majesty. The queen wants the little princess taken care of, just like her brothers. She wants nothing between her and the throne of this country."

Marcus closed his eyes in pain as their words pierced his heart. He had feared for the princes' lives, as their journey to their allies in Callarda would have taken them near the borders of Malanna as well. It sounded as if his fears had been realized. He held the precious bundle tighter as he mourned her brothers.

Once the enemy knights finished talking, there was a moment of tense silence. Thankfully, the princess stayed quiet the entire time. Eventually, the knights resumed riding, never seeing their quarry hidden just a few lengths into the trees. Yet, Marcus didn't draw a deep breath until long after he could no longer hear them, at which point he cautiously made his way to the road.

Seeing and hearing no one, he hurried in the opposite direction of the riders, grateful they were moving west. Deciding speed was more important than cover, and the leaves making it difficult to stay quiet in the forest anyway, he decided to travel the road.

With nothing but the open road before him, which was laid nearly straight for a good distance, he ran. He ran until he couldn't run any longer, as the setting sun seemed to carry with it the last of his strength. Then he ran even more. His own life meant nothing compared to this mission, especially with what he had heard from the riders.

He finally reached his destination an hour after the sun had set. He pounded on the door, exhaustion mixed with fear making him knock harder than necessary. The door opened almost immediately, with a short woman standing behind it. Her red hair and green eyes caught the light of the lantern she held. Those eyes went wide as she recognized the person pounding on her door so late at night. "Marcus!"

Marcus staggered past her and collapsed, his legs succumbing to fatigue. To his relief, his friend's sister had a fire going, and, still holding the baby, he crawled toward it. He then opened the bundle. Finally free of the blanket, the little princess sat up and looked around. Her wandering eyes paused when they fell on the fire, and she sat, watching the flickering flames as if in a trance.

"Marcus, what is the meaning of this?" the woman asked as she helped Marcus onto a chair. "You pound on my door and force your way in, then open up a blanket to reveal a child!"

"I need you to take her, Brianna," he said simply, trying his best to catch his breath.

She narrowed her eyes. "Who is she?"

Marcus sighed. "It might be better for you if you don't know."

Brianna huffed. "Does she at least have a name?"

Marcus would have chuckled had he the energy to do so. "I have given her the name of Lilia. She found a lily of the valley on the way here and was quite taken with it." He looked up into her unbending gaze. "You know I wouldn't ask if it wasn't of the utmost importance."

Brianna rolled her eyes and huffed again. "Very well, I will take care of the child." She then put a hand on Marcus's shoulder. "I understand the knowledge might kill me, but I deserve to know who she really is."

Marcus sighed again. He knew Brianna was never one to give up easily. It was one of the reasons he had thought of her to be Lilia's adoptive mother. In that moment, he felt too tired to fight with her, so he motioned to the little girl and said, "Brianna, may I present Her Royal Highness, Princess Kalysta."

The woman sobered at the pronouncement, her anger and frustration seeming to immediately leave her. "I wondered." She curtsied to the little girl. "It is a pleasure to meet you, Your Highness."

The little girl, who was still watching the fire, offered a regal nod, as if she knew exactly who she was. This made Brianna smile. "She is quite the precocious little thing."

Marcus managed to chuckle a little as he nodded. "She really is." He then frowned as the words the enemy soldier had said returned to his mind. "The princes... they've been..." he choked on the words, unable to utter them. Tears leaked from the corners of his eyes.

Brianna put a hand on his shoulder. "You don't need to say anything. I've heard. The town was searched this morning. The Malannan knights couldn't stop boasting about it. I'm so sorry, Marcus. I know how close you are to the royal family."

Knowing he didn't have time to cry, but unable to help himself, Marcus let out a little sob before he was able to control his tears. He wiped his face. He then fished in his pack and pulled out a pouch of money and handed it to Brianna. "This is to help you buy anything she might need. Knowing you, you'll probably be able to stretch that enough to buy something for yourself as well." He also pulled out his water skin and drained it into his mouth.

Begrudgingly, she took the pouch. "I'm only taking it because I don't have many of the things she will need."

Marcus managed a small grin as he nodded. "I know. You are a good woman, Brianna, which is why I'm entrusting you with one of the king's greatest treasures."

"What are your plans now?"

They both turned to stare at the child. "I must leave, before they find me here."

She returned her focus to Marcus, who pulled himself to his feet, preparing to leave. "Safe travels, my friend."

"I wish you the same, for you should probably leave the area," he replied. Without thinking, he put his hands in his pockets. His eyes went wide as he remembered what he hid there. He pulled out a necklace with a pendant suspended from it. "The king's crest." He handed it to Brianna. "You should probably keep this. Do not give it to her until...well, until it is safe."

Brianna nodded and gingerly took the pendant from his hand. She closed her fist around it and looked up at him. "I will protect her, Marcus. Do not fear."

He nodded and returned to the princess's side, unable to leave without saying goodbye. He picked her up and kissed her cheek before pulling her in for one last embrace. Tears leaked from his eyes as he said, "Be safe, my princess. We will need you." His voice broke as he spoke to her.

"Mawcus." She put her little hand on his face, as if to dry his tears.

The tears ran faster as he put her back down. "Goodbye, sweet princess. I will probably never see you again. If I do, it is because it is safe for you to return."

She nodded and returned her attention to the fire.

He wiped his face again, even though he knew it was fruitless to do so. "I love you, Princess," he choked.

She looked up at him once more. Along with the patience he had seen in the grove, he also now saw sadness in her eyes. "Love Mawcus."

Marcus managed to get out the door before the tears returned in earnest. Even though he was still exhausted and now in emotional pain as well from their parting, the fear of being found too near her hiding place carried him away from Brianna's house for a few hours. When he again could barely keep his feet, he decided to get off the road and get some rest.

Looking around, he recognized the spot where he had returned to the trail earlier, the place burned into his memory from the tense moments spent hiding from the knights. He found his way back to the grove, picked up the lily of the valley that Lilia had played with, and lay down near where it had fallen. He brought it to his nose, breathed in its sweet aroma, and then allowed his exhaustion to overtake him.

One

SEVENTEEN YEARS LATER

Thank goodness this is the last town, Sir Calem thought as he shifted on his horse. The movement made his armor clink together. *And I'm going to get some better fitting armor once we return home.* He had owned a properly fitted set, but it had been stolen several days ago. The set he had obtained to replace it was made for a much larger man than himself.

It was still something of a wonder to be calmly riding through Katniona as they were. King Kelvin had been fighting to retake the throne for most of the last seventeen years, and had finally secured victory late in the previous fall, largely thanks to his allies in Callarda. Now that the war was finally over, he was sending knights to discover if any of his children, whom he had sent into hiding, had survived.

The king wanted them home for several reasons. Obviously, he wanted to see them again, but he also hoped to cement the newfound peace with their neighbors with an alliance by marriage.

All of the Katnionan royal children would now be of marriageable age, while Malanna had a princess, and Callarda had two princes. The Katnionan princes had already been located—alive and well, despite Malanna claiming to have eliminated them soon after Katiera first fell—but there was still no news of the princess.

It was mid-afternoon when Calem started to nod off. He and his companion were still a couple of hours from the next town. The warmth from the sun was making it difficult to stay awake.

The horse ahead of Calem stepped to the side rather than straight. He looked up sharply. He chuckled quietly at what he saw. His companion's head nodded as he, too, fought to stay awake, or at least upright, in the saddle.

Calem had been waiting for his friend to do this. He pulled a rock out of the pouch at his waist and threw it at the other knight's back. It struck the larger man squarely in the middle. The knight yelped and sat up straight, all sleepiness abandoning him immediately. He looked around for a moment. It wasn't long before he put the pieces of the puzzle together and shot Calem a glare. "Not funny, Calem," he growled.

Calem barely suppressed the chuckle that threatened to escape, although he couldn't prevent the grin. Humor colored his voice as he spoke. "On the contrary, Gerald. Besides, you needed it. What use will you be to anyone if you fall off your horse and get yourself trampled?"

Gerald held up a hand in surrender. "Fine, fine. I deserved it. Thank you for keeping me from getting trampled." The heavy sarcasm in Gerald's voice nearly made Calem laugh aloud.

To dispel his mirth, Calem pulled out his map and consulted it. "We'll reach the inn soon enough, my friend. It can't be more than two hours away. We'll be able to rest there. If you remember what the earl in the last town told us, there are likely a few prospects in this particular village. We should be able to shed our armor for at least a couple of days."

Gerald rolled his shoulders. "I sure hope so. I'm growing stiff. I know that it protects us, and whoever stole your armor proved that we still need to be on our guard even with the war over, but sometimes I wish we didn't have to wear it."

"I completely understand, my friend. It has been difficult for both of us."

Gerald nodded his head in acknowledgment. "I imagine you are likely more tired than I am, being half my size with armor that could fit me. I still don't know how you became a knight," he said with a grin.

Calem raised an eyebrow. "Do we really need to practice our swordplay again?"

Gerald's grin became a scowl as he faced forward again. Calem chuckled to himself. The last time they had practiced, Calem had beaten the larger man soundly. Calem thought of their practice sessions more as training sessions for the larger knight, for Calem had yet to find his equal among the Katnionan people.

After an hour or so, the knights decided to dismount and walk for a while, both to rest their horses and to stretch their own muscles. Calem moaned with relief as he stretched his legs. Even better, after a few minutes of walking, they came upon a conveniently located stream running along a bend in the path.

They had just paused to allow their horses to drink when they heard hooves approaching, followed by wagon wheels. Looking up the road towards their destination, they saw a wagon barreling in their direction. While the wagon *was* moving with alarming speed, it was something else that caused Calem's eyes to widen in horror. Seemingly unaware of the devil driving towards her, a young woman was walking down the path as if on a stroll only a few lengths away from where he and Gerald stood.

When the wagon was almost upon the woman, who still hadn't even moved to the verge to give the wagon more room, Calem sprung into action. He ran and threw himself into the young woman, taking them both to the ground. He felt the air of the wheels as the wagon hurried past them.

As Calem heard the wagon slow, he also became aware of the woman in his arms, finally taking a good look at her. She was the most beautiful lady he had ever seen, notwithstanding her simple country clothing, and while he was sure he had never seen her before, she looked remarkably familiar somehow.

A shadow drew over them and Calem looked up to see a stranger near his own age standing over him and the young woman. To Calem's utter confusion, the stranger looked annoyed. Angry, even. "What ye be doin'?" the stranger asked rudely.

Calem scrambled to his feet and, despite being shorter, stared down the angry stranger. "Rescuing this young lady from your careless driving!" he barked.

The stranger was visibly cowed by his anger. "I weren't gonna hit 'er," he grumbled. "'Tis a game we play."

Calem could hardly believe his ears. He was about to respond when he remembered his manners. He turned back to the young woman and offered his hand to help her stand. She looked at his outstretched hand with a puzzled expression before standing without his assistance. He dropped his arm, both amused and a little put out that she had refused his help.

Then she looked at him again. Her eyes were mesmerizing. At first glance he had thought they were brown, but now he saw that while the portion of the irises right around the pupils was a light brown, there was a ring of green surrounding each, just along the outer edge of the iris. This gave her hazel eyes a watery quality, like looking into the clear stream where his horse still drank.

The stranger again pulled Calem's attention from the young woman. "Tell the knight," he huffed, apparently asking her to back up his story.

Calem shook his head to drive off the trance of the woman's eyes. Needing to focus on something other than her, he returned his gaze to the stranger. "I don't know what kind of game you are playing, but it is very dangerous. That," he motioned to where the cart stood nearby, its horses panting heavily, "is no way to treat anyone, especially a lady."

Calem nearly jumped when the young lady, who had remained silent until this point, let out an unladylike snort. "You 'hear that, Bob? 'E thinks I'm a lady."

Both she and Bob laughed. "That's crazy talk," he said after a moment, shaking his head in amusement. He then stepped between Calem and the young woman, who had backed up a pace without Calem noticing, a look of challenge clear on his face. The move was predatory, as if he was claiming the young woman. Calem's eyes found hers again, looking to see how she felt about her companion's actions. He could almost feel her annoyance as she rolled her eyes at Bob's back.

"What ye be doin' in these parts, knight?" Bob asked, his irritation back in full force.

Calem took a deep breath to cool his rising temper before responding. "We are searching for someone."

Bob brightened instantly. "Oh, is that all? Who ye be searchin' for? Lia, here, knows everyone near town. We can 'elp ya, then ye can be on yer way." His tone left Calem with little doubt that his sudden generosity stemmed from feelings of rivalry; the man apparently felt threatened by Calem and would assist as much as he could if it meant the knight would leave so he could have Miss Lia all to himself again.

Calem took another deep breath to help him respond in a civil manner. "For the moment, we are searching for the inn. We will likely be in the area for at least a few days, on top of hoping to rest for the night before beginning our search in the morning."

Bob scowled at the news and placed an arm in front of the young woman, as if he knew she would try to step forward, but she just glared at him and stepped around it. "I'll take ya there meself, Sir Knight. Ye said 'we', where be yer companions?"

"Just one companion, and I am him," Gerald cut in before Calem had a chance to respond. He approached from behind Calem. Calem idly wondered what the taller knight had observed. Gerald stepped past Calem and toward the young woman. In one smooth move, he took her hand, bowed over it, and placed a kiss on the back of it. "We are indebted to you, young lady, for your kindness in showing these weary travelers where they might rest their tired bodies."

Bob let out a hiss at the knight's sweet, flirtatious tone, and Calem ground his teeth. While Bob's reaction wasn't surprising in the least, Calem's surprised himself. While it wasn't the first time Gerald had made pretty speeches to the fairer sex, it was the first time Calem felt angry, rather than embarrassed, at his companion's actions. In fact, he had an almost overwhelming urge to wipe the stupid smile off of the other knight's face.

Fortunately, he didn't need to, for the young woman snatched her hand away, even as she brought the other hand around to slap the larger knight across the face. "I don' like yer way of thanks, knight. Keep yer lips to yerself."

Bob glared at Gerald before leading, almost pulling, the young woman towards his wagon. As he all but forced her up onto the seat, ignoring her protests that she could climb up on her own, Calem looked over at Gerald.

His eyes widened in surprise to see a bruise already forming on Gerald's face. It took a lot to make a bruise like the one he saw on the larger knight's face, as Calem had observed over a series of practice bouts between them. Not that he had aimed for the man's face, but between a few unintended strikes and multiple falls, Calem hadn't ever seen a bruise like this on his companion before. His estimation of the young woman rose even higher after witnessing her strength.

By the time Calem was done inspecting Gerald's face, Bob had pulled the wagon around and had rolled past them. Once they were out of earshot, Gerald rubbed his face and grinned. "I like this one. It feels like she left a serious mark." Calem nodded to indicate that she had. "Perhaps once we are done..."

Calem shook his head. "I suggest you leave that one alone." He tried to convince himself that this warning was for his friend's safety and nothing more.

Unfortunately, Gerald was not convinced, and his grin grew wider as they returned to their mounts. "Why? Because you are thinking the same thing I am?" Of course the man had to choose *that* moment to be annoyingly astute.

Calem glared as he mounted his horse, hoping the action would cover the heat rushing to his face. "How many woman does this make that you have suggested going back for once we finish our quest?"

Gerald swung into his saddle and set his horse in motion before answering. "I don't know," he replied honestly, "but this one is different from all the others. She didn't fall for my charms or try to win me over."

Calem spurred his own horse into a trot, quickly coming even with the other knight. "And I doubt she ever will try. She seems to be an excellent judge of character, and I believe you have just lost any respect for you she might have had."

Gerald grinned and shrugged, making Calem again consider hitting him. "It will be a challenge, but one I will win. Have you ever seen me lose?"

Calem thought of all the time they had spent practicing their swordplay over the last two months, and raised an eyebrow. "Only when I fight against you," he replied archly.

Gerald scowled and rubbed his shoulder, as if he, too, remembered their sparring. "Well, yes, there is that. However, you've never won where women are concerned."

There was a glaringly obvious reason for that. "Probably because I've never tried." Tiring of the conversation, Calem spurred his horse faster until he drew even with the wagon seat.

Of their own accord, his eyes kept flickering to the young woman. He even saw her look back at him a couple of times. Once, they made eye contact for a moment before she quickly turned away. Although she tried to hide it, he could see a beautiful blush on her cheeks that nicely complimented her long, light brown hair, which hung loose and wild down her back. He found himself comparing her to a woodland fairy, for not only where her eyes and hair hued in rich, earthy tones, she was also dressed in the colors of the forest, in a green dress and a brown cloak. *If she is a fairy, that explains why I can't keep my eyes from wandering to her*, he mused. She seemed to have cast a spell over him.

Roughly an hour later, the group reached the inn. When Miss Lia made to get down from the wagon, Gerald swung out of his saddle and rushed to assist her. Bob saw what the knight was intending, and he quickly jumped down and ran around the wagon to help her down himself. Bob got there first, and he seemed to bask in the chance to lift her from his wagon. His hands lingered on her waist for much longer than necessary, and Calem saw a flash of annoyance cross her face. Obviously tiring of him touching her, she pushed free, stepped away, and darted into the inn.

A pair of stable boys worked near the door to the inn, and they approached with the horses and wagon. The knights handed their reins to one boy, then followed the young woman into the establishment. Calem could hear her speaking to someone before he could see her. "...they be questin' for someone, so they'll be needing' a room or two for a few nights." By the sound of it, she was apprising the innkeeper of his and Gerald's business.

"Many thanks, Lia," the stout man replied. Miss Lia smiled and nodded.

Gerald smirked and raised an eyebrow at Calem, issuing a challenge, before putting on his winning smile and approaching the young woman. "Yes, thank you indeed, Miss Lia," he said with a deep bow.

Miss Lia met Calem's eyes and she shared a look of long-suffering with him that he understood all too well. The larger knight had become something of a brother to Calem during the two months or so they had been paired together. In spite of this, or perhaps because of this, they seemed to be at odds with each other more often than not. Thinking about his relationship with his own brother, Calem decided it was probably *because* they had grown so close, for there were few other people he had so many disagreements with.

Miss Lia looked back at Gerald as he rose from his bow. "Yer welcome, knight," she replied cordially. "If you be needin' anythin' anyone here knows where to find me."

Even in profile, Calem could see distress remained on her face, so he stepped forward to rescue her. "You are most kind, my lady," he said with a much more appropriate bow. "Please let us know if there is anything we can do to return the favor."

A sparkle of mischief lit her eyes, making them seem as if they were dancing. She raised an eyebrow and grinned at him. "Anythin'?" she asked teasingly

Her sudden playfulness drew a smile to his face. "Anything within reason, of course."

His comment brought heat to her cheeks. He had a better view of her blush than before, and he felt even more strongly that the color became her very well. "I weren't gonna suggest anythin' improper, Sir Knight," she replied, ducking her head.

Calem coughed to cover a smile. "I didn't think you would, my lady."

Miss Lia looked up at Calem through her eyelashes, and his heart seemed to stop as her hazel eyes held him captive. Her spell only broke when Bob took her by the arm and led her away, straight towards the exit. He turned back at the door and shot a glare at Calem. Calem held his gaze for a moment before Bob looked away, turning back to the door and pulling Miss Lia outside.

Gerald's sudden chuckle startled Calem and made him start breathing again, which he realized he hadn't done since being caught in her gaze. "Those eyes of hers are very powerful, aren't they?" the large knight asked jovially.

Heat flooded Calem's face, making both Gerald and the innkeeper laugh. This earned Gerald a scowl from Calem before he turned to the innkeeper. "We each need a room, sir," he stated gruffly. "Like Miss Lia said, we will likely be here for a few nights."

The innkeeper drew a pair of brass keys from behind his counter and set them on top of it, rather than handing them to the knights. "First, mind telling me about this quest little Lia was talking about? I'd be glad to help in any way that I can. Other knights were just here, but wouldn't speak with me about it."

Gerald leaned on the counter as well, and Calem found himself wondering how well the wood could hold both of the large men's weight. "We're looking for a young woman, about Miss Lia's age, that would have come here about seventeen years ago, and may have been taken in as an orphan. Do you know anyone that fits that description?"

The innkeeper rubbed his chin as he thought. "Is that all you have to go on?"

Gerald sighed and nodded. "Unfortunately, yes."

The innkeeper heaved a heavy sigh. "I can think of four young women, right off, that fit your description. Miss Lia will know all of them and maybe one or two others that don't come to mind. I don't know how much she'll cooperate with *you*, however," he said to Gerald. "She seems to have taken a particular dislike to you, sir."

Gerald let out a confident laugh. "Nothing I can't handle," he said with a smirk.

The innkeeper raised an eyebrow, obviously not believing him. "You've never met Lia."

The smirk remained firm on Gerald's face. "We'll see."

As Bob pulled Lilia away from the inn, she couldn't help glancing back at the establishment. When Bob noticed what she was doing, he yanked on her arm to force her to face forward to avoid falling. She glared at him as she regained her footing. "What was that for?"

"Yer better off avoidin' them, Lia," Bob replied, glaring at the inn.

"Why?" she huffed, offended on the knights' behalf.

"They seems likes trouble." His gaze remained fixed on the door they had just left through.

Lilia rolled her eyes at the back of his head. "I can take care of myself, Bob. You knows that as well as anyone." Considering the scrapes she'd gotten him out of time and time again, if he *didn't* know that, he was more dense than she thought.

Bob continued as if she hadn't spoken. "An' I don' likes the way you was lookin' at *him*. We's as good as married, Lia, so you shouldn't be lookin' at him tha' way."

Lilia bristled at his words. She'd had enough. She yanked

her arm free of Bob's grip. The force of her pull left him face down in the dust. "We is *not* as good as married, Bob." Her voice was like ice as she looked down at him. "I telled ya, plenty times, I don' wanna marry ye."

He sneered as he stood. "Well see what yer pa says about it, then. Me thinks he'll be on my side." He grabbed her arm again. "Let's go ask 'im now, shall we?"

Lilia planted her feet and yanked free again as Bob started pulling her towards her home. "No. Papa would never make me marry some'un I don' wanna. He loves me too much fer that."

"If'n he really loved ya, then he'd getcha married off fast so he knows ye'll be taken care of." Lilia dodged two more attempts to grab her by the arm before Bob grabbed at her hair instead. She deflected his grab only to find it was a feint, and he grabbed her arm again instead. Tightening his grip, he began dragging her towards the blacksmith's forge.

"Haven' I already told ya I can take care of meself?" she protested as she tried to break free once more.

"Ye're outta yer mind if ya thinks that, Lia. Only a man can take care of a woman proper like. Ya need ta get married."

"I don't think so. Me pa *will* take me side on this. I'll not marry you Bob! Ever!" Changing tactics, she ran past Bob, pulling free from his grasp as she pulled in the opposite direction she had been previously, surprising him. Instead of going home, she ran as fast as she could to the one place she was sure Bob wouldn't be let into, if he managed to keep up with her. She didn't even bother knocking on the door of the duke's manor, she simply opened it and stepped inside. "Yer Grace!" she called from the empty entryway.

The man appeared a moment later at the top of the grand staircase, his broad smile evident, even at a distance. "There's my favorite girl!" He exclaimed before running down the stairs and pulling Lilia into an embrace. "How are you, little Lia?" he asked after releasing her. "I wish you would come visit me more often."

She dipped into a curtsy. "It's good ta see ye as well, Yer Grace. I've come ta tell ya that there's more knights in town. I imagine they'll be stoppin' by, just like them others."

He nodded, causing his shoulder length, slightly curly hair to bounce. "That is good to know, thank you. Did you catch their names?"

She was about to answer, but another figure appeared at the top of the stairs. Lilia scowled. It was Genevieve, the duke's ward. While her outward appearance was beautiful, with pale blonde hair and vivid blue eyes, her inner self was much less attractive. "Lia," she almost spat. Her dislike of Lilia was as strong as Lilia's was for her. "What are you doing here?"

Lilia stood straight, putting on her most regal bearing as she did so. "I came ta tell 'is lordship that there be more knights."

Genevieve gave them an exaggerated sniff. "Well, you have done your duty. You may leave now."

"Genevieve!" the duke hissed. "Behave yourself, or else I will send you to your room."

She raised an eyebrow, again exaggerated to make sure they saw. "I, at least, actually *have my* own room to be sent to, unlike *someone* I know."

Rather than be offended, Lilia simply rolled her eyes. Her parents didn't dwell in the largest of homes, but they filled the space they had with love, which was more valuable to Lilia than her own room to sleep in at night. "If ye'd excuse me, Yer Grace, I ought to 'ead home. Me parents will be wonderin' where I am." She gave the man another curtsy before dipping an insincere one towards Genevieve. The girl glared in response. Lilia then glided out the door.

On the way home, Lilia passed the inn. Her mind wandered to the two knights she knew were inside. The taller of them was undeniably handsome, with his dark curls and sharp blue eyes. He looked as if a sculptor had chiseled him from stone.

Despite how handsome the taller knight was, the shorter of the pair more frequently occupied her thoughts. His hair, which he kept short, was as black as a raven's feathers. While he also had a handsome face, it was specifically his eyes that drew her attention the most. They were blue with flecks of gold and green, but in the short time she had seen them, they had shifted between blue, green, and gray in different lighting.

While his eyes were mesmerizing on their own, what really made her catch her breath was their expression. There was a serious maturity behind them that indicated he had likely seen more than his share of the war. It reflected in his bearing as well. Despite the fact that she was as tall as him, if not taller, he had a commanding presence that mace him seem twice his size, as if he had a large soul stuck inside his small frame.

In short, she was certainly more impressed with the shorter knight than his companion, even if the taller of them hadn't acted like a fopdoodle.

She couldn't think of the shorter knight without remembering their first meeting. The feelings that accompanied it returned to her. When he had pulled her down so Bob wouldn't strike her, his arms had been fully around her. In his arms, she had felt a degree of safety beyond anything she had felt before. Not even her father's arms offered such a strong feeling of protection. Then, when their eyes met after they had regained their feet, she felt more flustered than she could ever remember feeling. Time had seemed to stretch between them, well, until Bob intervened and broke the spell.

For the life of her, she wasn't sure if she was mad or grateful for the interruption. She had been so unnerved that she'd fully retreated into her rustic accent and persona, trying to use humor to defuse the moment. If only the knight, or Bob for that matter, knew how ladylike she could really be.

Lilia was so lost in her thoughts that she didn't realize she had already reached her father's forge. She entered to find him hard at work, his long, dark hair sweaty. He usually kept it tied back, but it was presently untied. She waited patiently, watching him work, until the large blacksmith looked over at her. He smiled when he saw her. "There's my girl," he said, his brown eyes twinkling. He set aside his tools. "We've been wondering when you would come home."

"Forgive me, Papa. Two more knights are passing through the village, so I went to inform His Grace of their arrival." She had been looking around the forge as she spoke. When she saw a familiar weapon on the wall, she frowned. "Speaking of the duke, did he not like his sword?"

The blacksmith heaved a heavy sigh. "He said it was a good sword, but that it was a little too short for his liking. He said it didn't feel quite right in his hand. He has, at least, given me permission to sell it."

Lilia nodded in understanding. "It does seem a little shorter than usual. I'm glad that he released you to sell it rather than demanding it be remade." As she studied the blade, a vision flashed in her mind. It was of a particular short knight wielding the weapon. She thought the shorter sword may work very well for someone of his height.

She shook her head to dismiss the image. "Does Mama need my help making supper?" she asked.

Her father nodded. "Even if she doesn't really need the help, she'll appreciate it. Go help her. I'll be in as soon as I've finished the day's work." His large strong hand patted her on the head before returning to his tools.

Entering the house, Lilia found her mother preparing the vegetables for the evening meal. She looked up at the sound of the door opening, smiling when she saw her daughter. "There's my princess." Lilia smiled. From the sound of her voice, it was obvious her mother was happy to see her. Her mother set down the knife and embraced Lilia. Once she released her daughter from her embrace, she motioned to the knife and vegetables. "Now, can you help me finish? My hands aren't as good as they used to be."

Lilia nodded. "Of course, Mama." She finished chopping the potatoes and carrots while her mother prepared the rest of the soup. Once the vegetables were mixed in, they put the pot over the fire

While the meal cooked, Lilia's mother took a brush to her daughter's hair. Lilia winced. Her mother set down the brush. She plucked something from the tangles. "What did you do to get sticks in your hair?" she asked, holding one of the sticks for Lilia to inspect.

Lilia sighed. "Bob was playing his 'game' again." Frustration at his antics was evident in her tone. Her tone changed completely, however, as she continued. "Today something different happened, though. I was rescued before Bob could pull me up into the wagon. A knight tackled me to the ground, thinking Bob might run me over. He wasn't entirely wrong, for it felt like the wheels were just inches from my feet." She growled as she added, "I wish that farm boy would understand I'm not going to marry him, and that his little game is just making his case worse."

"I know, dear," her mother said in a soothing voice. She had returned to the brushing. "I must say, whomever this new knight is, I like him already. Did you catch his title?"

Lilia shook her head. "No, we never ended up introducing ourselves. There was something odd about this knight. He was traveling with only one other knight, instead of three like we've seen the others do. Why do you think that is?"

"I don't know, dear," her mother said with a sigh. "Did you ever find out what the other knights were searching for?"

"I was never told specifically, but considering the types of girls they were meeting, I suspect they are searching for the princess." She started to shake her head, but then remembered that her hair was still being brushed. "Why more have arrived, I don't know, especially since I'm certain that Her Highness isn't here. I suppose they are more intent on being thorough than being coordinated."

To her surprise, her mother's hand shook, forcing her to put the brush down for a moment. "Oh, my silly hands are shaking again."

Lilia's eyes widened. "Again?" she asked, frowning.

Her mother nodded. "Yes. They have been shaky from time to time over the last few weeks. Anyway, I suspect you are right about the knights searching for the princess. With the war ended and the princes found, it is only natural they would search for her as well. I hope they find her." Her voice broke as she spoke, which Lilia thought a little odd. However, her mother cleared her throat and continued as if nothing strange had happened. "Speaking of princesses, how is *my* princess?"

Lilia grinned. "I'm fine, Mama. Tired, though. I think I'll sleep well tonight. I've had an exciting day."

"Then I suppose we should eat soon so you can sleep on a full belly. Will you please go tell your father supper is ready?"

Lilia nodded before going to deliver the news. She found her father putting away the last of his tools, his work finished for the night. He joined them inside shortly afterward, and they all ate together around their humble table.

Once dinner was done, Lilia cleaned up the bowls. After that task was done, she took a pillow over to the fire, lying down on the rug in front of it. She watched the flames dance on the logs. Usually, this was enough to lull her to sleep, but the memory of the knight's intense eyes kept intruding. The look behind those eyes could only be described as awareness, awareness of her in that moment. She felt she could loose herself in the fire of his gaze as easily as she usually did when staring into the flames in the hearth. Despite her exhaustion, thinking of his eyes held sleep at bay, and it was a long time before she finally fell asleep.

Three

When Calem awoke the next morning, he looked out his window to see the sun just peeking over the treetops. The light seemed to pierce through his eyes, making his otherwise minor headache spike. He turned his gaze away from the window. Despite the day before being long and exhausting, he'd slept little. His mind had refused to steer away from the memory of the mysterious Miss Lia and the look she had given him.

As he was shaving and washing his face, he considered how he would dress. He decided that he would leave his armor where he had placed it the night before, instead donning a simple gray tunic and breeches. Once he was ready for the day, he headed down stairs and out to the stables. He meant to check on his horse, Stoneheart, and perform his morning exercises.

When he entered the stables, however, all thought of exercise fled. Actually, every thought fled. He heard the voice that had been dancing through his mind the night before. When he grew closer to Stoneheart's stall, he was able to make out the words she was speaking to his horse. "...worry none, I'm sure he..." She must have heard him approach, for she broke off and turned to look at him. She dipped a curtsy. "Mornin', Sir Knight."

He offered her a bow in return and smiled. "A good morning to you, my lady." He walked closer and leaned against Stoneheart's stall door next to her. "You are here rather early," he remarked. At the height of summer, few beyond farmers were up at the crack of dawn, let alone out and about.

Yet, she just shrugged and rubbed the horse's nose. "Too much ta do ta sleep in, sir," she replied. "Gotta get food on the table somehow." While still rubbing the animal nose, she glanced at him. "What can I do ya for today?"

He watched her continue to interact with his horse for a long moment before answering her question. "As I mentioned yesterday, we are here searching for someone, a young woman about your age. She would have come here about seventeen years ago, probably as an orphan."

Miss Lia's response was a quiet chuckle. His heart raced at the sound. "Ya hear that, boy?" she asked the dapple-gray Andalusian stallion. "He's lookin' for a girl." Calem's ears started to burn. "Though, me thinks it's 'is friend tha' usually gets 'em." With those words, her face fell and the laughter left her tone. "Pretty words usually go far, from what I seen. Not for me, though. Neither does barreling' down the road at me, not that Bob cares." She let out a frustrated sigh. "You remember Bob, don'cha?" she asked the horse.

He bobbed his head, as if responding to her question.

"He been tryin' ta get me ta marry 'im for a while now, but I jus' can't." She moved her head to look at the horse from the side, and her eyes met Calem's. He watched as her eyes grew wide and her face reddened, a look of horror and embarrassment filling her face. Apparently she had forgotten he was standing there.

Calem couldn't help the quiet chuckle that escaped. He then cleared his throat and asked, "Do you usually take care of the horses?"

Miss Lia nodded. Her cheeks were still a little pink, but she seemed to relax, obviously grateful for the change in subject. "One o' me jobs is helpin' look after 'em whenever the inn has visitors. In return, we gets some of the spare food from the kitchen."

Calem nodded. "Sounds like a good deal to me." He then pushed a way from the stall door and stood straight, ready to get down to business. "Now, about this young woman we are searching for..." he prompted.

He watched as she, too, straightened. She nodded. "There's four 'round here, sir. We can easily do the first two today, as they lives close by. The third is out a ways, so it's be best to plan a day jus' for that visit. The last one is away right now, but she'll be back in two days time."

Calem nodded, making mental notes as she spoke. "We also need to add 'visit the local lord' to the schedule."

She nodded again. "Luckily, he be the keeper of one of them girls, so ye'll already 'ave that chance." She then grimaced and he wondered if the man was unliked. "I'll not be helpin' ya with that one. I ain't welcome there."

Calem was surprised by that. He couldn't imagine why this woman wouldn't be welcome somewhere. "Why ever not?"

"I should say it's the little miss that don't welcome me," she replied, shrugging nonchalantly.

Calem crossed his arms across his chest. "Well, you would be welcome there as my guide, surely. I would prefer for you to come with us so that you can identify the young woman in question."

A smile split Miss Lia's face. "I don' mind goin' with ya, when ya puts it like tha'. I like 'is lordship well enough." Her smile turned into a frown. "It's 'is ward I ain't on friendly terms with.

Calem was relieved to hear the that local lord was liked, at least, by Miss Lia, whom he suspected to be an excellent judge of character. "So, his lordship is good and fair, I take it?"

She nodded without hesitation. "Fair as they come."

He smiled. "I'm relieved to hear it. I have met too many noblemen who are not."

Miss Lia nodded and then went silent. Calem wondered what she was thinking. She looked in the direction of the stable doors and sighed. "Are we havin' ta wait for the other knight?" She then scowled. "I don' like the way he been treatin' me."

Calem fought a grin. He had no objections to spending a little time alone with Miss Lia. Even if Gerald was awake, he would likely be slow to show his face with the bruise she had given him. Calem cleared his throat. "If he makes you uncomfortable, then far be it from me to force you to be in his company."

Miss Lia flashed him a dazzling smile. His heart raced in response. "That's good." She then turned towards the stable doors. "Let's go." And just like that, she was off. On foot.

Calem had to jog to catch up with her, and needed to walk at a brisk pace to keep up. He wasn't sure if he found the surprise pleasant or frustrating. In most of the towns he and Gerald had visited, there had been an 'epidemic' of slow-moving women. The knights had known what was happening, and Calem had barely kept his temper at check. He didn't exactly blame them for wanting to linger with the knights, but for a man of action like himself, it had been agonizing.

Now, here was a young woman that he would be more than content to take a long walk with, and he had to exert himself to keep up with her. The irony was tangible, and he shook his head in amused frustration.

After a half hour of their brisk pace, something that made Calem rather grateful he had left his armor behind, they reached the duke's manor. It was easily the largest residence in town, but it didn't stand out like a sore thumb. Calem had seen many a nobleman's residences that were much too grand compared to the other houses in village, and was relieved that the duke didn't find it necessary to do the same.

Miss Lia gave him a moment to admire the building and catch his breath before striding up the walk and pounding forcefully on the door. Calem felt a great deal of shock when, rather than waiting for a butler or footman to respond to her summons, she opened the door herself, walked inside, and proceeded to shout, "Yer Graaaace!"

From where he remained out on the front steps, Calem could hear hurried footsteps coming from the upper story of the building. A moment later, a tall, bearded man came into view, stopping at the top of the stairs. He smiled down at his unconventional guest. "Hello, Little Lia, it's good to see you again so soon." As he reached the bottom, he noticed Calem standing beyond the open doorway. "Come in! Come in!" He beckoned. Then he turned to Miss Lia. "Who is this that you have brought with you?"

Calem stepped inside and looked to Miss Lia to perform the

introduction. The look she shot back at him reminded him that he hadn't actually introduced himself to her yet. "Sir Calem, at your service, sir," he said, bowing to the man.

The duke bowed in reply as Miss Lia curtsied. "Good ta finally get yer name, Sir Knight. An' I introduce to you 'is Grace, the Duke of Farreden."

"Well met," the duke replied. "Now correct me if I'm wrong, but I assume that you are here regarding the king's search?"

Calem nodded, unsurprised the duke already knew of the quest. Thus far, the higher the rank of the nobles they had met with, the more likely they were to have heard about it.

"Therefore, you will likely wish to speak with my ward..." the duke was cut off by a door slamming upstairs. He grimaced. "Prepare yourself. She is coming."

Once again, there was the sound of footsteps echoing from above their heads. This time they were lighter and more rapid. Soon, the sound produced a very beautiful young woman who, like her guardian before her, also halted at the top of the stairway. Her long, light blonde hair hung in ringlets, framing her diamond-shaped face. The face was presently marred by a look of extreme annoyance. "Lia!" she huffed, her expression clearly stormy. "I thought I told you not to—" She cut off as she realized that a stranger to her stood in the crowd below. Her annoyance instantly fled. Her expression and tone became flirtatious. "Who is this?" she purred.

The duke sighed heavily. "Genevieve, this is Sir Calem. Sir—"

Genevieve spoke before he had a chance to complete the introduction. "A knight." She had a wide smile as she glided down the stairs. She stopped right in from of Calem. He was unsurprised to discover she was taller than him, even without the heeled shoes her footsteps indicated she wore. Her smile faltered as she seemed to come to the same conclusion. "Where are your companions? Don't knights always have companions?"

"Genevieve! Manners!" The duke hissed the scold. He then sent Calem an apologetic look. "Sir Calem, this is Miss Genevieve, my ward."

"Forgive me," Genevieve purred. She dipped a curtsy in response to her introduction, and Calem bowed slightly in reply. "I'm just always so eager to meet everyone, and I have never known of knights on official business traveling alone."

Calem was quite grateful that he didn't meet with the young woman's approval. He gave a small nod to acknowledge her statement. "You are correct. I do have a companion, but he is still resting from our journey at the inn."

Her eyes lit up at his response. "I see. Well, it is still a pleasure to meet you. I do hope you will visit again with your companion."

Not if I can help it. Calem was starting to recognize why Miss Lia and Miss Genevieve didn't get along. Aloud, he said, "I will inform him of your desire to meet, my lady, but I cannot guarantee our return. We have much to do." Unintentionally, Calem dipped into a flourishing bow, something of a signature move of his he hadn't intended to utilize during this quest.

He then winced at what happened next. Out of the corner of his eye, he saw a look of recognition cross the duke's face. The man's eyes widened in surprise. "Sir Calem, a word, if you please."

Calem nodded and they moved away from the women. They had begun to bicker, which was alright with him, for he would rather they not overhear the conversation he had hoped to avoid.

The duke tried to rein in his amazement, without success. "Are you..."

Calem sighed. It wasn't too surprising that he would eventually be recognized. A duke would be the most likely to do so, after all. "Yes, I am. We have indeed met before." He hoped his word choice was enough to prevent the duke actually saying who he was.

It seemed to do so. "What are you, of all people, doing here?"

Calem narrowed his eyes. "You know our task. You know how important it is."

The duke scratched his head. "Yes, but certainly there are enough other knights for the task. After all, even as remote as we are, you are the second party to arrive here. So why..."

Calem held out a hand to silence the duke. "I am concerned for the missing princess, and for this kingdom. King Kelvin has declared that she is to marry the crown prince of Callarda, if she can be found. As a knight of this kingdom, I have offered him my services."

The duke nodded his understanding. "Of course." Then his look grew ponderous. He studied the young women for a moment, as if needing something else to look at while deciding whether or not to say what was on his mind. He turned back to Calem. "Perhaps it is providence you are searching. Were it anyone else, I would not share this information, but I feel like you should know. If you are truly to speak with every likely maiden and her guardians, you should include Miss Lia. She is not actually related to the people she calls her parents."

Calem frowned as he considered what the duke had just

revealed to him. "Why did she not tell me this herself? She has been nothing but helpful in the time we have been acquainted."

The duke shook his head. "I don't believe she knows." Calem's eyes widened at the news. "That being said, I would use your greatest discretion in regards to her. I would rather you not act on this information at all, but if you do, it may be best to ask her parents without involving her."

Calem took a moment to ponder this latest revelation. "May I tell my companion?"

The duke frowned in concern. "Who is he?"

"Sir Gerald." When the duke's frown turn from concern to confusion, Calem added, "Also known as the Flirting Knight."

The duke scowled. Unsurprisingly, Sir Gerald's reputation preceded him. The duke shook his head. "No, I think it best to keep this from him, at least until you truly need to tell him."

Calem nodded in agreement. Gerald wasn't exactly loose lipped, but this was particularly sensitive information. The fewer who knew the secret the better.

The duke studied the women for another moment before turning back to Calem with a grin. "You know, it would be prudent for the both of you to practice against Miss Lia while you are here. Her father is not just a blacksmith, but perhaps the best swordsmith in the north. She is as skilled at using swords as he is at making them. No one in the region can best her."

Calem followed the duke's gaze and grinned. "No wonder she is so strong. I witnessed her strength first hand yesterday, when the Flirting Knight tried a little too hard to get her attention. If he's not still resting, he is probably trying to figure out a way to hide the bruise she gave him."

The duke let out a hearty laugh which drew the young women's attention. "Yes, Mis Lia is not to be trifled with. If you want a show, have your companion challenge her. Wooden swords, of course. We don't want her to do lasting damage to anyone." Miss Lia grinned cheekily at them, as if to say that she wouldn't mind doing exactly that. Then Miss Genevieve said something that drew her attention back with a fiery glare.

Calem joined the duke with a chuckle of his own. "Thank you, Your Grace, for the information. I believe it will prove useful." He glanced at Genevieve. "Considering your knowledge of the search, I assume that Genevieve is not our quarry?"

The duke nodded. "You are correct, though part of me wishes she was, so I'd not have to care for her anymore." He grimaced. "I love the girl, but she is frequently just too much. The staff have taken to calling her 'Miss Grievance' when she is not present. I can't blame them, either," he added with a sigh.

Calem nodded. "Well, forgive me for saying so, but I'm glad that she is not the person we are searching for, as many would not appreciate a princess with that kind of attitude."

The duke waved his hand. "Nothing to forgive. I do suggest that you take Miss Lia soon, however, before she decides to chop off more of Genevieve's hair."

Calem's eyes widened in shock. "More?!"

The duke nodded, an amused twinkle in his eyes. "They were seven years old. Miss Lia was showing me her knife-throwing skills. Genevieve was standing next to the door with a scowl on her face. She said something particularly rude. So, Miss Lia threw her knife and expertly cut off a lock of Genevieve's hair." He chuckled. "She's been my favorite person ever since."

Calem let out a laugh. "She seems kind, but I agree she is not to be trifled with." *Excellent qualities for a princess to have,* he mused.

The duke grinned. "Exactly."

Calem smiled. "Well, then I shall take the good lady away. Thank you, again, for your time and information."

The duke nodded. "You are most welcome." They bowed to each other again. Then Calem turned towards the women to let them know it was time to part ways.

Four

WHILE THE MEN SPOKE PRIVATELY, LILIA WAS FORCED TO lend Miss Genevieve a patient ear. The girl told her of the latest happenings at the duke's manor. "One of the knights who was here last month came and dined with me nearly every night. I thought he would take me away from this dreadful place, but, alas, he was on a quest. He did promise to come back once they completed their quest and take me away to the capital, however. Can you just imagine it, Lia?"

Lilia barely refrained from rolling her eyes. "No, Miss Genevieve." *Actually, I can, and have even dreamed of what it may look like. I know you have no interest in listening to me, though, so I'll not even mention it.*

Genevieve let out a huff. "Of course you can't, you ignorant thing. Not that you'd even know the capital when you arrived."

Lilia raised an eyebrow. "Don't it 'ave a castle?"

Genevieve gave her a look that conveyed how much she thought the question, and likely the questioner, lacking. "Yes, it does."

"Then I reckon I'd at least guess." Lilia folded her arms across her chest, daring Genevieve to contradict her.

Genevieve simply raised an eyebrow and said, "Perhaps. You wouldn't be welcomed, though, looking like that." She gestured with one hand towards Lilia's less than refined attire.

Lilia shot her flat stare. "Of course not, Miss Genevieve." *As if I would go anywhere important without tidying myself up.*

The other girl continued as if she hadn't spoken. "I, on the other hand, would be welcomed everywhere," she said as she ran a hand over her hair and down to finger the fine fabric of her blue gown. She always wore blue. "I am beautiful, I know how to carry myself..." she cut off as the duke laughed loudly enough to draw both of their attention to him. He spoke loudly enough for them to hear him suggest to Sir Calem that he should challenge Lilia to a training match with wooden swords. Lilia shot them a cheeky grin to say that she approved of the idea.

To reclaim Lilia's attention, Genevieve continued speaking. "I also know how to behave like a lady," she said cuttingly, which drew Lilia's eyes back to her with a glare. "I also know how to speak properly." This last attribute was recited in a particularly haughty manner.

Her words made Lilia burn with anger. She was frustrated that, even though they had grown up together, this girl didn't actually know anything about her. Lilia straightened her shoulders and looked Genevieve in the eye. "Oh, I know, quite well, how to speak properly when I want to, " she said, all hints of her rustic accent gone. "It is just easier not to, especially since people like you underestimate me when my speech is less than refined."

In that moment, Genevieve was the one who looked roughly raised, her mouth hanging open in shock. "Your... your speech is flawless!" the girl stammered. "Why would you ever choose to speak like an commoner when you have such a refined tone?"

Lilia continued to stare her down. "One can't be too careful when one almost lives in the gutters, Miss Genevieve." *We are not actually that poor, but Miss Genevieve would certainly think so, were she ever to deign to visit our home.*

In the next moment, the look that crossed Genevieves face raised a small amount of alarm for Lilia. It spoke clearly of unfriendly, even selfish, calculation. "You know," Genevieve drawled, "I *could* offer you a position as my personal maid. You would no longer have to live anywhere near the gutters. Or the smithy." She scrunched up her nose as if she had smelled something terrible. "All the smells of the forge…" she shuddered, "I don't know how you can stand it."

Lilia ground her teeth. *You will not speak of my family that way.* "I can't *stand* it, I *enjoy* it, because I have a mother and father who love me. I'll not leave them and become your *maid,*" she spat the word, "just to have better food on the table." *If it is actually any better than Mama and I make anyway.*

Genevieve raised an eyebrow. "Even though I could also provide better food for them as well?"

Recognizing that she wasn't getting her point across on her own, Lilia withdrew the knife she kept on her at all times. She calmly began to clean her fingernails with it. Genevieve's eyes went wide, and she took an involuntary step back. She put a hand on her hair, as if remembering their little disagreement from when they were children. "I have actually had this discussion with them," Lilia replied nonchalantly. "They don't want me working as a maid, either, especially for someone like you."

Genevieve took another step back and hissed, "Put that thing away, you—"

To Lilia's relief, Sir Calem suddenly appeared at her elbow, cutting off what was likely a very unladylike reply. "Pardon the interruption, ladies, but my business here is concluded." His eyes flashed to the knife and he raised an eyebrow. "Would you please lead me to the next candidate, Miss Lia?"

Lilia almost jumped for joy, she was so grateful for the offered escape from Genevieve's presence. She gave the knight a grateful smile. "O' course, Sir Knight," she said, her 'vulgar' accent back in full force. She turned to the duke and dipped a curtsy. "Farewell, Yer Grace."

The duke gave her a smile and a nod. "Until we meet again."

If only every meeting with him didn't have to include seeing her, Lilia thought as she turned to Genevieve. She offered the girl a polite nod. "Farewell, Miss Genevieve." Despite their constant animosity, she sincerely did wish the girl well. She also wished not to have to cross paths with her again anytime soon.

Genevieve returned the pleasantry with a glare. "Miss Lia," she responded through gritted teeth.

Relieved that the farewells were over, Lilia turned and left the manor without a backwards glance. Her stride was even faster than when they had arrived. Sir Calem was on her heels once again.

As soon as they were out of sight of the manor, Sir Calem suddenly took her by the elbow. "Miss Lia, wait."

As she turned to face him, she also took a step towards him, misjudging how close he already was. This left them altogether too close, and as she looked into his stormy blue eyes, her heart raced. "Yes, Sir Knight?" Her voice was hardly recognizable. It had an almost airy quality to it that she'd never used before.

He seemed as stunned as she felt and he held her gaze for a moment, studying her eyes, her face. Then, he took a deep breath and let it out, creating emotional space between them, if not physical space. "The visit appears to have caused you distress."

That's putting it mildly, Lilia almost said in reply.

"I would like to make certain you are well before we return to the inn."

His concern made her heart beat even faster. Needing to escape his gaze, she looked down and took a subtle step back. "I'm feelin' better now that I ain't in her presence," she mumbled.

Since she was looking down, she saw his hands balling fists momentarily at her words. He was silent for a moment before replying. "Was she unkind to you?" His voice was strained, as if he was offended on her behalf.

"Yes, but not more than usual, so I'm used to it." She sighed. "There be no need to worry over me." He didn't respond, which drew her gaze back to his face. His jaw was clenched, and he took a couple of deep breaths in an obvious attempt to control his anger.

After a moment, he said, "Very well. I will do my best not to worry." He took another breath, and then managed a small grin. "Besides, I have fewer options for saving you from a lady than I do if it were a gentleman." He chuckled a little, which seemed to help him release more tension. He then stood straight again. "Alright, where are we headed now?"

She sighed with relief at the change in topic and return to formality. "We be headed ta visit a friend o' mine, a Miss Gloria." She turned around again and resumed her quick pace. "She lives on the far side o' the inn from here, so we can stop an' get yer companion on the way if you'd like," she tossed over her shoulder.

He caught up with her quickly, matching her pace to walk beside her. "I told you that I wouldn't make you suffer his company, Miss Lia. Besides," he said as a grin appeared on his face again, "I am not sure he will be at all willing to leave his room, sporting the bruise you gave him."

Lilia couldn't prevent the smirk that forced its way onto her face. "Had it comin' 'e did."

Sir Calem let out a laugh, the sound making her heart skip a beat. "You'll get no argument from me on that score. He has embarrassed me more than once these past two months going on like that, though I believe you are the first to be offended rather than flattered by his attention."

"Oi, that be a long time to endure some'n like 'im."

"True," he replied with a nod, "but he has also become a brother to me in that time. Thinking of him that way has helped me to more easily endure him."

Lilia nodded in approval. "Sounds like a good strategy, Sir Knight." Recognizing he had given her the choice of how to proceed, she pondered just how she wanted to continue. Her pondering was interrupted by a grumble of her stomach, reminding her that they'd departed without breakfast. "Well, we probably ought ta stop at the inn for somethin' ta eat, whether we bring him along or not." The mention of food seemed to make the knight's stomach grumble in reply, and he nodded in agreement to her plan.

When they reached the inn, Sir Calem inquired after the other knight, and was informed that the man had yet to make an appearance. Glad that she didn't have to deal with him at the moment, Lilia shrugged and requested some of whatever they had for breakfast. Sir Calem did as well, and then glanced at the stairs. He wore a concerned frown. Lilia sighed and took his hand to guide him to a table. "What be on yer mind, sir?" She asked, despite having a good idea what, or at least whom, he was thinking about.

"I've naught seen him sleep this late," he replied. "I hope he is feeling well."

"I'm sure he be fine," she replied. Then she grinned. "Like you said, 'e be nursin' a sore face."

The smile she had seen hints of, the one she realized she'd been waiting for, finally made an appearance. He then chuckled heartily. "That is quite true. Actually, even he was impressed with how hard you hit him. He's not likely to be thrilled with you, though. He likes to keep his face unmarred, unless it is by marks of battle. Those he uses to gain sympathy from the ladies."

Lilia rolled her eyes at the picture he had painted. "O' course 'e does. I'd wager he'd be angry for bein' nicked from shaving because it ain't a proper wound, rather than on account of it hurtin'." Sir Calem chuckled at the suggestion. She joined in. After their laughter calmed, he found herself unable to hold back from asking, "What of you, Sir Knight?"

Without missing a beat, he replied, "I avoid attracting the ladies' attention as much as possible."

"Shame," she replied. He looked at her, then, and searched her face. She wondered if he found what he was looking for. She felt her cheeks redden slightly, but she continued. "Ye should be lookin' for a bride."

"Well, if things were different, I would hope to attract someone with more intelligence than most of the women I've met on this trip have displayed." Seeming to realize how rude he had sounded, he cleared his throat. "Forgive me. They have all been more intelligent than what I said makes them sound. It's just... nearly all of them deliberately hid their intelligence, because they think all men wish for an obedient wife that thinks only what her husband wants her to think. Which, admittedly, many do."

Like Bob, she thought grimly. "An' you don't?"

He held her gaze as he shook his head. "I would rather wed a woman that can and will argue with me over anything we disagree on, one that isn't afraid to voice her opinion. I want fire I cannot shape and needs to be respected, not lifeless clay I can mold into whatever shape I want."

Lilia sat stunned, and as his words sank in, her heart beat faster. *Him. He's the kind of man that I have been waiting for, someone that will love me for me, like how Papa loves Mama.* Unsure of what to say, she looked down, noticing for the first time that their food had arrived. She stuffed a bite into her mouth so she wouldn't feel the need to answer, although he didn't seem to be waiting for a response.

Without warning, they heard a thump, followed by a groan, come from upstairs. Both of them turned their attention to the staircase. When no one appeared, they returned to their food, eating in silence. After several minutes passed, they heard footsteps, and soon the larger knight lumbered down the stairs. By all appearances, he had just awoken minute earlier. He still seemed to be shaking off the last of his sleepiness.

Lilia searched his face. Sure enough, an ugly purple bruise covered a large part of it. Seeing the damage, Lilia felt bad about how hard she'd hit him. Sir Calem, however, didn't seem to share her sorrow. Instead, he laughed at his traveling companion's condition. "So, you are among the living, then, Gerald?"

Sir Gerald glared in reply. "Silence, Calem."

Lilia looked over at Sir Calem to find him smirking, his eyes full of mirth. She could also tell he was thinking about something. He cast a quick glance at her before saying, "You look like you could use some practice to wake up, my friend."

Lilia sat up straighter and jumped into the conversation. "Mind if I be 'is opponent?"

Sir Gerald scoffed. "You?"

Lilia stood and put her hands on her hips. She raised an eyebrow and said, "Ye doubt me? Even after..." She mimed her slap from the day before.

Sir Gerald raised and eyebrow. "You're still a girl, and I'm a trained knight."

The conversation had drawn the attention of others in the room. "Oh, boy," the innkeeper moaned. He turned to Lilia. "Miss Lia, I ask that you please take this outside."

Lilia saluted the man and grinned. "O' course!" She then turned to Sir Gerald. "Come on, knight." Brimming with confidence, she strode outside into the stable yard. The inn's patrons, which included many of the residents. of the village who stopped in for their morning meal, all followed them.

All but Sir Calem, she quickly realized. However, he appeared a moment later with a pair of wooden swords. She shot him a curious look, as she was expecting a fisticuffs match. He nodded his head towards the duke's manor, and she remembered what the duke had said to him earlier. She smiled and nodded in reply. Now was as good a time as any for this.

Sir Calem expertly wove through the crowd, which was growing by the moment. People out and about their business seemed to notice the hubbub, and wanted to watch as well. He approached the spot where she and Sir Gerald stood already facing one another. Sir Calem presented a sword to each of them. Sir Gerald was slow to accept his. He seemed even more loath to take up a blade against a girl than to engage in a fistfight. So, Lilia took hers first and settled into a ready stance.

This was enough to convince Sir Gerald that she knew what she was doing, and he took his blade as well.

"Five hits, or until one yields or is disarmed," Sir Calem declared. The audience, now seeing they were to be treated to a sword fight, backed away further, to give the combatants sufficient room to work with. Sir Gerald also stepped back a pace as he settled into his own stance.

Sir Calem held his hand above their blades. "En guarde," he announced, filling Lilia with excitement. It had been a long time since she had faced a truly skilled opponent, and she relished the opportunity.

Sir Calem glanced at both. Seeing that they were ready, he dropped his hand and shouted, "Allez!" He backed out of the way.

Lilia was on Sir Gerald in a second, pressing her attack hard. The large knight stepped back in surprise, and she saw a hint of doubt enter his gaze. She gave the normally cocky man a malicious grin as she stepped back. *Let him think he knows what he's up against now.*

Either her grin served to motivate him, or he thought he saw an opening, for he launched into his own attack. His cocky smile dropped into an angry glare as he did so.

She easily blocked his initial thrust, and danced away from his follow up, taunting him with a feigned yawn. He slashed at her, but she stepped away again. Another slash. This time, she swung as she dodged, halting her blade inches from his face. Even a dull wooden sword, could have blinded him had she followed through and struck him. They both stood frozen for a moment. Sir Gerald's eyes were wide and full of surprise and fear.

"A hit," Sir Calem announced quietly, for the maneuver counted a such.

The surprise in Sir Gerald's eyes was replaced with determination as he returned to his stance. He attacked again, faster and stronger now. He was easier to read, though, and she parried or dodged each blow. She also landed three more hits in quick succession during his angry volley. One hit his arm, another his leg, and the last his side.

Sir Gerald realized his predicament and backed away, allowing her a moment to look around. The crowd had grown even larger. As she and Sir Gerald began to slowly circle each other, she spotted her parents among the spectators. She could see that both of them wore concerned frowns, as they usually did if they saw her using a sword.

She generally hated to disappoint them in any way, but in this, those frowns gave her courage. *I'll show you this really is something I can do well,* she thought as she saluted them with a grin, even as she danced away from another attack. Her mother's look turned questioning, and she nodded towards the two knights, then to Lilia. Lilia understood. Her mother had some questions for her once the fight was over.

"You are formidable," Sir Gerald panted.

His words made Lilia grin. "I've had many years to practice."

"As have I," he replied with a glare, "and I shall show you them now!" He launched himself at her again, another flurry of strong attacks. He nearly penetrated her guard this time, and she twice blocked him with her sword braced against her body, just managing to get it in place ahead of his strikes. She now recognized that he had still been holding back, and only now was he showing his full strength. When he went for an overhead strike, she blocked and sidestepped at the same time. As she let her blade fall away from his, the loss of resistance sent him off balance, and before he could recover, she had her blade resting against his throat.

"Five hits!" Sir Calem called out.

The crowd cheered, elated that their hometown hero had bested the large knight.

Lilia looked over at her opponent and was surprised to find that, though still visibly frustrated, he wasn't angry. She raised a questioning eyebrow, to which he responded with a malicious grin. "You have bested me, fair maiden. Now you must face my second."

Lilia's eyes widened. "Who is that?" she asked, even though she already knew the answer.

Sir Calem stepped forward, eagerness clear on his face. Sir Gerald handed him the wooden sword, which he gladly accepted. "I am," he replied, a genuine smile on his face.

Lilia's heart skipped in her chest. Something told her this man was not on the same level as his companion. No, he was far better, as if she had been facing the apprentice and now faced the master. She closed her eyes and took a deep breath. When she let it out, she forced her nerves to leave with it. She opened her eyes and held up her sword.

Five

Calem was filled with excited anticipation. From the moment the duke had mentioned Miss Lia's skills with a weapon, he had looked forward to having a chance to face her. He felt somewhat indebted to his friend for giving him the chance so soon.

Calem and Miss Lia both took their ready stances, and Gerald held up his hand. Calem tensed as he waited for the hand to drop, expecting Miss Lia to press a hurried attack as she'd done with Gerald. Looking at her, though, he saw nothing but patience in her posture. It was as if she planned to wait for him to make the first move.

Sure enough, when Gerald gave the signal, neither moved towards the other. Instead, he began to circle to the left, wanting an idea of her footwork. She copied the movement with fluid grace. Their gazes met, and he stared into her eyes. He searched those eyes for any clues, any tells she might expose.

"Are you afraid, Miss Lia?" he asked. If she was, she hid it well. "Why do you not come at me as you did my companion?"

She raised an eyebrow, as if finding his accusations ridiculous. "My intuition has never failed me."

He let out a small smile. "And what does your intuition tell you about me?"

She stopped pacing. She held her sword in a defensive position, as if sensing something from him. "To be cautious. That you have more natural talent that he." Calem noticed that she spoke in refined tones, no trace of her usual countryside lilt. However, he was still in a fight, no matter that they were both motionless at the moment, so he tucked that information away for later.

At the same time, Gerald let out a bark of laughter in response to Miss Lia's verbal jabs at him. "That he does, little lady. Have you ever heard of the Lightning Knight?"

Miss Lia's eyes went wide and she let out a gasp. A murmur of similar reactions spread through the crowd of spectators. "You are he?" she asked Calem.

Calem's small smile turned into a grin, and he nodded. Taking advantage of her surprise, he launched into an assault. He didn't gain much advantage, however. Miss Lia's eyes narrowed in concentration as she blocked or deflected every blow. Nothing could be heard but wood on wood and grunts of exertion for a full five minutes. Then, as if on cue, they both stepped apart at the same time. They even panted in unison as they recovered from the barrage.

Once sufficiently recovered, Miss Lia stepped into a more aggressive stance, but stumbled. Seeing her off balance, Calem grinned again and went in for another attack. He was surprised to find it had been nothing but a feint, and suddenly he was blocking *her* attack. He found himself surprised by the flurry of strikes she let out that rivaled what he had just dealt to her only a few moment earlier.

As he defended himself, he watched for any sign of weakness, any opening he could exploit. When they again parted a few minutes later, he felt he had found one. She fought in something of an erratic pattern. She repeated the same dozen or so attacks in sets. It was slightly unpredictable, for they were always in a different order, but she always executed all of the moves before starting again. This gave her attacks a long rhythm that he may be able to break.

Once again, a grin broke out on his face. "My friend was right, you are a formidable opponent." He searched her face before he continued. "However, you have a weakness."

To his astonishment, her expression didn't change at all. The only indication she had heard him was the slightest dip of her sword. "Very observant, Sir Knight."

He was surprised to realize that she was completely aware of her shortcomings, yet able to remain confident. She was so confident, in fact, that he wasn't sure he could actually use that opening after all.

She must have seen his hesitation, because she launched at him again. Her attacks were faster this time, something he hadn't thought possible. It took every ounce of skill he possessed to keep her blade at bay. However, the pattern was still there, and he saw his opening. Her final move of a set would be an overhead strike. Instead of blocking, like he normally did, he stepped in and caught her sword arm with his off hand, bringing his own blade around for a similar strike.

Yet, she seemed to anticipate this, for her hand was there to catch him before he could land his blow.

There they stood. They were breathing heavily, inches

apart. Their left hands held their opponent's right wrists, with right hands holding swords.

"Draw!" Gerald called.

Calem barely heard him as any sound but their breathing faded from his awareness. This fiery lady's gaze held him captive, except for a small moment when his eyes flicked to her lips instead. His eyes snapped back to hers. He realized then that, were he not who he was — a knight with years of chivalry ingrained in him — he would have closed the scant inches between their lips.

Realizing the direction of his thoughts, he quickly sobered. It didn't matter how well matched he and this woman were. Nothing could ever come of a relationship between them. He was already betrothed, and he wouldn't dream of breaking the arrangement.

"You fight well," he rasped, his mouth suddenly dry.

Still unable to look away, he watched as a mask flew over her countenance. "As do ye, sir." There she was, back to her rough speech again. He wondered if it was something she used to defend herself.

He regretted the mask, but he knew it necessary, so he nodded and said, "Thank you for the practice."

She grinned. "Ye're most welcome, Sir Knight."

He looked towards the inn. "I find myself famished after that." He returned his gaze to her. "Would you care to join me?"

She glanced away, then shook her head. "I'm afraid I can't, sir. Me parents 'ave need of me at the moment."

He nodded. "Of course. Are you still able to direct me to Miss Gloria's residence later? Or should I have someone else take me there?"

She glanced around and nodded her head towards the road.

He looked to find a very irritated Bob sitting atop his wagon. "If yer needin' ta get there sooner than I can show ya, Bob can take ye." She lowered her voice. "Don't count on his bringin' ya back, though."

Calem grinned his understanding. "Thank you for the warning. I shall make sure to remember the way back in case he doesn't wish to wait around."

She nodded once more. Then she turned and walked towards a man and woman still lingering where the crowd had been standing. She had mentioned they were her parents, but he would have been able to tell without the warning. She didn't look much like either of them, but their expressions showed they clearly loved her. While her mother pulled her into an embrace and kissed her cheek, her father placed a hand on her head and gave her a fatherly smile.

At the sight of the happily gathered family, Calem had to turn away. The sight had made him painfully homesick for his own family. It had been over a year, nearly two, since he'd left home. He found himself wondering what his younger sisters and older brother were doing. A melancholy mood settled over him as he thought about how old his sisters would be when he saw them again.

His grumbling stomach interrupted his sad musings, and he found himself able to come out of it. His quest was almost over. He would see them soon. The thought made him smile, and, as he returned to the inn, he had a spring in his step.

He found Gerald waiting at a table with an extra plate of food, likely expecting Calem to be hungry. "I thought you'd be hungry after that," Gerald said, confirming the assumption.

Calem nodded his thanks as he sat down and started eating. "Thank you, I am," he said after swallowing his first bite.

After Calem had eaten a few bites, Gerald leaned towards him across the table. "You seem well matched with that one," he said quietly.

Calem couldn't help but agree, though he tried to keep his expression unaffected. "It does appear that way."

Gerald raised an eyebrow in disbelief. "That's all you have to say?!" he growled. When a couple of heads turned in their direction, he lowered his voice again. "I saw that look in your eyes, Calem. You wanted to kiss her, and I'll bet that only years of having chivalry hammered into you prevented you from doing so."

Calem was unable to keep the heat from his face, so he looked down at his food. "Nothing can come of it," he grumbled.

Gerald frowned. "Oh, yes, I remember now. Something about you being betrothed." He grinned. "Well, you're not married yet. Perhaps there's still a chance for you to choose your bride."

"And you think I should choose Miss Lia." Calem's tone was flat, even to his own ears.

"Yes." Gerald nodded for emphasis. Then he grinned again. "My fight with her has officially pushed her from my list of ladies to pursue. I could never marry a woman with the upper hand." Calem rolled his eyes. "But you... you two are a perfect match, Calem."

Calem's jaw tightened as his frustration with his companion rose, his earlier excitement at the thought of seeing his family forgotten. "I will not back out, Gerald. The cost would be too great. There are things at play here that I can't tell you about, not yet."

Gerald gave him a sad frown. "Don't you deserve to be happy, Calem?"

Calem gritted his teeth and slammed the table. This sent his cutlery clattering to the floor. "I told you it's not happening! So, stop!"

Obviously taken aback by the sudden outburst, Gerald's eyes went wide. He recovered quickly, however, and studied the smaller knight for a long, silent moment. "You're not looking forward to returning home, I'd wager. Not entirely, at least. As soon as you do, you'll be married off to whomever you're betrothed to. It seems to me that your anger stems from panic. Well, this girl you are promised to might change her mind, you know. You might get lucky."

Calem rubbed a weary hand over his face. "It's not that simple."

Gerald scowled. "You keep saying that. I wish you would tell me why," he grumbled.

Calem let out a sigh of resignation. "I cannot."

Gerald also sighed with resignation. "I know, I know."

They finished eating in silence before Calem brought up a new subject. "Now, would you like to go with me to visit the next lady?"

Gerald shot him an annoyed look. "What do you mean by 'next'? Have you already visited one of them?"

Calem nodded without apology. "Yes."

Gerald scowled. "Why did you not alert me?"

Calem held the man's gaze for a moment before answering. "Because my guide was displeased with your actions yesterday and didn't wish to be in your presence.

Gerald chuckled in understanding. "Ah, Miss Lia. I bet you enjoyed your walk with her," he said with a raised eyebrow.

Despite the heat rising to Calem's face, he scoffed. "Walk? If you must know, it was more of a run. She kept a quick pace that made me grateful to have left my armor upstairs."

Gerald stared at him. "You mean she hasn't caught on that walking slowly with a knight is what is expected of a young lady?" he asked with theatrical dismay.

Calem couldn't prevent the grin that escaped. "I don't think Miss Lia cares about what is expected of a young lady."

Gerald laughed. "No, I don't think she does. Well, tell me about this girl you've already visited. Would I like to take a look at her?"

Calem rolled his eyes. "She would be more than happy to receive you, but I have already said it may not happen."

Gerald's eyes widened. "She was that bad?"

Calem leaned across the table to keep his voice low. "She is the same age as Miss Lia, but she behaves like a spoiled child. I believe even you would be hard pressed to remain congenial in her company. What does it say about her that her guardian wishes to be rid of her, but at the same time, would not wish her on anyone?"

Gerald nodded his understanding. "Message received. I'll steer clear."

Calem nodded his approval. "Good. Now, let us go visit Miss Gloria."

To Calem's surprise, Gerald's eyes widened in tortured fear. "Miss Gloria, you say?"

Calem studied his friend for a moment. "Do you know her?"

Gerald became oddly distracted. "I know someone of that name, but it is a common enough name..."

Calem narrowed his eyes. "What are you not telling me, Gerald?"

The large knight hung his head, almost looking...defeated. "I met a young woman in Katiera that I fell quite in love with. If she ends up being the princess..."

Calem nodded, understanding. "I see. Well, the best thing we can do is go and see."

Gerald gave a distracted nod, then stood and exited the inn. Calem followed, more than a little concerned for his friend.

They found Bob waiting for them in the lane, sitting atop his wagon. "Knights," he said, nodding almost civilly to them. The knights returned the greeting. "Miss Lia says ye might be wantin' ta visit Miss Gloria."

Calem stepped forward, saving his friend for needing to answer. "Yes. Would you be so good as to direct us to her residence?"

Without changing his expression, Bob jerked his thumb at the wagon bed. "Hop in." Once the knights were both aboard, but before they were settled, Bob flicked the reins. The horses started forward. He was probably hoping to throw the knights off balance. Fortunately, they caught their balance easily enough, leaving Bob to grumble under his breath as they headed towards the edge of town.

Six

"WHO WAS THAT MAN YOU WERE SPARRING WITH, LILIA?"

The question made Lilia cringe. She knew, quite well, her mother's thoughts on fighting. Her mother liked neither fighting in general nor Lilia's swordplay. Her mother had told her to stop fighting every knight that came through town, but she just couldn't help herself. None of the men in the village would spar with her anymore. Even if they would, only the knights passing through were able to give her the challenge she craved.

Lilia was grateful that her mother at least waited until they were home to scold her.

"It was the legendary Lightning Knight, Mama."

Instead of the rebuke Lilia was braced for, her mother's eyes widened in amazement. "Oh!" It seemed even her mother understood just how much fighting him would mean to her. "How splendid for you! How did he measure up?"

Lilia's heart raced as she remembered how the match ended, how close they had been. She'd been unable to look away from his eyes. And then those eyes had flicked to her lips... "Neither of us could land a blow, Mama, so he measures up well."

Her father leaned on the table as he joined the conversation. "So..." he said, a look of pondering on his face, "a perfect match, eh?" He rubbed his chin. "Do you happen to know whether or not he's... unattached?"

Heat flooded Lilia's face. She looked between her parents. The look they were sharing made her feel something akin to panic. "Is this what you have called me home to discuss?" she demanded. "His eligibility?"

"Yes and no," her father replied. He sank into a chair and rubbed a weary hand over his face. "I'm getting on in years, princess. I want to make sure you are taken care of, and that you can take care of your good mother, if possible."

Now feeling concerned, Lilia sat at his knee and frowned. "So, are you angry with me for turning down Bob and all the other men in this village?" she asked quietly.

"No, sweetie," her mother replied. "None of them have been good enough for you." Her mother bent down and put a finger under Lilia's chin. She guided her daughter's head so their eyes met. "What we're saying is..." she took a deep breath, as if gathering courage, "we want to take you to Katiera."

Lilia's eyes widened as she shot to her feet. "You...what?!" She couldn't believe this was happening. "You want to take me..." Visions of what the grand city might hold swam through her head. She'd seen paintings of the royal palace in the duke's manor, but she couldn't imagine seeing it for herself. She thought of the grand balls, the beautiful gowns, and the handsome suitors that Genevieve would go on and on about. It was enough to set her heart racing as her head danced through the clouds.

Then her feet reminded her of their shoes, and she came crashing back down. Here, in her little village, she had her loving parents and her dear friends. The thought of leaving them all and never coming back brought tears to her eyes. "I don't want to go," she cried.

She then took a deep breath and paced as she sorted out her thoughts. Her parents had taught her to lay out her arguments logically and in an orderly manner. "I want to stay here with you. If I go to Katiera, I'll likely be married off to someone who will never let me see you again, lest he has the means to do so." She paused again, her emotions surging. "You cannot make me go!" She turned and ran before either of them could stop her.

Only the familiarity provided by many years of living in her humble home enabled her to escape, for as she rushed form the house, tears blinded her eyes. She heard her parents call her back, but she ignored them. She didn't want to say something she'd regret without having time to calm down first.

Instead, she ran towards the center of town. She needed some space, needed a friend to talk through with this. She paused and wiped her eyes as a thought struck her. She needed Gloria.

Grateful for a direction, she turned and started towards her friend's house at a dead run. Not long after leaving the village, she passed a startled Bob heading the same way, his wagon holding two passengers. He called out to her, but she wasn't in any mood to speak with him, so she kept running.

When she reached her friend's house, she was out of breath, but not out of tears. They still streamed down her face. Her friend must have either heard or seen her approach, for just as she was about to knock on the door, the lady herself pulled it open. She had a very worried expression on her face. "Lilia! What's wrong?"

When she tried to answer, Lilia was struck by the realization of how far she had run. She put a hand to the pain that flared in her side as she panted heavily. Gloria must have realized that her friend needed a moment before she could answer, for she gently pulled Lilia inside. She guided her to the drawing room and helped her into a chair.

Once Lilia was sufficiently recovered from her run, she began to speak, though emotion was still thick in her voice. "My parents..." she began.

Gloria sighed, cutting her off. "Want to take you to Katiera," she finished for her.

Lilia looked up sharply, surprise cutting off her tears. "How did you know? *Why* did you know before they told me?"

Gloria sighed again and settled onto the adjacent chair. She put a hand on her hair, as though checking to see if it still looked acceptable. She took longer than necessary to arrange her skirts. *Is she stalling?*

Finally, she took a deep breath and met Lilia's eyes. "They came to visit me yesterday."

Lilia's eyes went wide. "Really? Why?"

Gloria nodded to answer the first question, then said, "As you know, I only just returned from a stay in the capital. Your parents also knew this, and came to ask me if there were many eligible men there that might suit you. I told them that there were several whom I met, and likely many more I did not. They also asked about the state of the country, but I hadn't paid much mind to political talk, so I had little to say to reassure them on that score."

After another sigh, she continued. "In the end, I told them

all I could about that grand city. By the time they left, they were convinced you ought to go and seek out a husband. I told them you wouldn't take the news well. Judging by the manner of your arrival, they didn't listen to me."

Lilia wiped the tears from her eyes and gave her friend a watery smile. "I'm glad you understand me so well, Gloria. Speaking of your visit to Katiera, is now a good time for you to tell me about it?"

Gloria's next sigh was full of longing. "I absolutely loved it there, and I would go back without a second thought. The places I went, the events I attended, and most of the people I met were absolutely wonderful. I even fell in love." She sighed again, this time wistful. "Alas, he was in the midst of a quest for the king. He did promise to come find me once his quest was over, however."

Lilia smiled at her friend's starstruck expression. "What is the name of this man who has stolen the heart of my dearest friend?"

"Sir Gerald," Gloria said with a dreamy smile.

Lilia's eyes widened. *There's no way...he couldn't possibly be the same man.* "Do you happen to know if he is also known as the Flirting Knight?"

Gloria's eyes also widened in shock. "Why, yes," she replied slowly. "He is indeed. How could you possibly know that?"

Before Lilia could respond, Gloria's butler entered the room. "Sir Gerald and Sir Calem to see you, my lady," he said in his proper, stately tones.

Both women froze. Lilia had completely forgotten she had sent the knights this way. They must have been the passengers in Bob's wagon! Which meant they might have seen her crying...

She cringed just as Gloria said, "Let them in." The lady

almost succeeded in speaking normally, despite the emotions warring on her face.

The men entered, Sir Calem first, then Sir Gerald. Lilia's eyes were drawn to Sir Calem. Judging by his concerned expression, he *had* seen her crying as she had ran past them. She turned away as her face flooded with heat at her embarrassment.

This brought her eyes to Sir Gerald. He, however, only had eyes for the golden-haired beauty sitting next to her. "Gloria," he croaked, emotion thick in his voice.

Lilia studied him in surprise. They way he said her friend's name spoke deeply of his sincere love for her. His expression alone made his ridiculous flirting with her the day before pale in comparison. She had seen through his too-charming smile and flowery words on the instant, and she'd known his interest in her was not genuine. This was nothing like that.

It took a moment for Gloria to recover from her surprise enough to speak. "Gerald!" she exclaimed. "What on earth are you doing here?"

The larger knight got down on his knees in front of her and took her hands. "I will tell you, but first I must ask; who are your parents?" Lilia could hear desperation in his words.

Gloria hesitated, obviously confused by his sudden interest in her family history. "My father was the grandson of the Baron of Lankin, his father being the younger son. He had money and land, but wasn't anyone of consequence outside of his immediate circle."

"And you have proof of this?" Sir Gerald pressed.

"Yes, of course," she replied. "His brother owns this house and is my guardian. He has papers about my birth and his guardianship in his study."

Sir Gerald released a heavy breath and brought her hands to

his lips, kissing them gently. "You have no idea how relieved I am to hear it."

Gloria stared at him, again in obvious confusion. "I'm glad you have no objections to my family, but how does that relate to why you are here? I don't understand."

He looked back up at her, his face full of joy. All traces of desperation had vanished. "Do you recall that I was departing the capital on a quest, which prevented us from marrying then?" She nodded. "Well, the quest has brought me here to Farreden, to you. When I heard you might be the person we are searching for, I was worried I may have lost you."

His explanation obviously did little to relieve *her* confusion, but Lilia thought she was starting to understand. "Gerald, you still are making little sense. Who is it you are looking for, who matches my description? And why would you have lost me if I were her?"

Sir Gerald looked to Sir Calem. "May I tell her?"

Sir Calem studied first Gloria, then Lilia. His gaze lingered on her. He nodded. "Miss Gloria need not remain in the dark, and I trust Miss Lia with the secret." Lilia blushed at the unexpected compliment.

"You are certain?" Sir Gerald asked.

All eyes were on Sir Calem, but it was Lilia who held his gaze. Their eyes met for a long moment before he responded. "Tell your lady, Sir Gerald."

Sir Gerald's face and posture spoke of palpable relief as he turned back to Gloria. "Have either of you heard about how, early in the war, the king sent his young children into hiding?"

"Yes," Gloria said slowly. She still looked quite confused. Gerald looked to Lilia as well, and she nodded that she had heard the tale as well.

"Well, the princes have all been found and returned to the capital, but the princess is still missing. The man who took her from the castle was eventually captured by Malanna, but he had already delivered her to safety. They never were able to get her location out of him, from what we could learn. With the country now secure, we have been sent to search for her."

Realization dawned on Gloria's face. "And all that you have to go on is that she would be an orphan around my age, it seems."

"Exactly," the knight replied. "The king is rather desperate to find her, or to find out what happened to her. Not one of his loyal knights will rest until we can take him knowledge of her fate, if nothing else."

While the news satisfied Lilia's interest in the quest itself, it didn't explain why the knight had been so worried moments before, so she asked, "And what'll happen to 'er if she be found?"

Lilia jumped when Sir Calem was the one to answer. His tone was bitter as he said, "She will be taken to the palace to be reunited with her family for a time. Then she will be married off to the crown prince of Callarda, cementing the alliance that helped win the war."

Lilia didn't envy the girl her fate. "Poor girl," she muttered. Her eyes went wide and her hand flew to her mouth when she realized she'd spoken her thought aloud.

Sir Calem studied her for a moment. "What makes you say that?"

Lilia's cheeks flamed and she looked down. "Forget I said anythin'."

From the corner of her eyes, she saw Sir Calem's hand

clench at his side, then slowly relax, as if he was forcing himself to stay calm. "I'd genuinely like to know, Miss Lia."

Unsure if she believed him, or whether she should, she looked up into his eyes. His stormy blue eyes. There was no mocking in them; rather, she felt as if he truly wanted to know, needed to know, her opinion on the subject. She took a deep breath and said, "Who wants ta be a princess and marry someone she's never met?"

He raised an eyebrow. "I daresay most girls would be perfectly happy marrying someone they've never met, if that someone is a prince. That is partially why we've been so secretive about our mission."

She rolled her eyes. "Well, I *daresay* most o' those girls don' know what it's like ta be loved enough ta wish for it for themselves."

He was silent for a long moment and she couldn't look away from his eyes as his gaze turned probing, even piercing. "Is that what you wish for, Miss Lia?" His tone turned husky, his gaze intense. It was the end of their fight all over again, except nothing to interrupt them. She could feel energy rolling off of him in waves, something that heightened her awareness of him, and his of her, she was certain.

Rather than shrinking at the sensation, she felt stronger, able to stand proud and meet his gaze with her own. His gaze didn't drift to her lips this time, but she felt certain he was exercising every ounce of self control to keep himself from pulling her into his arms and kissing her. Part of her wished he didn't keep such a tight hold on his self control, for she almost ached for that embrace, that affection.

"With all me heart," she replied softly after a long moment.

Another long intense silence stretched between them until

he turned and strode to the window, breaking the spell that held them bound. She released a breath she hand't realized she'd been holding as her rational mind tamped down on the longing for his touch, his kiss... *Heavens! Am I in love with him?*

When he spoke his tone was clipped. "Then I wish you luck. It seems, however, that your luck in that regard has run dry here. Have you considered searching elsewhere for the love you seek? Perhaps you could find it among the eligible young men in Katiera, for instance."

She frowned. Katiera again? Why was everyone trying to get her to go to the capital? Never mind how quickly Sir Calem had closed himself off again. Setting that question aside, though, she voiced another, more pressing question. "Would they let me come back here ta visit me parents?" She tried to make the question sound casual, but she could hear the tremor of fear in her voice.

He continued peering out the window. "I am certain that, if you found someone who loves you as much as you hope for, he would move mountains if you asked him to. Coming back here would be a simple enough request, provided he has the means to see to it."

Lilia pondered the idea for a moment. Perhaps he was right. Perhaps her parents were right. The fact that both he and they had suggested traveling to Katiera without any connection between them made the idea worth considering, at the very least. Gloria did speak in glowing terms of her own time there...

Thinking of her friend reminded Lilia that Gloria and Sir Gerald were still both in the room. Turning to them as if she hadn't forgotten all about them for several minutes, she addressed her friend. "What think you, Gloria? Would I like the capital?"

Gloria's eyes lit with excitement. They dimmed slightly, however, as caution entered her expression. "I don't know about you finding a husband there, though there is certainly a chance, but I do think you would enjoy going regardless. There are so many things to do and see there! If you do decide to go, let me know! Though I've just returned, I already long to go back." She smiled widely as she continued. "I could take you around to all the wonderful people I met! It would be so much fun!"

Fun. The idea of going for fun took root in the cracks of her resolve to stay in Farreden. She wouldn't be turning her back on home if she was just taking a trip there. If, by chance, she did make a match there and return home with a husband, or at least betrothed, so much the better. She made up her mind in that instant to only accept a man who would respect her attachment to her home. "I'll think about it."

Gloria clapped her hands with glee.

Seven

"ARE YOU DAFT MAN?!" AFTER VISITING MISS GLORIA, THE men had returned to the inn. Gerald had obviously wanted to speak with Calem, for he followed the shorter man into his room instead of proceeding to his own. At least Gerald had waited for Calem to get comfortable before hounding him. After Gerald's initial outburst, he went and stood by the window.

As for himself, Calem laid on the bed and closed his eyes. He deserved the rebuke, he knew that, and he was grateful his friend wasn't afraid to deliver it. "I lost my head," he mumbled, the most justification he could come up with.

"You most certainly did, you fopdoodle!" In any other situation, Calem would have taken offense at being compared to a mindless donkey. However, this was milder than what he had been calling himself since forcing himself to walk away from Miss Lia rather than kiss her. Gerald's well-founded exasperation laced every word as he continued. "Will you *please* tell me what is keeping you from courting that girl?!"

Calem stared sightlessly at the ceiling. "I have already told you that I cannot."

Gerald growled. "What's so important about this union that you cannot break it for the sake of happiness?"

Calem sighed. He knew he had to give the man *something*, otherwise, he would never hear the end of it. "All I can say is that lives would almost certainly be lost if I were to renege. I cannot tell you more than that. Indeed, I have been *forbidden* from telling anyone about it." He sighed again, his thoughts feeling even heavier. "Once I am no longer obliged to keep it secret, you will be the first to know."

Gerald huffed, which was an improvement from the growl, at least. "I should hope so. You have been terrible company almost since the moment we came upon that girl. You have bounced between excited and miserable, with miserable being dominant. Do you have any idea how difficult you are to be around when you are miserable?"

Calem pinched the bridge of his nose. He did, in fact, know he was an absolute bear to those around him when he was miserable. "I'm sorry, Gerald."

"As well you should be," Gerald grumbled in reply. After that, silence lay between them for several minutes. While Gerald appeared to be watching the street below, Calem continued berating himself silently as he stared, once again, at the ceiling. Gerald took a heavy breath to calm himself before turning toward Calem. "Now, what is the plan for tomorrow?"

Calem sat up, grateful to change topics away from his stupidity and on to business. "There is another girl who lives far enough distant that Miss Lia did not think it wise to visit her today as well. Then, there is another girl who is due to return the following day."

Gerald nodded, but then pinned Calem with a studying gaze for a long moment. "Do you think it wise to spend so much time with Miss Lia?" he asked, his question quiet but penetrating. "Perhaps it would be wiser if I were to ask Miss Gloria to accompany *me* and Miss Lia to visit the next candidate."

As much as the suggestion stung, it made sense. While Calem didn't wish to be out of her presence for so long, it would be wise to do so. As he considered the plan, another idea formed, one that actually required that both his friend and Miss Lia be occupied elsewhere. "That may be the wisest plan. I could probably use a reprieve from both the search and our guide. Besides, I have been wanting to visit the blacksmith anyway." He looked up and grinned. "You know I can never pass up the opportunity to find my perfect blade." Gerald nodded. "So, while you accompany Miss Gloria and Miss Lia, I will see to a few things around here."

As he made the suggestion, he saw a foolish grin spread across Gerald's face. He was obviously excited to spend more time with his lady. "Well then, I had best go ask my love if she is available." He stood and moved to the door, but turned back before opening it. "Do you have plans for the rest of the evening? I daresay there are several hours yet before the sun goes down. There may not be enough to meet with this other friend of Miss Lia, but surely there is something you can do."

Calem was struck with a sudden bolt of inspiration. He quickly climbed off the bed. "Actually, I have some business I wish to discuss with His Grace." He considered Gerald for a moment before continuing. "If I am not back here yet by the time you return from speaking with Miss Gloria, you may join me there. However, I suggest you do not."

Gerald grinned, obviously remembering what Calem had

told him of His Grace's ward. "I think I'll pass on the invitation. Now that you know where my heart lies, I no longer wish to keep up my Flirting Knight persona around you, or anyone, if I can help it." He sighed as if a weight had been lifted from his shoulders. "It was useful when we were in need of information, but I hope to be able to resign from it when we return to the capital."

Calem let out an amused chuckle. "I always wondered why you kept it up."

Gerald stared at the younger man. "You knew it was a ruse?"

Calem shook his head. "Not at first. However, we've been together long enough that I was able to see the annoyance you hid even as you sounded perfectly sincere."

Gerald let out a chuckle. "You really are quite observant. Miss Lia hit the nail on the head with that observation."

Miss Lia...the name made Calem freeze in his tracks, which made the other knight chuckle again. Face red, Calem glared at his friend. "I'm leaving now. I'll be back in time for supper, if I don't return before you do."

Gerald laughed. "Good luck, old boy."

They exited the inn together, stepping into the stable yard. Calem's head was still full of thoughts of Miss Lia, and he jumped when she stepped out of his horse's stall as he approached. "Miss Lia." He couldn't hide the surprise in his voice, and he hoped she wasn't offended by it. After discussing her not long ago, he wasn't prepared to see her at that moment.

To his relief, she didn't seem to be too offended. She simply nodded to him. "Sir Knight." Why did he like it so much when she called him by that moniker, especially since now it was a sign of her annoyance with him? "I were just seein' to the horses. Did you need yours? I can saddle 'im for ya."

"No, thank you. I like to do it myself." He went and took the saddle from the tack wall, then proceeded to enter the stall and throw it over Stoneheart's back.

Instead of leaving, she stepped over to Gerald's horse. "And you?" she asked.

"Yes, please," the other knight replied.

She nodded and grabbed the saddle from where it sat next to Calem's. "Judgin' from yer grin, I'd say yer goin' back to see Miss Gloria," she said with a glance back at Gerald. Then she met Calem's eyes over the rail between the stalls. "What 'bout ye?"

"I have some business to discuss with His Grace," he replied quickly.

She grimaced. "Good luck avoidin' Miss Genevieve."

Despite his resolution to keep things neutral between them, Calem couldn't help but chuckle. "Thank you."

She responded with a dazzling smile. Maybe she wasn't as upset as he thought.

Feeling the sudden need to be out of her presence before he did something rash, Calem quickly finished saddling Stoneheart and left the stables. As he rode to the duke's manor, he couldn't help but remember his journey there that morning. He shook his head, trying to find a moment where he *wasn't* thinking of her. The fact that she was the subject of his discussion with the duke made the problem even more difficult.

There was a stable boy waiting to take his horse as he entered the courtyard around the duke's home. He dismounted and handed over his reins. He went to the door and knocked. A staid butler showed him into the drawing room to wait for His Grace.

The duke appeared swiftly. "Sir Calem, what brings you back so soon?"

Calem took a deeb breath. "Sir, I need help."

The duke's expression grew concerned. he shut the door, likely to ensure privacy. "Is something wrong?"

Calem sook his head. "On the contrary. I have come up with a scheme that involves achieving my objective without a *certain someone* becoming aware of the real plan."

The duke raised an eyebrow in surprise. He took a seat, and motioned for Calem to do the same. Once they were both seated, he replied. "If you are referring to Miss Lia, you have no idea what game you will have to play. She is more observant that anyone I have ever met."

Calem nodded. "I have seen as much. Seeing as you know her so well, I hope you can tell me whether my plan has a chance of success." Reading the tension in the duke's posture, Calem decided to sweeten the pot. "My plan would likely take your ward off of your hands for a little while."

The duke leaned forward in his chair. "I'm listening."

Calem grinned. "Good." He stood and started pacing. "First, while she seems unaware that she is not originally a blacksmith's daughter, I think Miss Lia is the object of our quest."

The duke's eyes widened. "You think she is the princess?"

Calem gave a sharp nod. "Yes. When I first met her, she looked vaguely familiar. However, it took seeing her fighting back tears to finally realize she looks exactly like Her Majesty, the Queen."

The duke stroked his chin and stared at nothing for a

moment before nodding. "Of course, I see it now. I've rarely seen Miss Lia downtrodden — especially as an adult — which is a too familiar look on Her Majesty. Still... I should have seen the similarity before now."

Calem chose not to comment on the duke's reply. "So, I have come up with a plan that may get her to the capital." He stopped pacing and turned to meet the duke's eyes. "She isn't thrilled with the idea of going to the capital to find a husband, but she is otherwise at least intrigued with visiting there. So, if you were to ask her to go as companion to, no, *protection* for Miss Genevieve, she is unlikely to refuse you."

The duke gaped, then laughed aloud. "Of course! That should work splendidly!" He took a moment to catch his breath, but he was still beaming. "Lad, you are the first person I have ever met that knows how to deal so perfectly with Miss Lia. Her parents, or more properly her guardians, have recently expressed their desire to send her to the capital. We were at a loss as to how to achieve that end. You, who have only just met her, have figured her out completely." His eyes narrowed for a moment as he studied the young knight. "How is that, I wonder?"

Calem looked down and flushed, wishing he could hide his feelings from *someone*. "It matters not how that is." He met the duke's eyes again. "Now, are you willing to send your ward away?"

The duke let out an incredulous laugh. "Willing?! I will gladly pay for a whole new wardrobe for both her *and* Miss Lia if it means a few weeks without her here!" His expression then sobered. "Don't get me wrong, I care for the girl, but she is also quite a trial. Now, I imagine you will need a carriage."

Calem nodded. "It will likely be more comfortable for the ladies, sir."

The duke nodded. "And are you depriving our little village of anyone else?"

"Miss Gloria and my companion have an understanding from her own time in the capital, sir. Since the quest will soon be over, they will be able to wed soon enough. Aside from that, she also expressed a desire to return to the capital, and her presence would serve as extra incentive for Miss Lia to go."

The duke sighed and pinched the bridge of his nose. "I hope you realize you are taking two of the best women this village has to offer."

Calem nodded. "I do, sir, even if I haven't known either of them long."

The duke sat back and took a deep breath. "Well then, I will have to make sure Genevieve has sufficient money to be outfitted once they arrive. I would also like to see if I can persuade the blacksmith and his wife to allow me to do the same for Miss Lia."

Calem raised an eyebrow. "She'll not likely thank you for that, sir."

The duke chuckled again. "Probably not, lad, but she more than deserves it, and I am more than willing to give it to her." He sighed heavily. "That child has worked too hard over her lifetime here to be given anything less than a royal wardrobe."

"I agree," Calem replied with a nod. "Well, I will leave it to you to inform your ward."

He turned to leave, but to his surprise, the duke stood and stepped over to the door. He opened it and yelled, "Genevieve!"

Realizing the duke intended for him to wait, Calem remained where he stood. After a couple of minutes, Miss

Genevieve appeared in the doorway. "Yes, Your Grace?" she asked, her tone a little too sweet.

"I have some good news for you. I have finally received word from my sister that she is willing to let you come for a visit. Sir Calem, here, has agreed to accompany you, as his business will soon be finished. With him and Sir Gerald acting as your protection, I have decided to send you to the capital."

The girl's expression grew genuine and bright. "Really?!" Then her eyes narrowed. "What's the catch?"

The duke grinned. She knew him well, it seemed. "I'm going to be asking for Miss Gloria and Miss Lia to accompany you; Miss Gloria as your companion, and Miss Lia as your protection."

Calem watched her expression begin to crumble at the mention of Miss Lia's name. He was sure that, had he not been there, she may well have refused outright. She schooled her expression after a long moment. "Well," she huffed. "I cannot promise to get along with Miss Lia, but I will gladly put up with her for a few days if it means getting out of this dreary backwater." With that, she turned and gracefully stormed from the room.

The duke sat down and sighed, relief apparent on his face. "That went much better than I was expecting." He remained in his chair for only a moment, then stood again. "Now, I will go speak with the blacksmith."

Calem put a hand up to stop him. "If you would like, you could just write him a letter, sir. I plan to visit his forge tomorrow, and can deliver it to him then."

The duke nodded. "That is a good idea. After all, I now have a great many things to do, thanks to you." He grinned at the younger man. "Thank you. I'll write out the letter in my study and be back in a moment."

Calem nodded. As His Grace strode from the room, he retook his seat to wait. Only a few minutes passed before the duke returned with a letter in his hand. Calem stood and accepted it from him. "You have likely just saved me from insanity," the duke said, his sincere smile belying the jest of the words. "If there is something I can do for you in return, please let me know."

Calem grimaced. There was really only one thing he wanted for himself at the moment. "If you can figure out a way that I can end my blasted betrothal without restarting the war, I would consider your debt paid in full, and then some."

The duke's eyes went wide when he realized just was Calem was asking. "You speak almost treason," he whispered.

Calem rubbed both of his temples with the thumb and index finger of the hand that wasn't holding the letter. "I know."

The duke narrowed his eyes and studied the younger man for a long moment. "It is Miss Lia, isn't it?"

Calem dropped his gaze and nodded, his face heating. "She is unlike any woman I have ever met, and not just because she fought me to a draw with our swords."

The duke studied him for a moment longer, then grinned childishly. "I will see what I can do."

Eight

WHEN LILIA ARRIVED AT THE INN THE NEXT MORNING, SHE was surprised to find both Gloria and Sir Gerald waiting for her, seated in the common room. Sir Calem, on the other hand, was nowhere to be seen. Lilia stared at her friend in confusion. "Are we all goin' ta visit Miss Angelica?"

While Gloria nodded, it was Sir Gerald who answered verbally. He stepped forward and executed a much more appropriate bow that he had given her thus far. "Yes, good lady. If you have no objections, Sir Calem has requested that I accompany you and Miss Gloria to visit the next lady today. He, unfortunately, won't be joining us, as he has some other business to see to."

Lilia hoped her disappointment didn't show. "I guess I'll git us a ride, then," she replied, turning to search out someone with a wagon.

"There is no need," Sir Gerald said. "I have already secured us a ride."

Lilia felt a pit of dread build in her stomach. "Don' tell me…"

"Y'all ready ta go?" The three of them turned to where Bob had called for them just outside of the door.

"We are," the knight replied. He stood and helped Gloria to her feet, then crossed to the entryway. "I asked our friend Bob to assist me in retrieving my darling this morning. It only made sense to ask us if he could also convey us to our next destination," he told Lilia as they passed where she stood rooted in place.

She mutely felt into step behind them. Not only was Sir Calem not joining them, but Bob *was*. She and Sir Gerald assisted Gloria into the wagon, but as the knight went to assist Lilia in as well, Bob cleared his throat. "I need Miss Lia ta sit in the front, Sir Gerald," he said. "The seat ain't broad enough for you an' I ta both fit, an' there ain't enough room in the back for three."

Lilia looked in the back of the wagon, praying he was wrong and hoping her rising annoyance didn't show. Sure enough, with his other goods and tools in the wagon, there was only space for two to sit comfortably. She knew from experience that sitting perched on the back rail was trouble, otherwise she would have attempted it. She could also see that Sir Gerald was broad enough that he would likely hinder the equally-broad Bob's ability to control the reins.

Resigned to her fate, she cast Gloria a long-suffering look. She received an apologetic one in return. Then she rounded the wagon and climbed up next to Bob, ignoring his outstretched hand. She tried to settle herself in such a way that she wasn't touching Bob, but he was sitting nearly centered on the bench.

In order to keep their legs from touching, she was forced to loop an arm through the one he offered her in order to stay balanced.

"So, where to?" Bob asked once Lilia was settled. "Sir Gerald said you was the one who'd know who yer gonna visit."

Lilia closed her eyes and counted to ten before opening them. "Ta visit Miss Angelica," she replied with a sigh.

"Perfect! I been needin' ta see her uncle, anyhow," Bob replied He looked toward the yard of the inn. "Is the other knight not comin'? I figured he'd be ridin' alongside."

Lilia shook her head. She mentally cursed Sir Calem for leaving her in this situation with now more explanation than having "other business".

Bob smiled like a cat who'd got to the cream, then flicked the reins to set his mismatched pair of horses walking through town, the wagon rolling behind them.

Between the uncomfortable arrangements and the sorry state of the road in the forest, the next few hours were sheer torture. Lilia endured it largely by imagining the various ways she would thump an apology out of Sir Calem the next time they crossed blades.

Lilia almost shouted for joy when she saw the home of the local apothecary through the trees. The man alternately lived in the forest, where many of his herbs grew wild, and above his shop in town so he could tend to the residents. Occasionally, however, he had to travel further afield to purchase supplies not found near Farreden. He had been doing so the last few days, which had delayed this meeting. The smoke rising from the chimney reassured her that he had returned on schedule.

By the time they arrived, it was nearly midday. Almost before the wagon fully stopped, Lilia leapt from the seat, all but slapping Bob's hand away in the process, and ran inside. "Uncle 'Arry!" she called.

The apothecary appeared a moment later. "Miss Lia!" He gave her a one armed embrace, as his other arm was full of some herbs. "How wonderful to see you today! I thought you were coming tomorrow."

Lilia motioned outside. "You 'ave some visitors today, sir. Two knights arrived in the village a couple o' days ago, lookin' fer someun'. One of 'em is 'ere ta speak with ya."

Harry, or Uncle Harry as nearly everyone called him, adjusted his spectacles and looked out at the wagon. "Ah, I see. They wish to speak with me about Angelica's past, no doubt. I heard about the search in my travels."

Lilia nodded. "Just so, sir."

He studied her for a moment. "Do you know who they are searching for? I have an educated guess, but I'm not entirely certain."

Knowing he would be able to see through any lie she might attempt, she nodded. "I do know, but I'm not at liberty ta say."

Uncle Harry nodded in understanding. "I see. Well, bring them in."

Lilia returned to the wagon. Making sure to stay out of Bob's reach, she smiled at the occupants. "The apothecary bids ye welcome!" she announced theatrically.

Sir Gerald smiled and nodded, then jumped down from the wagon. He then turned to help Gloria down. His hands lingered on her waist for a moment, causing the young woman to blush. She gave him a smitten smile once he released her, then turned and walked toward the house.

Lilia walked along with her, hooking her arm through that

of her lovestruck friend. In a low voice, she asked, "So, is it official? Is you twos gettin' hitched?"

Gloria stopped and looked behind them. Lilia followed her gaze to find Sir Gerald watching them. The man winked at the pair of them. Gloria giggled. "Yes, Lilia, we are," she replied, turning to face forward again.

"I'm so 'appy for ye!" Lilia said with a wide smile as they resumed walking.

Gloria sighed more heavily than Lilia was expecting. Lilia turned her head to look at her friend while not slowing their pace. "Thank you," Gloria told her. "I was afraid you may be angry or upset, since it means I will be leaving for the capital again, for good this time."

Lilia shook her head. "I know what I said yesterday, but 'tis my feelin's for m'self. I knew ya prob'ly wouldn' always be here. Life goes on."

Gloria stopped again, turning so that she and Lilia faced each other fully. "Please come to Katiera and see me wed!" she requested. Her face shone with eagerness at the idea. "I would absolutely love for you to be part of the wedding. You are my dearest friend, Lilia."

Lilia frowned, the words filling her with twin desires: to see the capital and witness her best friend's big day, and a strong anticipatory longing for home. "I don't know, Gloria," she replied, her distress making her drop her rustic tone. "It's a long way from home."

Gloria let out a heavy sigh, but nodded. "I know. For now, just promise me you will think about it."

Lilia nodded. "I will."

Gloria looked about to respond, but a noise from the house drew their attention. A moment later, a bubbly girl emerged from the house, effectively ending their conversation. She smiled brightly when she saw Lilia, and began waving her hands excitedly. *You weren't supposed to come until tomorrow!*

Lilia could read the meaning of her gestures easily after years of practice. She released Gloria's arm so she could reply in kind. *Hello, Angelica. These people had some things to discuss with your uncle, and as I have been helping them, I decided to come with them. I'll try to come back tomorrow as well, but I may not be able to if they need my aid again.*

How intriguing! Angelica signed in reply. *What's going on?* Her hands moved almost too quickly for Lilia to read, as they often did when excited.

The stranger is a knight. He and his companion, and most of the knights by the sound of it, are looking for someone. A girl our age who was orphaned as a baby.

Well, I doubt they are too interested in me, since they are probably looking for a foundling and we know who my parents were.

I agree, but it is still best to check everyone.

"My dear, I am pretty sure they are saying something with all of those gestures, but for the life of me, I have no idea what." Lilia had been so engrossed in the conversation that she hadn't heard Sir Gerald approach.

Gloria wrapped her arms around one of his. "My love, this is Miss Angelica, the girl we have come to visit."

His eyes widened momentarily. "Is she deaf?"

Gloria nodded. "From birth, as I understand."

The knight looked more than a little concerned. "Do you think she is who we are searching for?"

Gloria shook her head. "No, but she does meet the qualifications, and you ought to be thorough.

He let out a sigh of relief. "That is true. Now, considering Miss Lia's shout earlier, I assume there is someone I can actually speak with without a translator who can answer my questions."

Gloria nodded and led him to the house. "Yes, her uncle is our resident apothecary. He is likely expecting us." Lilia and Angelica fell into step behind the couple. Lilia knew, without turning to see, that Bob was following as well. She could almost feel him watching her.

Gloria led them to a small drawing room, which was empty when they arrived. Before they were able to find seats, however, the apothecary appeared in the other doorway from the room. His eyes lit up when he saw Gloria among his company. Hers did as well. "Uncle Harry!" she said with a smile. "It has been an age."

Uncle Harry, as he was known to even those in the village older than himself, smiled. "Indeed it has been, dear Gloria, but seeing as how that means you and your uncle's house have been in good health, is that not a good thing?"

"It is indeed," Gloria replied with a laugh. She then turned and motioned to the knight, who still held one of her arms. "Uncle Harry, this is Sir Gerald. He is needing to know about Miss Angelica's past."

Uncle Harry pushed his glasses up his nose and turned to Sir Gerald. The men shook hands. Uncle Harry then motioned for the ladies to take a chair. Once they were seated, he offered Sir Gerald to do the same. After everyone was seated, the older man began, "Presumably, you need to know of her identity."

Sir Gerald nodded.

The older man continued. "Well, while most everyone calls me 'Uncle Harry', Angelica is my only actual niece, my brother's daughter. His wife died in childbirth—Angelica nearly did as well—and he himself fell in one of the earliest battles of the war. I was there for her birth, and have taken care of her ever since she was born."

Sir Gerald rubbed his chin in thought. "She is truly the daughter of a soldier?"

The older man nodded. "He was technically a farmer and an apprentice apothecary, but yes. He heeded the call of his king and died defending his country."

Sir Gerald gave the man a compassionate smile. "Well, then, that is the end of my questions. Thank you for your time. We will not keep you from your duties." He prepared to stand, but Gloria nudged him and tilted her heads toward Miss Angelica. The girl was signing rapidly to her uncle. Sir Gerald patiently waited until the signed conversation between the two ended before speaking again. "Or, perhaps not. What did she say?"

Uncle Harry smiled. "She has asked that I invite all of you to stay for the noon meal. Which I would have without her asking, especially when I have visitors at his hour. Considering our distance from town, I imagine you will be quite famished by the time you return to the inn if you do not."

Sir Gerald grinned in a way that made Lilia roll her eyes. "Far be it from me to refuse such an invitation. Is everyone else in agreement?" He looked to Gloria, Lilia, and even Bob for confirmation. Lilia reluctantly nodded. "Wonderful. Breakfast was several hours ago for me, and likely for Bob here as well, with how early we first set out."

The apothecary nodded, then stood. "Please, feel free to remain here and chat while I prepare it. Besides, Angelica has something to finish for Miss Lia, as she is here a day early. Since it would not do to make her return so soon, I cannot let her leave until Angelica is finished." The last he said with a mischievous wink and a smile before stepping from the room.

Angelica rose and departed as well, likely to finish her project. Gloria gave Lilia a confused frown. "What is she working on for you?"

Lilia smiled. "Every week, she 'as a new story for me to take and read to the children in the village. They 'ave quite come to depend on those stories, actually," Lilia knew her pride in her friends work shone in her voice. "I love 'ow I've been able to 'elp 'er find 'er voice and a way for our neighbors to come to know 'er."

Gloria and Sir Gerald both smiled. "How amazing!" Gloria replied. "I never knew either of you did that. A product of me living on the other side of town, I suppose. Do you have any of her previous stories that I could read? I am quite intrigued now."

Lilia chuckled. "Not with me. I do copy 'em, but I bring the originals back ta Uncle Harry, so he can keep 'em. But I warn ya, they are tough ta read. 'Er grammar is rather poor, ta put it mildly, so I always have ta do a bit o'...refinin' ta make them really make sense. I'm 'appy to interpret for ya, however. The stories themselves are beautiful, an' the children just adore 'em." She got to her feet. "I'll go ask where 'e keeps 'em.

Before she reached the doorway, however, the apothecary returned. "The food is ready, if you would all follow me." Once everyone was standing, he led the way to the kitchen, where four bowls of stew sat steaming. "Go ahead, eat up. I'll wait and eat with Angelica once she is ready."

Gloria, Sir Gerald, and Bob each took their seats, but Lilia waited a moment. "Uncle 'Arry, could ya bring us one of Angelica's stories while we eat? Gloria 'as expressed an interest."

"Of course. I'll be back in a moment." He left the room and Lilia seized the chance to move her bowl from the place next to Bob around to the foot of the table to sit adjacent to Gloria. She could tell he was not happy with the change, but he chose not to be rude and react to her retreat.

Uncle Harry returned a few moments later with a story, and between bits, Gloria attempted to read it. Her interpretation was rather horrid, making both Lilia and Sir Gerald laugh often.

Bob, on the other hand, sat quietly in his corner and mostly watched Lilia eat. She could feel his eyes on her again. From the corner of her eye, she could see his territorial gaze. It made her burn with anger. She had never given him *any* reason to believe his suit was being welcomed, yet the thick-headed buffoon seemed to be convinced she would eventually agree to marry him. *Well, he has no idea who he's up against,* she thought as she turned her focus back to Gloria.

Just as Lilia swallowed the last of her stew, Angelica appeared from the hall to her bedroom, where her writing desk was. She was waving a handful of papers excitedly in front of her. *I'm done!* she signed with her free hand.

Lilia got to her feet and accepted the papers. *Wonderful! I'll tell it to the children tomorrow.*

Thank you, Lia. You are a true friend.

Her words warmed Lilia's heart. She set the papers on the table to free up both hands. *You are as well. I do hope you will come to see the children some day so they can meet you. I'm certain the will love you*

Angelica blushed. *I don't know.* Her posture grew stiff and timid.

Just think about it, Lilia signed with a reassuring smile. Angelica visibly eased. Then a thought struck Lilia. *I might soon be going to the capital for a while, though, so if you want me to be there, it will have to be before I leave or after I return.*

The capital? How exciting! I promise to work up my courage so I can be ready when you get back.

Lilia smiled. *That sounds wonderful. Farewell, Angelica.*

Farewell, Lia. Safe travels.

Thank you. Lilia turned to retrieve the story and found Gloria and Sir Gerald watching her in confusion. She realized with where she had been standing, Gloria couldn't see most of what was said, and Sir Gerald, of course, didn't know what they meant. "I was jus' tellin' 'er she oughtta come to story time ta meet the children."

"Ah," Gloria said. "Yes, she should." She looked around. "Are we ready to go?"

It seemed they were, so they all made their farewells to Miss Angelica and Uncle Harry, and made their way to the door. Sir Gerald and Gloria led the way again, which put Lilia next to Bob. She was about to move away from him when he grabbed her arm. In hushed tones, he said, "Why'd you not tell me yer goin' ta the capital?

Lilia cursed silently. She'd forgotten Bob also knew how to converse with Angelica. "What's it matter ta you?" she challenged.

"If'n we was married, it'd matter a great deal."

Lilia scowled. "Well, we ain't."

He raised an eyebrow and smirked. "Not yet."

It took all of her restraint to resist the urge to wipe the smirk off of his face with her fist. When he attempted to assist her into the drivers seat, she broke away from his grip and quickly climbed into the back. Fortunately, he had been telling the truth about having business with Uncle Harry, as some of his load had been removed. There was just enough room for her to join Gloria and Sir Gerald.

"Git up here," Bob called from his bench.

"No," she snapped in reply. "You know I gotta concentrate ta memorize this story fer t'morrow."

He scowled back at her. "You got plenty o' time later."

"No, I ain't. I got chores ta do." Still, he refused to pick up the reins. "Don' be like this, Bob. It's for the children."

The way Bob's eyes lit up, Lilia knew that she'd said the wrong thing. "Alright. Get settled, then." Lilia's face burned, and she scowled at the back of his head. Then she settled in, barely registering her friend and the knight doing the same. Once the wagon was moving, she relaxed and let herself get lost in the world Angelica had created.

Nine

Calem watched from his window at the inn as Miss Lia emerged from below. She followed behind Gerald and Miss Gloria. He watched as they loaded into Bob's wagon. Miss Lia attempted to sit in the back, but was persuaded to sit in front, instead. He couldn't help but smile when she climbed onto the bench while refusing Bob's offered hand. Moments later, though, his hands clenched as Bob moved over so far that Miss Lia was forced to hold onto his arm to stay seated.

Calem tried to convince himself that he was angered by seeing any woman being mistreated. He told himself his reaction would be the same had Miss Gloria or Miss Genevieve been the one on the bench. However, he knew it was more than that.

As soon as the wagon was out of sight, Calem exited the inn and went in search of the blacksmith. He had asked the innkeeper for directions earlier, and was then following them. He found the man hard at work in his forge. "A good morning to you, sir!" Calem called over the noise.

The man looked up at the call. Seeing he had a customer — a new one at that — he set his hammer in its place and lay the metal he was working with onto a nearby work table. He removed his gloves as he approached Calem, set them on the counter, and extended a hand. "Good morning, sir." Calem shook the offered hand, then the smith continued. "My name is Derrick. What can I do for you today?"

This was Miss Lia's father? His speech was impeccable, with no hint of country accent. Calem then remembered that small moment during the fight when her speech had changed. *Interesting.*

"Sir Calem," the knight replied. He took a moment to admire the small arrangement of display pieces nearby as he extracted the letter from the duke. "I have come for a few reasons, one of which is to deliver this letter from His Grace to you." Calem held out the letter to the smith. The man's eyes had gone wide when he'd mentioned who had sent it. "I've also come to look at your fine wares. I've long searched for a sword that is a good fit for me," he gestured to indicate his shorter stature, and the man nodded in understanding, "and I make it a point to visit any smith I can in search of it."

Derrick looked over the letter for a moment before turning back to the knight. "Well, help yourself. If you would excuse me, I had better see what His Grace wants."

Calem nodded and approached a rack which held several swords. He picked one up and grinned. It was perfectly balanced. After a couple of swings, however, he realized it was longer than what he was looking for. So, he put it back and drew another. It, too, was perfectly balanced, but though shorter, it was still too long. Judging by the look of them, the others on the rack were all about the same length.

Deciding to try a different approach, he looked around. The entire front of the smithy held various pieces: horseshoes and hinges, chains and cookware. He scanned the entire room. There was nothing jumping out at him from where he stood, so he began wandering the shop.

In the very back corner, something shining in the light of the embers caught his attention. It was an elaborate scabbard. The length of the scabbard was too short for all of the other swords he had seen thus far. It looked more ornamental, rather than real, so he tried to dismiss it. The sword was not to be ignored, however. As if it was calling to him he went and picked it up. He withdrew the sword and attempted to hold back a gasp.

While the sword was real, this was not what caused his reaction. As with the other sword he'd tried, the balance was perfect, but what amazed him was how it felt in his hand. It felt...right, as if it had been made especially for him. The grip of the hilt felt fit to his fingers. When he swung it, it felt like it was truly an extension of his arm. The length was perfect. The balance was perfect. The hilt was perfect. The sword was perfect.

He couldn't hold back his grin as he faced the blacksmith. "My good sir, is this blade available for purchase?"

"Hmmm?" The blacksmith looked up from his letter. When he recognized the blade, he nodded. "Oh, yes. I made it for His Grace, originally, but he found it too short for his liking. He has given me permission to sell it, so no need to worry on that score."

Calem's grin widened. "I must have it. What is your price?"

Derrick's attention had returned to the letter, so it was a moment before he responded. "I'll leave it to you to suggest a fair price. Just understand that if I think it's too low, I can refuse."

Calem was thrilled by the man's words. Whenever he thought of his personal quest to find his perfect sword, he hoped he had the chance to name his price. He drew a large purse from his belt and set it heavily on the counter. The blacksmith's attention was immediately captured again. "I'm willing to give you fifty gold pieces for this blade."

The astonished blacksmith let out a whistle as the letter he'd been holding floated to the ground. "Surely you jest, sir. Name a lower price, I beg you. No blade is worth that much."

Calem looked the other man squarely in the eye. "Sir, I have been searching for this blade since the first day I held a sword as a boy. I'll not offer you less. You have asked me to set a fair price and I say that fifty gold pieces are the value of finding the blade I've sought for so long."

The man turned away, suddenly, and yelled, "Brianna!"

A moment later, a stout woman with fiery red hair and sharp green eyes appeared in the doorway. Calem assumed her to be the man's wife. "Yes, my love?" she asked.

Derrick pointed an accusatory finger at Calem. "This man is offering *fifty* gold pieces for that blade!"

She let out a gasp. "Fifty? That's far too much!"

Derrick nodded. "That's what I told him. The duke himself would only have paid ten for it, had it been to his liking."

"In all fairness," Calem cut in, "the duke isn't a swordsman. Not a true one, anyway." He took a deep breath before folding his arms across his chest and staring them down. "I will give you no less. I *must* have that blade. A lifelong friend is worth everything I am offering and more. I can and would offer more, but I know you'd be even less likely to accept. So, please. Take what I have offered."

The woman studied him, likely searching for some way to

persuade him to pay what she felt was a more honest price. "You are certain?" He could tell from the tone of her voice that she was beginning to waver. Calem replied with a decisive nod. She was silent for a moment before saying, "Then we will accept your most generous offer."

Calem let out a breath, his stern expression leaving with it. His grin from before returned. "Good. Thank you." He pushed the bag towards them, then took the sword and deftly belted it on. He stepped away from the couple and smirked at them. Then he drew the sword and quickly ran through a practice series that wouldn't bring him close to anything he could hurt. With a flourish, he tucked the sword back into its scabbard.

The blacksmith and his wife applauded. "You are right. I can see how comfortable that blade is in your hand," the smith said, his voice filled with a little awe.

"No wonder you are called the Lightning Knight," his wife added. Calem gave her a quizzical look, wondering how she knew who he was. "We saw your duel with our daughter. That was the name she gave you when we spoke of it after."

He nodded, remembering then that Miss Lia had returned home with them after the duel. "Ah, I see. Well, I have always said that I traded stature for speed," Calem said with a laugh. "Now, I do have some other business with you, as well. It regards that letter," he added, indicating where it had fallen, "So perhaps you should both read it first."

"Of course," the blacksmith replied as he bent to retrieve it.

He handed it to his wife, who scanned it briefly. She then looked up. "Let us all go into the house while I read this," she told them. Both men nodded, and Derrick removed his apron. He hung it and his gloves near the hearth, then offered his arm to his wife. She took it and they led the way from the smithy.

Calem followed them into their house, which sat adjacent to the forge with enough distance between the stonework of the forge and the wooden beams of the house to be considered safe.

They entered into a common room, and Derrick retrieved a chair from the table, setting it nearby. His wife sat on it. He moved two more chairs over to it, placing one next to it and the other a pace away, facing the other two. He took the seat next to his wife and offered Calem the remaining chair. Calem sat down.

The men waited for a moment for Brianna to finish the letter. When she did, she folded it back up and laid it in her lap. "So, what do you have to speak with us about?" she asked. "The letter is fairly straightforward, as is typical of His Grace."

Calem considered them a moment, pondering how to best proceed with the topic on his mind. He concluded that a direct approach would be best. "I actually wish to speak with you about the princess."

Both of them jerked back, obviously not expecting him to bring the subject up. Brianna was particularly wide-eyed, with a tremor of fear in her countenance. "What about her?" she asked cautiously.

Calem narrowed his eyes, studying her. She was trembling slightly, and under his gaze, she began to wring her hands. *Best to just rip off the scab*, Calem reminded himself. "Miss Lia is Princess Kalysta, correct?" he asked quietly.

The woman gaped at him for a moment. "How—" she cut herself off. "What makes you say that?"

"Among other things, the primary reason is that she looks just like Her Majesty, the Queen. Her voice is quite similar, too, when she isn't hiding behind her mask of a farm girl's illiterate speech."

Brianna was visibly shaken. Her husband wrapped his arms around her. She leaned into him, drawing several shaky breaths. Once her breathing was more even, she replied, "You are correct. Lilia is Princess Kalysta." She began to finger her necklace absently. "I knew this day would come. Once we received word the war was finally over, I knew it would come very soon." She fought back tears, but a few escaped in spite of her efforts. "That is why we wanted to take her to the capital, you see, though when I told her yesterday, she not only refused the idea, she fled the house in tears. Perhaps that was because I brought it up in terms of seeking a husband. She expressed fear that she would never return here."

"I see," Calem replied. He felt for this woman, who obviously loved the girl she had raised. "I believe I spoke to her soon after that when we were visiting Miss Gloria. She expressed a similar concern. In truth, it was seeing her sad at the time that allowed me to make the connection to Her Majesty, as the queen has had little to be happy about in the years I have known her." He took a deep breath. "Apart from your word, do you have any proof of her identity?"

Brianna didn't reply right away, but she did reach behind her neck and removed the necklace she had been toying with. "This was given to me the night she came into my care. I was asked to give it to her to remind her of her true identity once it was safe for her to know."

She handed the necklace to him with its pendant hanging free. He took it up with his other hand to study it. He immediately recognized the king's crest carved into its surface. He had seen an identical pendant before, around the neck of the queen. "Who was it that brought her to you?"

Swallowing hard, she replied, slowly. "He was a personal

scribe of the king, and he became a good friend of the royal family. His name was Marcus." Her voice broke on his name.

Calem closed his hand around the pendant, and closed his eyes as they became watery. "I suppose you have heard of his passing?"

She nodded, even as the pain in her eyes grew.

"Malannan guards caught him trying to re-enter Katiera from the south. He was likely trying to obscure your location. After that, it wasn't clear what happened, whether he was taken captive or killed right then. Either way, he never revealed to them the princess's location." He opened his eyes and looked at his hosts.

Brianna let out a sob, and Derrick wrapped his other arm around her, pulling her into his embrace and letting her cry on his shoulder. "Word got around that he'd been killed, but they understandably skimped on the details," he replied. His wife sobbed again, and he began stroking her hair to soothe her. Obviously seeking to change the topic, he asked, "What are your plans for Lilia, then? I assume His Grace knows about her as well?" He indicated the letter, which had again fallen to the ground. Calem nodded. "Are you planning to take her all the way there without her knowing the real reason?"

"I feel it may be best, yes," Calem replied. "She has expressed her disdain for the pampered lifestyle of a princess, as well as for traveling so far to perhaps find a husband. Hence the need for this ruse. I believe that upon meeting the queen, she would recognize the truth for herself, and that may be the way she needs to find out in order to accept it. I feel that if we just tell her, she will run as far as she can in the other direction."

Brianna let out a watery chuckle as she wiped the last of the tears from her face. "I believe you are correct, sir. You have taken her measure well for such a short acquaintance. She will not refuse to act as Miss Genevieve's protection, especially with the request coming from His Grace directly."

Calem nodded. "I thought not. If it puts your mind at ease, Miss Gloria is going as well. Amusingly, I learned yesterday that she and my companion actually met during her recent trip to the capital. Before he and I departed on this quest, they developed feelings for one another. They wish to wed as soon as His Majesty allows the practice again. This also means that Miss Lia will have a friend by her side, and will not be subjected to Miss Genevieve's exclusive company. I know they do not get along well."

"Which is sad," Brianna replied. "When they were little girls, Lilia and Genevieve were quite close, too, but they had a falling out some ten years ago, and have barely had a civil word between them since."

"Did it have something to do with a throwing knife, or did that happen afterward?" Calem asked, remembering the story from his first visit to the duke's manor.

Derrick chuckled ruefully. "That was probably the most memorable part of the fight, but they started bickering before then."

Brianna nodded in agreement. "As Lilia put it then Genevieve was becoming 'unsufferable', as she had never been one to just tolerate someone taking advantage of her." She sighed heavily, then turn back to Calem. "So, when will you be leaving?"

"Our current plan is the day after tomorrow."

Brianna nodded. "We will make sure she is ready to go by then."

Calem nodded and they all stood. He held out the necklace

for her to take, but she closed his fingers around it and pushed it away. "Keep it and give it to her when the time is right."

Calem nodded. "I will." He put it around his own neck to keep it safe until then. "Is there anything more I can do for you?"

Brianna looked at him, and the light caught the streaks of the tears still glistening on her face. "Just make sure our girl is happy, please."

Calem was sure that she had no idea just what she was asking of him, but he swallowed past the lump that formed in his throat and nodded. "I will do my best."

She studied him for a moment. "I believe you."

Calem tried to hide his blush as he made his farewells to them and left the house. He returned to the inn briefly, then set out for the duke's manor to tell him what he'd learned from Miss Lia's parents. He supposed that calling them her guardians was more appropriate, but in truth, they were her second parents, having done everything to raise her when her birth parents could not.

He had not gone far when he met the duke himself, walking in the the opposite direction. "Your Grace!" he hailed, catching the man's eye.

"Sir Calem." His stiff tone hinted that something was bothering him. "I'm just taking a stroll..."

Calem grinned as he sensed the reason for the other man's discomfort. "Away from Miss Genevieve?"

The duke slumped. "Is it that obvious?" he groaned.

Calem nodded. "To me, at least."

The duke sighed, then stood straight again. "Oh well. At least this time it is because she is in high spirits." He turned to fully face the knight. "Seeing as how you seem to be headed towards my manor, we may as well speak here. What can I do for you?"

Calem chuckled at the duke's candid manner. "I have just spoken with Miss Lia's parents," Calem replied. "They are in agreement with our plan to send her to the capital with Miss Genevieve."

The duke nodded, then gave Calem a curious look. "Did they say if she is really the princess?"

"Yes," Calem replied with a nod. He pulled out the pendant and showed it to the other man. "Everything fits."

The duke's eyes widened when he recognized the crest. Calem then tucked it away again. "To think, all this time..." his shoulders sagged again. "I don't believe I have ever treated her or her family poorly, but I could have treated them better, had I known..."

Calem put a hand on the duke's shoulder to stop him, and nodded in understanding when their eyes met. "True, but life doesn't usually let us know everything. That is just as true for those of rank as for those without. Besides, from what I have seen of her in your company, and what she has said of you, she has been generally happy under your care. She speaks highly of you and seems genuinely pleased to be able to be so informal with you. I know few people who could walk into a duke's manor, shout 'Your Grace', and still expect a warm welcome in return."

The duke's expression brightened again at his words. "I'm glad that she will remember me fondly, then."

Calem replied with another nod as a spike of envy pricked his heart. He was certain that she wouldn't remember *him* very fondly once she learns of how he was plotting behind her back. Shaking off the thought, he said, "I wonder if you buying her wardrobe will improve or sully her memory of you."

The duke laughed. "I should hope that even she would be glad that I am buying her those fancy dresses rather than Derrick and Brianna." Calem smiled at the thought. "I think I will go and talk to them about that now, actually. Until we meet again, Sir Calem." Calem returned his farewell. Then the duke set off in the direction Calem had come with a spring in his step.

Calem considered returning to the inn, but he suddenly felt restless, so he decided to wander for a time instead. Lost in thought, he wandered for quite a while. When he looked up at the sky, he found that it was nearly noon. His stomach growled with displeasure at the realization.

An hour later, he had returned to the inn and finished a light meal. He then went up to his room and tried to rest, but thoughts of Miss Lia kept intruding. He scowled as he remembered how he'd last seen her, forced to hold on to Bob to stay on the cart. The idea of that man marrying her made him grit his teeth. The realization of just who would actually marry her once she was presented as the princess made his blood boil. To stop his thoughts from continuing down that path, he forced himself to sleep. It was a useful technique he'd learned for when memories of battlefields kept him awake during the war.

He was awakened some time later by the noise of a panicked horse. No, of *his* panicked horse. Knowing his horse well, he knew the meaning of those noises, so he flew down the stairs.

Ten

Once the wagon reached the edge of town, Lilia rose to a crouch. She offered a quick farewell to both Gloria and Sir Gerald. When Bob slowed to almost a stop for someone or other in the road ahead of him, she deftly leapt off the wagon and quickly made her way home.

She was surprised to find her father in the house when she arrived. It was still early enough that he was usually still in the forge. Instead, he was sitting at the table, a letter in his hand and a distracted look on his face. "Papa, what do you have there?" she asked as she took her seat across from his.

He shook off his distracted haze and turned to her. "It is a letter from His Grace, Lilia. He has decided to send Miss Genevieve to visit his sister in Katiera. He is asking for you to accompany her as protection. They plan to depart the day after next." He paused, meeting her with a stern look on his face. "I have told him that you will go with them."

Lilia slumped in her chair as she tried to find a silver lining. "I suppose it won't be all bad," she sighed. "Perhaps Gloria will be able to go with us, as she is returning there soon anyway. We can all ride together." She knew her words sounded flat, but she couldn't force herself to feel happy about the subject.

Her father nodded. "It sounds as if she already is. While he didn't say as much, perhaps her engagement is part of why he is arranging the trip."

Lilia nodded as well. "Perhaps." She was then silent as she considered whether or not to ask what was on her mind. She decided to take the plunge. "Why did you not discuss this with me first?"

Her father held her gaze. "Because we are your parents and have the right to make decisions on your behalf when we think you are not making the correct ones."

She closed her eyes and took a sharp breath. His words caused her no little degree of pain. He was disappointed in her. It had been a long time since she'd felt the shame of disappointment from her parents. "I understand," she whispered.

She felt his hand on her. She opened her eyes, looking back at his. They were gentler, now. "My princess, this town is too small for you. You *need* to see more of this world."

That struck a chord. As much as she loved her little village, she had also dreamed of seeing the world beyond it. Yet, she still hesitated. "Do you know why they are going now?"

He looked back at the letter for a moment before answering. "Well, Sir Gerald and Sir Calem are at the end of their quest, seeing as there are no more towns or villages north of here. They will also be returning to the capital, so you won't have to be her only protection."

"If she has two knights, why do I need to go?" Rather than arguing anymore, she was genuinely curious about the situation.

He paused, as if considering how to answer her. "Even if

your services aren't needed on the journey, you can still protect the other young ladies' reputations. You know it is not good for a single, young woman to travel alone in the company of men. Also, they will not be able to stay with her in the capital, or come back with her." He grinned before adding, "Besides, I think the knights would be thankful to you for protecting *them* from Miss Genevieve."

Lilia chuckled at the ridiculous picture he'd painted. "You're probably right, Papa. I suppose I should take pity on those poor men. They don't deserve to have to deal with her."

He let out a bark of laughter. "That is very true." He smiled at her again. "There's a good girl. They're leaving in the morning of the day after next. I expect you to be ready and not keep them waiting."

Lilia nodded and headed towards the stairs, intent on deciding what she would pack. "I will be ready, Papa. I'll not disappoint you. If anything I'll be left waiting for *them*," she added with a wink.

Her father laughed again, then stood and walked over to her, planting a kiss on her head once he reached her side. "I know you won't disappoint us, my child. Thank you for not digging in your heels too much."

She wrapped her arms around him, the way she had since she was little. He returned the embrace. "Gloria has already asked that I be part of her wedding party, so I have many reasons to go." Looking past him to the table, she noticed a money pouch sitting on it. She turned him and pointed at it. "Where did that come from? Did you sell something while I was gone?"

When he saw what she was pointing at, he released her and went to pick up the pouch. "As a matter of fact, yes, I did. Sir

Calem came to browse my wares and was quite taken with the sword I made too short for His Grace. He gave us enough that I could retire today."

Her eyes widened in shock. "Just for one sword?!"

He nodded and stared at the pouch in his hand as if unsure what to do with it. "Apparently, it is the sword he has spent his career searching for, and he insisted on us taking his money."

She stared at the pouch, trying to figure out how much coin it held. "How much did he give you?"

To say her father looked overwhelmed as he examined the pouch was an understatement. "Fifty gold pieces."

Her eyes widened in shock. "Fifty!" she shouted. "What was he thinking?"

He scowled, as if frustrated with the sudden windfall. "I don't know. We tried to persuade him to give us less, but he wouldn't hear of it." He shook his head as he set the pouch back down, walking away from it. "Well I've had enough talk about this. I'm quite exhausted emotionally, if not physically, so I'll retire early this evening. If you want supper, I suggest you head to the inn. The innkeeper wishes to speak with you anyway." Lilia nodded then embraced him once more before heading out the door.

When she reached the inn, she started for the main entrance, but then she remembered she was supposed to care for the horses that evening. She headed into the stable yard, just in time to see Bob suddenly fly through the air. She looked to the stall he had flown from to find Sir Calem's horse bucking angrily. She hurried into the stall and calmed the horse enough to prevent further injuries, then went to check on Bob. He had fought his way to his feet, but he rubbed his chest as if in great pain.

"Bob! What you be doin'?!" she howled at him.

He scowled in reply. "Nothin'!"

She glared at him. "Rubbish! This is one o' the best trained horses I ever seen. I'm fair certain he wouldn't've kicked ya like this 'less you did somethin' ta provoke 'im!"

Bob said nothing, just continued to scowl. Lilia wasn't going to let him get away with anything, however, so she grabbed his ear and dragged him towards the inn. Before they got there, though, Sir Calem bolted out of the door into the yard. As he took in the scene, she dragged Bob over to him. "Yer horse jus' kicked Bob in the chest. What woulda caused 'im ta do that?"

Sir Calem stared Bob down. "Whether or not it was your intention, Bob, the horse thought you were trying to steal him."

Lilia let go of Bob's ear as she spun to face him. "What the matter with you, Bob? You ain't never been the kind o' bonehead ta steal a horse."

Bob's face was red with anger. "You been spendin' all yer time with him the last few days!" He jerked his thumb towards Sir Calem. "I enjoyed not havin' 'im around today. I figured that, if I set the 'orse loose, it'd get 'im away for a while 'n we could do somethin' together."

Lilia glared at him. "Yeah, an' that somethin' would've been helpin' the poor knight track down his horse!" She studied him. "Why are you doin' this?"

"'Cause I were jealous!" Bob shouted. "An' its all yer fault! If'n ye'd just marry me already, I wouldn't feel the need ta resort ta this!"

Her eyes went wide as she tried to figure out if she'd heard him correctly. "Yer blamin' *me* for all o' this?"

"Yes!"

Sir Calem's sudden, sharp intake of breath told her that he

knew what her thoughts were on what Bob had said. She whipped out her knife and held it to Bob's throat. His eyes went wide in terror. "You listen ta me, Bob. It's obvious you don' really love me, 'cause if you love someone, you *never* blame them for somethin' you did, and since you don't love me, I'm *never* gonna marry you!"

To her surprise, the fear left his face, replaced by rage. He grabbed the wrist of her knife hand and pushed it away from him. Then he grabbed her head with his free hand, pulling her face to his. In reply, she jammed her knee up between his legs. He doubled over in pain. She slammed the same knee into his head, holding back just enough to keep him conscious. She stormed back over to the stable as he collapsed in the muddy yard.

The horses seemed to sense that she was upset, for they poked their heads out to see if she was alright. She went to the nearest one, which happened to be Sir Calem's, and patted its nose. She took comfort from a motion she'd used to calm the same horse only moments before.

A second later, she heard footsteps. She turned to find Sir Calem coming towards her. While she was relieved it wasn't Bob, who was likely still curled up in the mud, she also remembered that she was angry with the knight, as well. "What were ya thinkin', offerin' so much for one blade?"

Obviously not expecting her anger, he froze in his tracks. Then he sighed. "You're complaining as well? I thought you, at least, would be happy to hear that your parents are settled for life."

She scowled at him. "What makes ya think me Pa wants that?"

He raised an eyebrow. "I never said he did, but think about

it. He never has to worry about putting food on the table again. He can keep forging to his heart's content, without relying on it to get by. Don't you agree he deserves every penny of what I paid him?"

Lilia held back another retort and seriously considered his words. She actually did agree with him. Her Papa did deserve it, especially since he had always been generous with his customers. She let out a sigh of resignation, letting her anger flow out with it. "I suppose he does."

Sir Calem looked ready to say something more when they were interrupted by a little boy approaching her. "Miss Lia?"

"Yes, Henry, what is it?"

The boy glanced at Sir Calem warily before stepping closer and saying, "Beggin' yer pardon, Miss Lia, but we heard ye been ta visit Miss Angelica today. Did ya bring a story back with ya?"

Lilia smiled and went to her knees so she was eye level with the child. "Yes, Henry. I did. Let the others know that I'll be tellin' the tale in the square tomorrow mornin'."

His smile was wide as he nodded enthusiastically. "Hurray!" He then ran off, likely to tell everyone the news.

As she watched him go, she felt someone's eyes on her. She looked up to find Sir Calem watching her. "What?"

He looked in the direction the little boy had gone. "You handle everyone well, don't you?"

She frowned in confusion as she stood back up. "What do ya mean?"

He continued to keep his gaze averted. "Everyone here loves you. Young and old, male and female...everyone I have spoken to has mentioned you with high praise at some point in the conversation. Well, all except Miss Genevieve, of course," he added shaking his head ruefully. He then looked back at her.

"You encourage happiness wherever you go, but you make sure you're not treated unfairly in the process."

His words made Lilia blush. "I just like ta make people 'appy, is all, Sir Knight." She stepped away from Stoneheart. "Now I was on me way to speak with the innkeeper." She set into her usual quick pace. The knight kept pace beside her. "You headin' in, too?"

He nodded. "I have concluded all of my business for the day, and I find myself famished."

She looked at the sun and nodded. "It is gettin' near ta meal time."

When they entered the inn, they found Gloria and Sir Gerald seated at a table, deep in conversation. They fell silent as Lilia and Sir Calem approached the table. Lilia raised an eyebrow at them. "What's goin' on here?"

Gloria looked between them for a moment. "Nothing. We were just discussing the capital."

Lilia wasn't entirely convinced, but she let it go. "'Bout that, Gloria, Miss Grievance is also goin'. I think the duke expects all of us to ride together."

Gloria grimaced and let out a sigh. "I am to be confined to a carriage with Miss Grievance?" Then the rest of Lilia's words seemed to sink in. Gloria's face filled with hope. She took Lilia's hand. "Us?! You are coming, too?"

Lilia gave a nod and let out a chuckle. "His Grace has asked that I act as protection for 'is ward. It's a good thing ye'll be there, in case someone is gonna have ta protect 'er from me."

Gloria laughed. "Oh, this changes everything! I am so excited! Do you know when we are leaving?"

Lilia nodded towards Sir Gerald and Sir Calem. "Day after next, with the good knights here."

Gloria smiled wide. "Oh, this will be wonderful!" She stood. "I must begin packing at once!" She turned to Sir Gerald and gave him a smile. "Gerald, would you please escort me home?"

The knight stood and smiled. "I would be more than happy to, my lady." He took her hand and kissed it before tucking it into the crook of his arm.

Lilia and Sir Calem both turned to watch the couple walk, arm in arm, out of the inn. Lilia let out a happy sigh. "She sure is happy, ain't she?" She looked over to see that Sir Calem's expression was *not* one of happiness. Instead, he seemed almost pained as he watched their exit. She frowned. "Do ye not approve of me friend fer yours?"

He shook his head. "It's not that." He looked down. "I'm just feeling little envious of him. I haven't the luxury of choosing my bride. I'm one of the poor souls who must marry for something bigger than myself."

Lilia's heart sank at his words. He was betrothed. No wonder he kept shutting her out. She hadn't realized how strongly she had come to feel for him until hearing the news. She took some comfort in knowing that he wasn't pushing her away because of something about her, that, perhaps, he had actually felt the same pull she had. However, that only added to the sting of knowing he'd been right to keep his distance.

Nevertheless, she saw that he needed comfort at the moment more than she did. She pushed her own growing heartbreak aside and said, "I'm sorry, Sir Knight. Perhaps yer bride won't be as bad as ye fear."

He looked at her. She saw exasperation in his eyes. "There is an additional reason why I, personally, am on this quest. I am concerned for the princess, of course. However, as soon as I learned who I was betrothed to, I enlisted in the search to give me time to come to terms with the arrangement." He sighed and looked back at the doorway. "A missing princess seems a good excuse, don't you think? No one could blame me for prioritizing finding her." He looked down again. "I truly have no kind feelings for my betrothed; it is all advantage for our families. If you need a comparison, I'd rather marry Miss Genevieve."

Lilia's heart swelled for him. "How much longer is yer quest?"

He sagged. "As you said before, we are returning to the capital after this. Whether or not we, or any of the other knights, found the princess, *my* quest is over. I will marry one month after my return to the capital."

The poor man looked miserable, but she didn't think she could say anything to help him feel better. "I'm sorry, Sir Knight. I wish you luck."

He looked up at her with a feeble grin. "Thank you, Miss Lia."

"Lia!" called the innkeeper. While Lilia hated to leave the knight in this condition, she was almost grateful for the escape. Now that she knew he was unavailable, it was difficult to be around him. *I have fallen for him.* She had fallen and would fall further whenever they were together.

As she approached the counter, she remembered this was why she had come to the inn to begin with. "Yes, sir?"

The innkeeper leaned over the counter. "I hear you're going to be gone."

Lilia nodded. "Yes, sir. I leave day after tomorrow, along with Miss Gloria, Miss Genevieve, and the knights."

The innkeeper smiled. "How exciting for you! I just wanted

to let you know that I'll take care of your folks for you. You've done so much for all of us. I couldn't do anything less."

A tear leaked out of the corner of Lilia's eye. "Thank you, sir. I have been worried for 'em."

He nodded in understanding. "Well, you don't need to worry any more. I'll see to it that they are fed. I even have something of a surprise for your father. My nephew is interested in becoming a blacksmith, so I'm going to ask Derrick if he'd like to take the boy on as an apprentice.

Lilia smiled, knowing that her father had been considering taking on an apprentice. "I think he'd be happy to, sir."

The innkeeper smiled. "I'm glad to hear it. Now, let me know what food you all will need for your journey. I'll give you what I can and have it ready for you and your companions by the time you leave."

Lilia's eyes widened. "We can't have ya give us that much food! There'll be five of us goin'! Perhaps more!"

The innkeeper's smile turned a little sad. "I get the feeling that none of you will return for some time, so let it be my parting gift to you."

Lilia smiled as more tears escaped. "Thank you, sir."

After finally taking care of the horses at the inn, Lilia returned home. When she tried to sleep, however, it came only in fits and spurts. Anticipation for the journey and news of Sir Calem's betrothal made falling asleep difficult.

In the end, she used the time she was awake to study Angelica's story by the light of a nearly-full moon. She was relieved when the sky started to brighten. She hurried to get ready for the day, then rushed outside and waited in the square for the children to arrive. Deciding she probably had enough time to look over the story once more, she went to pull it from her pocket. It was gone! She looked around, but knew it would be too difficult to see something like that in the dim morning light. She would have to find it later. She was suddenly grateful for her restlessness, as she had basically memorized the tale.

By the time all of the children were assembled, it was an hour after sunrise. She stood and cleared her throat to get their attention. "Now, I know I'm a day early, but things've been strange 'round here the last couple o' days." She paused, dreading what she had to say next. "I need ta tell ya, this'll be the last story for a while, because I'm leavin' on a trip."

All of the children expressed their disappointment at the news. Some of the youngest even started crying. "Now children, be happy for me," she said, even as she still struggled to feel happy for herself about the journey. "I'm goin' on a grand adventure! If'n yer all good, I just might return and tell ya what happens."

That drew a cheer from all of the children, which made her smile. "That's better. Now, everyone take a seat, and I'll share with ya the story Miss Angelica created for ya."

The children immediately sat down. Once they were all settled, She gave them a big smile and began the tale. "Once upon a time..."

Eleven

Even with being able to force himself to sleep, Calem had a restless night. Waking even earlier than usual, he decided to go for a walk to try and clear his head. As he was approaching the town square, he heard something crumple under his foot. Bending down, he found a folded piece of paper and picked it up. Unfolding it, he realized it was actually a few sheets together. Though dawn was breaking, it was still too dark to read, so he hurried back to the inn, one of the few places with a fire and candles lit this early.

He could tell it was a story, but it was difficult to actually read it. Even so, he soon realized just what it was. Gerald had apprised him of the results of the journey to see Miss Angelica the day before, both about her solidly known parentage and about the young woman herself. Being deaf and mute, her grasp of grammar was likely different from people who could hear, even though she was obviously literate.

Recognizing the author also meant he knew who must have dropped it. With a grin, he left the inn and went to the town square. He found it charming that in Farreden the town square was actually a public lawn. Like most town squares, it sat at the central intersection of the town, with important buildings like the town hall and the inn adjacent to it. However, Farreden had actually built a fence with gates around what they called their square, preserving a pleasant green space in the center of the settlement. The center of the square was dominated by a large tree, which was surrounded by a curved stone bench. At that moment, Miss Lia was sitting on the bench, surrounded by a growing crowd of children.

Calem entered the square from the gate behind where Miss Lia sat, and sat further around on the bench. There, he could easily see her, but she was unlikely to notice him, as long as the children held her attention, as seemed likely to happen. He held on to the story, ready to give it to her in case she needed it. This didn't seem likely, though, as she seemed prepared to recite it from memory.

Once the crowd of children had swollen to twenty or so, along with a few adults standing in the back, Miss Lia stood and explained why the story was a day earlier than usual. She also told them how she was going on an adventure. The children were obviously sad she was leaving. When she told them she might come back with stories of her travels, however, they cheered up and settled down. Once they were quiet again, she stood on the bench and began the story.

Calem found her storytelling charming. She easily changed her voice to match the different characters. She even used a few props, such as a stocking on one of her hands to represent a dragon. He was strongly reminded of when he and his older brother would put on puppet shows for their younger sisters when they were little. The girls had loved them. The oldest had even joined in the telling by the time he and his brother had been forced to quit the stage by the call of duty.

He smiled at the memory and returned his attention to the lady in front of him. As she told the story, he followed along with the written copy. The story was about a dragon and a princess, who were actually friends. Every week, the dragon would come to visit and they would play together. One day, however, a knight came to visit the princess. He was still there when the dragon arrived. The knight was a dragon slayer, so he pulled out his sword — which Miss Lia showed as a stick — and ran at the creature. The princess demanded that he stop, but he insisted all dragons should die. The dragon fought back bravely, fiercely defending himself. Suddenly, the knight made a sneaky move and slashed the dragon with his sword. The dragon fell limp to the ground and did not move when the princess called out to him.

A hush fell over the children. A few even began crying.

Miss Lia continued. The knight went to the princess and proclaimed he had saved her. Because of this, she had to marry him. The princess tried to run away, but the knight was faster. He caught her and tried to kiss her. Suddenly, the dragon was there! He gobbled up the knight in one bite.

The children cheered loudly.

Miss Lia waited a moment for the children to settle down, then resumed her telling. After that, the dragon asked the princess to come with him to his lair. He always asked her that, every week when he visited, but she always told him no. This time, however, she was so grateful that he had saved her, and so happy the knight hadn't killed him after all, that she said yes. She climbed onto his back, and the dragon flew them away.

When the dragon landed, she realized that his lair was an

abandoned castle. The dragon let her down in the courtyard then asked her to wait a moment before disappearing inside. He returned a moment later with a golden crown, which he held on his tail. He presented the crown to the princess as a gift. She loved the gift and was so happy that she kissed the dragon.

Not knowing what he was about, but knowing what came next, Calem suddenly leapt up onto the bench next to Miss Lia. "Thank you, dear lady!" he shouted melodramatically. "You have broken the curse a witch put on me many years ago!"

All of the children gasped in surprise. So did Miss Lia, but she recovered quickly when she realized he was playing out the story with her. "You are *not* a dragon! You are a man! Please, sir, tell me who you are!"

Calem put hand on his chest and looked at the children. They were leaning forward, waiting eagerly for his reply. "I am a prince from a distant land! Only a kiss from a princess could break my curse." He turned toward Miss Lia and took her hand. "Now that the curse is broken, I beg you to marry me, my friend!" He went down on one knee as he said this.

Miss Lia blushed slightly, but turned to the children and asked, "What do you think happened then?"

"They got married!" they cried delightedly.

Miss Lia smiled and nodded. "They got married and lived happily ever after!"

"Hurray!" All of the children cheered as they stood and clapped their hands. Calem took a bow with Miss Lia, then helped her down from the bench before releasing her hand.

Once everyone was mostly calmed down, a little girl asked, "Who is your prince, Miss Lia?"

Miss Lia's cheeks took on a pretty shade of pink. "He's one of me new friends. He'll be makin' sure I'm safe on me journey.

He's a knight named Sir Calem." She then motioned to him. "Can everyone thank 'im for joinin' us today?"

"Thank you, Sir Calem!" the children replied in unison. Then, to his great surprise, they all surrounded him. He knelt down and embraced each child that approached him. It was one of the oddest things he had ever experienced, but one he knew he would never forget.

"Are you gonna marry Miss Lia?" one of the oldest girls suddenly whispered.

Heat rushed to Calem's face. "I don't know," he whispered back.

"Well, I hope you do. She looked really happy to see you."

Calem looked over at Miss Lia, who was also surrounded by children wanting hugs. She was far enough away that she couldn't have heard the whispered conversation, but she was watching him between embraces. He realized that, while she did look happy, she also looked pained. He understood, feeling much the same way. He turned back to the little girl. "What is your name?"

"Hannah, sir," she said with a gap-toothed smile.

"Well, Hannah, I want to, but I don't think I can. I'm supposed to marry someone else."

The girl smiled again and patted his shoulder. "I'm sure it'll all work out."

He smiled at her naïvety. "I hope so."

Once all of the children had hugged him, they went over to Miss Lia. Each of them gave her a hug and told her she would be missed while she was away and they hoped she would come back soon.

Feeling the love from these children, and feeling how it affected her, Calem understood why she was so reluctant to leave her little village. Here, she was loved. In the capital, she would have none of that. There, many people would hate her just because of her station. Even her own family there would be strangers to her. His feelings of guilt, which was already great enough to have robbed him of sleep, multiplied. Knowing he wouldn't be able to live with the regret of forcing her to go to the capital, he resolved to convince her to stay home.

Once all of the children had dispersed, he approached her. "Miss Lia," he began, but she cut him off.

"Thank you."

He frowned in confusion. "For what?"

She glanced to where the last few children now played together in a clear space of the square under the watchful eyes of their mothers. "For making the story that much better for the children. They all loved it, and many expressed their hopes that you might return and do it again." Calem noticed that her rough speech had slipped again, her flawless diction returning. She had done the same while telling the story.

He waved a dismissive hand at her comment. "It was nothing. It looked like fun, and I couldn't help myself from jumping in. I do apologize for not consulting you."

She met his gaze, her stare indicating that she needed him to understand something important. "It wasn't 'nothing'. No knight that has ever passed through this village has ever taken the time to know these children, or make them feel important. Most barely pay them any notice at all. It might have been nothing to you, but it was everything to me."

He fell silent as her words sank in. While they warmed him, they also reminded him of his guilt. "Miss Lia, if you don't actually wish to go to the capital, I am certain I can convince the duke to allow you to remain here. I've seen how much you care for everyone here, and how much they care for you. I don't feel right taking that away from you."

She held his gaze for a moment before saying, "Sir Calem, I have already decided. Even without the duke's request, I was prepared to make the journey. If nothing else, I wish to go so I can be with my friend on her wedding day. She has done so much for me over the years, and has asked for so little. If going with her is something I can do to repay her kindness, I want to do it." She suddenly grinned and brightly added, "Besides, who else will keep you safe from Miss Genevieve?"

He returned her grin, but kept his tone serious. "If you are certain. I don't want you feeling tricked or forced into this."

She gave a decisive nod. "I am." Suddenly her face fell, causing Calem's heart to lurch with concern. "Have I...been speaking..."

"Flawlessly?" he finished for her, chuckling as his concerns vanished. Her face went from pale to flushed, and she looked away. "Yes. Both during the story and during our chat now, although you were using your normal tone in between. Also during our duel, you slipped for a time." He paused waiting for her to meet his eyes again. "Why do you hide behind a rustic mask, Miss Lia?"

She hung her head. "It is generally safer for a young woman if people underestimate her. I only speak this way with a select few people. You were never meant to hear it..."

Calem grinned, then spoke in his melodramatic voice from earlier. "Well, then I shall pretend I heard nothing. As you have just witnessed, I am very good at pretending."

She let out a laugh that rang with true amusement and relief. The sound warmed his heart. "That ye are, Sir Knight," she said, returning to her rough accent. "Now, shall we go visit the last miss?"

It took a moment for Calem to remember there was still one last candidate to meet, the one who had been traveling. Even now that he knew who the real princess was, he knew he should still go meet this lady to keep up the ruse. "Lead the way," he told Miss Lia.

She led him to a house a few streets away. "Now, fair warnin', she's prob'ly not who yer lookin' for. She's a year or so older'n me, and I'm not sure if she's an orphan or not." Calem nodded for her to proceed, so she knocked on the door.

"Come in!" a woman's voice called form inside. Miss Lia pushed the door open and entered. Inside was a woman, facing half away from them, holding a newborn child. Had he not already learned who the real princess was, seeing this young woman with a child would have been rather concerning.

Miss Lia spoke up. "Isabelle? I've a knight here ta see ya."

The woman pulled her gaze from the baby's face, and Calem's eyes went wide. The woman let out a laugh. "Calem! What are you doing here?"

Calem laughed as well. "Hello, Isabelle! When you said you were moving far away, I didn't know you meant *this* far."

It was Miss Lia's eyes turn to widen in surprise. "You two's already met?"

Isabelle smiled and nodded. "We played together as children. When my father died, my mother and I were taken in by his brother's family here in the north. In years where the fighting wasn't fierce, I was able to visit during the summers. Towards the end, however, Calem began his knighthood training and had little time to spend with his family, let alone with distant friends." She turned to Calem. "Calem, it's so good to see you again. How is everything at home?"

He couldn't help clenching his jaw at the question. "A little frustrating, but well enough."

Isabelle's eyes narrowed. "I'm sure it is *quite* frustrating. I've heard you are betrothed."

Of their own volition, his eyes flashed to Miss Lia. He clenched his jaw and nodded. "Yes."

Perceptive as always, she had caught the subtle eye movement and mimicked it. "I see. I'm sorry." Then she smiled softly. "Would you like me to speak with your mother? She always did love me."

"Yes, she did, enough that if things had been different, she may have tried to make a match between you and I," he replied, forcing a smile and a light tone. Both of them fell flat. He sighed. "If only it were that simple, Belle."

Her eyes widened as she finally understood the situation. "Oh! No I suppose it wouldn't be simple with you being..." Calem cut her off with a look and a minute shake of his head. "Anyway, I truly feel for you. Especially since I imagine your brother is more to blame than your mother."

"Yes," he replied stiffly. "He has gotten himself betrothed, as well, but, as always, he has gotten the better share of the bargain." He clenched his jaw again. "Sorry to be so abrupt, but seeing as you are most assuredly not the person we are searching for, I really must depart. I have some things I must discuss with His Grace before our return to Katiera."

She nodded. "Of course." Then she looked over at Miss Lia. "I have heard that you will be departing with them."

Miss Lia, who had been watching them interact with the

eyes of a hawk, narrowed those eyes for a moment, then nodded. "Yes, I'll be travelin' to the capital with 'em."

Isabelle looked back and forth between them once more before saying, "Well, I wish you a safe journey." Her gaze settled on Calem. "I hope the both of you get what you desire."

Calem nodded stiffly. "Thank you. Now that I know where you live, perhaps I can come meet your little one and your husband another time. Farewell." He then turned on his heel and headed out the door without a backward glance.

Earlier, during the storytelling, he had been thinking of his brother fondly. Now he was angry, even furious, with his older sibling. He was frustrated by the whole situation, and he let his frustration carry him quickly to the duke's manor. He idly wondered if his speed surpassed that of Miss Lia's on his first journey there.

When he arrived, he pounded on the door. The duke himself answered it. "Calem?!" That was all he had the chance to say as Calem forced his way past and stormed into the drawing room, slamming the door behind him. He moved to the fireplace, which sat empty, and grabbed onto the mantle with both hands, gripping tightly to keep himself from channelling that frustration into something more breakable. After a few moments, the door to the room opened, then shut again. A glance over his shoulder told him His Grace had followed him. "What's wrong?" the older man asked, forcefully enough to convey that he expected an answer.

"This blasted marriage arrangement!" Calem shouted. "And even more than that, what we are trying to do to Miss Lia. It is wrong. All of it is wrong!" He pounded his fist on the top of the mantlepiece. The sting of the blow made him realize his head was now throbbing, so he lay his forehead on the cool stonework for relief. "How can I take her away from these people who make her so happy?" As the stone warmed from his contact with it, he pushed away from the mantle and began to pace. Surely there must be some way around the situation. "I could always tell His Majesty that she perished," he muttered, mostly to himself. "I could even give him the pendant as proof. She doesn't have to give up her life here. She shouldn't *have* to give it up!"

A moment of quiet passed before the duke spoke up. "You really love her, don't you." he asked softly.

"Yes, and I'm going to have to watch her marry another man while I marry the daughter of her father's sworn enemy!" His heated fury of moments before evaporated, and the words came out cold and hard. He sank to his knees in defeat as his realization of just how hopeless the situation was sank in. "I'm doomed to a life of misery in the name of duty, all because of the terms of a treaty."

The duke squatted down next to him and put a hand on the younger man's shoulder. "Calem, I'm doing what I can, though it will take time. Perhaps all is not lost. Go to your mother and explain the situation. Surely she can do something about it. I have a feeling that things are not what they seem at court right now. Also, treaties can be changed." He paused as though hoping his words sank in. "I think you should go. Things will work out."

I'm sure it'll all work out. The little girl's words echoed in his mind. "A little girl, Hannah, said nearly the same thing this morning."

"A little... Are you *trying* to cause yourself more pain?" the duke asked, aghast. Calem cringed. It seemed that His Grace was not impressed with Calem's judgement. "I'm certain that watching her tell the children a story only made your feelings stronger, and the situation worse."

Calem stood enough to slump into a chair and nodded. "It did." He pulled the story from his pocket. "And, to make matters even worse, I joined in at the end." He handed the pages to the duke. "You can only imagine what I did."

The room was silent for a moment as the older man deciphered the very strange story. When he finished, he shook his head and cast Calem a pitying look. "Calem, my boy, you are a fool."

Calem nodded miserably. "I know."

Twelve

LILIA SPENT THE NEXT HOUR AFTER SIR CALEM FLED —
she couldn't think of any other way to describe it — from
Isabelle's house with the woman. Somehow, Isabelle had known
Sir Calem longer that she had known Lilia, even though Lilia
had always thought of them as growing up together. Along with
general conversation and time holding Isabelle's little boy, Lilia
tried to pry more information about Sir Calem from her long-
time friend.

Lilia hadn't missed that Sir Calem had signaled Isabelle not
to reveal *something* about why his betrothal was so important.
However, Isabelle had always been someone to be counted on to
keep a secret. So, other than realizing his betrothal was
somehow political, Lilia knew no more than she had that
morning.

She spent the rest of the day getting ready, saying her
farewells to friends and neighbors — most of whom had some
kind of gift to give her — and packing her limited wardrobe.
Perhaps the most practical gift anyone gave her was a traveling

trunk. Bound in leather, it was, of course a gift from the village's tanner, and it was large enough that all of her clothing barely filled half of it.

That evening, Lilia bade her parents goodbye and went to Gloria's house for the night. Gloria had suggested, and Lilia had agreed, that it would be best for her to have a proper bath and clean clothes when setting out on such a trip. Lilia liked to think her parents didn't want for much, but one luxury she wished they had was a proper bathtub.

Once both of the young women were dressed for the night, Gloria came into the room Lilia was staying in. "Are you excited?" Gloria asked, her own excitement clear in her voice.

Lilia went to the window and looked out. The night was peaceful. The moon was nearly full, allowing it to illuminate the woodlands around Gloria's home serenely. "I don't know," Lilia replied after a moment. "I want to go on an adventure, to see new places, but I feel like it won't be that simple. I don't know when I'll return home and...that scares me." There were few things Lilia would admit scared her. She had learned over the last few days that leaving home without knowing when she would return was on the list.

Gloria took Lilia by the arm and gently, but firmly, led her to the dressing table, forcing her to sit in front of the mirror. She then began to braid Lilia's hair. "I understand, Lilia, I really do. I'll be getting *married*. Who knows if I'll ever make it back here? Not that my dear would ever stop me from coming, but I don't know whether we'll have the means to travel." She sighed then pulled herself together. "Aside from that, though, I am quite excited to see the capital again. The duke's sister, Lady Garnet, is one of the most wonderful people I have ever met. She is kind and graceful, but unafraid and unwilling to let others speak ill of her." She grinned at Lilia's reflection. "She reminds me of you."

Lilia snorted. "I am *so* graceful," she scoffed.

Gloria frowned. "Why do you doubt that? I have seen you fight. When you are using that sword, it isn't merely fighting. You *dance*. Your movements are fluid, as if the blade is really your dance partner."

Lilia pondered her friend's words for a moment. "I guess I see what you mean. I had just never thought about it like that, I suppose."

"Well, you are graceful, even if your manners are sometimes a little...coarse," Gloria insisted. "I cannot wait until you learn how to dance. I'm certain you will be a natural."

Lilia groaned. "I have to learn how to dance?"

"Oh, pish," Gloria scoffed. "Of course you do, but it is ever so much fun! I promise you will love it."

Lilia grinned. "If I don't, you owe me a gooseberry tart."

They both laughed at their age-old joke. Whenever one of them failed to deliver on a promise, they owed the other a tart of their choosing. They'd each only had one tart this way over the years.

"If you don't, I will eat my dancing slippers," Gloria replied confidently.

Lilia raised an eyebrow. "Is it really that enjoyable?"

Gloria nodded. "Indeed, it is. The handsome men, the beautiful women, the twirling and other movements...it is very exciting."

"What makes you think I'll be invited to an event where I'll be required to dance?" Lilia challenged.

Gloria grinned. "If I know the countess, and I do, we will be invited to *every* event. As soon as we reach the capital, you and

Genevieve will be properly outfitted. Then the dancing lessons will begin. Once the countess thinks you are ready, she will accept an invitation on our behalf to a small assembly. There, you will dance with courtiers of every shape and size. Some will, of course, be boring. Others will be ridiculous. Some will be charming, but you must watch out for those. They steal hearts they have no intention of keeping."

Lilia sighed as she thought about dancing with the person who already *had* her heart. She knew it was unlikely to happen, but that didn't mean she couldn't dream about it. "Is that how you met Sir Gerald? At a dance?" she asked, trying to deflect the conversation from herself for a moment.

Gloria nodded, a dreamy smile crossing her face. She had finished with Lilia's hair, so Lilia turned to face her. "I was getting some refreshment when the countess surprised me by introducing me to three knights. The first barely waited for introductions to be completed before whisking me away. He danced well, but I didn't particularly like him. Another one cut in, but he, though kind, was dreadfully dull. Sir Gerald claimed my next dance. While he may not look it with his large stature, he is a *divine* dancer. The magic of the ball wove its spell, and I fell in love with him that first night. He called on me every morning afterward, until he had to leave. That's when I decided to return home. Without him, there wasn't really anything holding me there. At least, not until we could marry."

Lilia smiled at her friend's expression. "I hope he knows how lucky he is to get you."

Gloria blushed. "I feel like the lucky one." Then, she yawned, prompting Lilia to do the same. "I suppose we ought to get some sleep," she said once the yawn had passed. They both stood. After a quick embrace, Gloria left the room.

Lilia sat on the edge of her bed and spent several minutes lost in thought. Everything she had learned that day, everything she wished she could have learned, and the coming journey all spun about in her thoughts. Finally, she pushed them all away and lay on the bed, suddenly exhausted. The last thing she thought of before she fell asleep was the look on Sir Calem's face as the children embraced him.

The next morning, the sky was clear, perfect for starting a journey. Better yet, Lilia had actually slept well. She only hoped she hadn't already used up her good luck for the trip with how well it was starting.

As had been agreed upon the evening before, Gloria and Lilia, in a smaller carriage owned by Gloria's uncle, traveled to the inn to meet the knights and wait for Genevieve and the duke's carriage. They also retrieved the food the innkeeper was giving them for the journey, making sure to thank him profusely.

A short time later, they heard the sound of the duke's carriage arriving. Lilia was mildly surprised, as she had expected Genevieve to drag out her departure at least half an hour longer. Perhaps the girl was more desirous to leave the village than Lilia thought.

Sir Gerald picked up their trunks and loaded them into the storage compartment before climbing into the driver's seat. He and Sir Calem would be taking turns driving the carriage, with Lilia as backup should the need arise. His Grace used the carriage so little that he didn't employ a driver. He simply called on one of the few people in the village, Lilia included, who knew how to handle it when needed.

Lilia was about to climb into the carriage when she heard her father calling out to her. She turned to find him jogging towards her with something in his hand. "Lilia," he panted when he reached her.

"Papa, I'm so glad you came to see me off."

"I had to give you this." He presented his parcel, a short sword and scabbard. "I'd been making it for your birthday, but I finished it last night. I think you might need it now."

Lilia took the sword. It was perfectly balanced, just as she expected. She looked the blade over. She gasped. There was a lily of the valley engraved into the hilt. "Oh, Papa...it's beautiful."

He smiled. "I'm glad you like it, princess. Keep it with you."

A tear leaked from her eye. "I will," she promised. She stood on her tiptoes and kissed his cheek. "Thank you, Papa."

He kissed her forehead in return. "You're welcome. Now, be good and be safe."

"I will, Papa. Thank you." She looked back at the carriage. While Gloria was waiting patiently, Genevieve looked annoyed. "I need to go now," she told him.

He nodded, hugged her briefly, and stepped back. "We love you."

"I love you, and Mama, too," she replied, another tear escaping her eye. "Give her a hug for me."

He gave her a tear-filled smile. "I will." Then he turned and ran in the direction he had come from.

Sir Calem stepped towards her. "We need to get going."

She nodded and turned towards the carriage. He held out his hand, which she took, and assisted her into the conveyance.

Once she was settled, he shut the door. A moment later, they were off.

They hadn't even reached the edge of town when Miss Grievance made an appearance. Gloria and Lilia sat together on one bench, and Genevieve had the other to herself. It seemed, however, that a whole bench was not enough room for the spoiled girl. "Lia, sit up straight! Your knees are running into mine!"

Lilia had no intention of putting up with this behavior for the entire trip, so she pulled out her knife and a stone. She began to sharpen the blade. "If you make one more complaint about how much room you don't have, I'm going to display my knife throwing skills again." She looked the other girl in the eye. "You are taking up half of the carriage as it is, while Gloria and I *together* share the other half. Aside from that, the backs of my knees are touching the seat. I cannot bring them back further. If either of us isn't sitting up straight, it is *you*."

Genevieve fell silent, looking at the knife fearfully and touching her hair protectively. Once she had been silent for long enough, Lilia put the knife away. Even then, it was still some time before Genevieve spoke again. "You could at least have bathed. the stench is horrible."

Lilia turned to Gloria. "Do I smell to you, Gloria?"

Gloria fought a grin. "Not at all. I daresay the bath you had at my house last night, along with the washing my uncle's servants performed on your clothes, took out any smell you might have had from your father's forge."

Genevieve obviously did not share Gloria's amusement with that observation. Her annoyance was written on her face, but she resumed her silence. It was another hour before she dared to speak again. "You could at least do as I tell you about sitting straight and behaving like a proper lady."

Lilia turned to her friend again. "Gloria, did any of the ladies you met in the capital address all of their insults at only one lady? If so, would you have called that behavior ladylike?"

Gloria fought another grin. "Oh, there were enough, but they were generally those women who were only invited anywhere because slighting them was a guaranteed way to have their venom directed your way. They weren't considered lady-like at all."

Genevieve seethed now. "Fine," she replied through clenched teeth. "If you know how to act like a lady, show me. Engage in small talk."

Lilia sat up straight and held her chin at the proper angle. She put her hands in her lap, and hid her amusement at being challenged to small talk when Genevieve had made no such attempts during the course of the journey. "The weather was beautiful this morning, did you not think so, Miss Genevieve? Oh, and Miss Gloria! How lovely you look today! Is that a new gown? It must be, for I've never seen you wear it before. Miss Genevieve, you look lovely, as well. The blue of your gown is a perfect match for your eyes."

Genevieve's mouth dropped open in amazement and she was blessedly speechless for a few minutes. Once she recovered, she asked, "Where does all of this come from?"

Lilia held the other girl's gaze. "My mother. She is very ladylike, and made sure I learned to speak flawlessly. While I learned how to defend myself with a blade from my father, I learned how to defend myself with words from my mother." She tsked. "I pity you, Miss Genevieve, for your inability to see past the end of your nose. I was quite honest before, you do look lovely, but your manners will never impress anyone."

Genevieve fumed, but fell silent again, something Lilia was grateful for. She was even more grateful that Genevieve remained silent until they pulled to a stop a few hours later. At that point, she looked out the window and frowned. "Are we already stopping for the night?"

Lilia was about to look out her own window when the door opened. Sir Gerald poked his head in. "We are stopping for a meal, if you are interested, ladies."

Lilia looked out the open door and recognized where they were, having driven the carriage through here before. It was a small village that didn't even have a true inn. There were a few homes that had beds to let, but they were mostly owned by older folk whose children had grown and moved out on their own. Lilia was sure the men planned to use their packed food rather than impose on any of them to prepare a meal.

Obviously grateful to be able to do so, Genevieve climbed out as fast as she could. Gloria rolled her eyes, but followed a moment later. Lilia remained where she was. After a moment, Sir Gerald poked his head back in. "Are you not coming, Miss Lia?" he asked.

Lilia shook her head. "Not right now. I need a few minutes without Miss Genevieve."

He cast her a commiserating look and nodded. "I understand. I will have Calem wait with you while I escort the other two inside."

Lilia nodded her thanks, and he shut the door. She leaned back against the cushioned seat and looked out the window. Sir Calem was pacing just outside, however, so she turned away.

The pain of having him so near, yet out of reach, was

becoming increasingly familiar. Yet she found herself unsurprised that the one man she might love was unable to return that affection.

Deciding she'd had enough time to sulk, she opened the door. Before she could climb out, however, Sir Calem began climbing in. "Miss Lia, there is something I need to speak with you about," he said as he shut the door behind him and took the opposite seat.

She sat up straight, surprised and nervous about this sudden turn of events. "Alright."

He was quiet for a moment after she responded, so she took a moment to study his face. His expression was tormented, holding fear, misery, and pleading. "Miss Lia, I have to warn you that you must *not* go to the capital."

Her eyes widened in shock. "Why ever not?"

"Because, if you do, you may never have the chance to return home to Farreden."

She stared at him in confusion, her own concern growing. "What are you saying?"

Without warning, he reached under his tunic and pulled a necklace from around his neck. "This belongs to you," he said as he handed it to her. "Your mother gave it to me, to give to you when the time was right."

She took it and studied the pendant. She recognized it as the one her mother usually wore, but she'd never been able to look at it closely. She traced the intricate design it bore with her finger. "What is it?"

"It is the king's crest." Her inhale was almost as sharp as the look she cast him. "Miss Lia, *you* are the princess we have been searching for."

Her body and mind went numb. *No! I can't possibly be the*

princess! I'm just the daughter of a blacksmith! She wanted to scream her protest aloud, but her lips wouldn't form the words. Her grip on the necklace loosened, and the weight of the pendant pulled it from her hand. He, apparently, anticipated the reaction, for he caught it easily. Then he stared at it cautiously, as if it might bite him.

"This whole trip was a scheme," he admitted slowly. "One of my making, I must admit. My plan was to wait until we reached the capital to tell you your identity, as you would be able to see it for yourself. You are the spitting image of the queen, you see. So, the proof would be irrefutable, even without the crest, which I didn't know about when I made the plan." He hung his head. "I hope you can forgive me for deceiving you."

She stared at him for a moment as she tried to sort through her feelings. Not just her feelings about herself and her new reality, but also her feelings about him. "Why the change of heart, then? If you wanted to get me to the capital, why are you telling me this now?"

He met her eyes, and seem to search them for *something.* She wondered if he found it. "Because I knew that you would never forgive me, nor would I forgive myself, if I didn't offer you the choice. And you do have a choice. Say the word, and I will take you back home. Right now. Then I will take this pendant to the king and tell them you had died young. You can return to your home with no one the wiser."

I can return to my family, my home, she realized. On its heels, however, came another realization. *I have another home, too. Another family. Another father and mother. Brothers, too.* She had always longed for siblings. Derrick and Brianna had tried for years to have more children, but each pregnancy ended with either a stillborn child, or one too weak to survive more than a month. *That's why Mama and Papa need me, though, because I'm all they have.*

Conflicted, she stared at the pendant in his hand. The crest reminded her, again, of who her parents were: a king and a queen. They likely wouldn't tolerate being made the fools. "What would happen if they found out you lied?" she asked hesitantly

"Nothing," he replied quickly. Too quickly.

She narrowed her eyes at him. "Don't lie to me."

He closed his eyes, anguish written on his face. "Such an action would be considered treason against the crown. The punishment for treason is either death or banishment." He opened his eyes again, the anguish replaced by pleading. "I beg you, though, don't let my fate sway your decision. I nearly destroyed you with this trap. I want you to do what is going to make *you* happy, Miss Lia."

How can I do that? How can I make a decision I know will make others miserable? Make others suffer? The thought of suffering brought up another point. The princess was promised in marriage as part of the treaty that ended the war, if she understood what Sir Calem had told her the other day correctly. "If it was learned that I had been found and not returned, would war break out again?"

He closed his eyes and nodded. "If it became known that I found you and then lied about it to the king, war would most certainly follow."

She sat for a moment, shocked. "You are willing to put your life *and* this country in jeopardy just to make me happy?"

Their eyes met, but he couldn't hold her gaze for long. He looked out the window instead. "Miss Lia, I saw how much the people of Farreden love you. Every person that heard you were coming with me told me to take care of you. You won't feel that amount of love in the capital. Many people will despise you simply because of your station. That is why I completely understand if you want to turn around and return to where you know you are loved."

Where I am loved.

The words echoed in her mind. Mama and Papa surely loved her, as did the children and her friends. However, did the king, her father, also love her? He had sent all of his knights to every corner of the kingdom searching for her. Then she remembered that Sir Calem received the necklace from her Mama. This meant that she knew. Mama and Papa knew, years ago, that someday she would return to her other family. Surely that was what they had in mind when they said they wanted her to go to the capital, before they ever met Sir Calem.

Mama and Papa are ready for me to go, and Mother and Father are anxious for my return.

Lilia gently took the necklace from his hand. His gaze flew to her face, shock evident in his eyes. "Well, Sir Calem, I can tell you two things that are *not* going to make me happy. It would not make me happy to see the country at war again, and it would not make me happy to see you die for my decision." She drew the necklace over her head, settling it round her neck. It felt...*right*. The weight of her birthright, symbolized by the pendant, filled a place in her she'd never known was empty until that moment.

The knight hung his head. "I am so sorry, Miss Lia." His voice broke when he said her name.

She shook her head. "No," she told him. He looked up in confusion. "You don't need to apologize. You were doing what you thought was right with the odds stacked against you. You were charged with finding a way to get a young woman who told you outright that she had no interest in being a princess to accept her fate. I've realized this is what I need to do, for myself and for everyone else involved." She frowned as another realization struck her. "My name isn't actually 'Lilia', is it?"

He shook his head. "No. Your given name is Kalysta." His voice broke again. "I wish I could take this burden from you," he whispered.

She put her hand on his and squeezed it. "You gave me the opportunity to have it taken from me, and I have refused. I appreciate what you have done for me, and especially what you were willing to give up on my behalf."

For a moment, he just stared at her hand on his, as if her touch both burned and healed him all at once. Then Lilia remembered he was betrothed, and she pulled her hand away. The hand she had held balled into a fist, a sign of his frustration at the whole situation.

Suddenly, he sat up straight. "My lady, we will be departing soon. If you wish for something to eat, I suggest you hurry."

Lilia almost cried at the return to formality, but she knew it was necessary. "Thank you, sir." She replied. He nodded and opened the door. He climbed down, then turned to help her descend. Just as she set foot on the ground, she saw the others emerge from the tavern. "It seems I am too late."

"Forgive me, my lady," Sir Calem said in a strangled voice.

She shook her head. "It's alright. I've rather lost my appetite, anyway," she replied in a whisper.

He nodded and assisted her back into the carriage. She was joined a moment later by the other two young women. Once they were settled, Gloria placed a handkerchief on Lilia's lap. Lilia opened it to find a couple of rolls. "I thought you could use something to eat, even if you didn't feel hungry enough to come in."

Lilia gave her friend a grateful nod. "Thank you, Gloria."

On the other bench, Genevieve narrowed her eyes. "Something feels...different. What happened?"

Not feeling up to revealing what Sir Calem had told her, especially to Genevieve, Lilia sighed and said, "Yes, something *is* different, but I'm not in the mood to discuss it at present."

Genevieve scoffed. "Since when did you decide you get to speak like a princess?"

Lilia stared and almost laughed at the irony. Genevieve couldn't have had any idea how right she was. Lilia stared her down until the other girl started to squirm. "Well, considering how you have spoken like one almost the entire time I've known you, I daresay I have the right to do so whenever I wish."

Genevieve huffed, but fell mercifully silent.

Lilia looked out the window and saw Sir Calem smirk. He had obviously overheard the conversation. Grateful that someone found humor in the situation, Lilia smiled and sat back in her seat.

Thirteen

SEVERAL DAYS HAD PASSED SINCE CALEM HAD TOLD MISS Lia that she was really Princess Kalysta. With his conscience clear, he had been able to relax and almost enjoy the journey. Whenever it was possible, he would listen to the princess and Miss Genevieve trading verbal barbs, which always ended with a cutting retort from Miss Lia — he still generally thought of her by that name, especially since that was all the others knew to call her. Those exchanges gave him something to actually smile about, even with their pending marriages to other people weighing on his mind.

They were retracing the route that he and Gerald had taken to reach Farreden in the first place, so he and Gerald knew where they could stop along the way. Generally, they had been stopping at the side of the road for a midday meal of bread, cheese, and dried meat the innkeeper in Farreden had provided them with. Some days, though, when they were near a town at midday, they would find an inn or tavern to eat at instead.

Rather than cram all five of them around tables that were

built for only four, the men would sit at one table and the women at another nearby. This offered just enough privacy for Gerald to comment on Calem's habit of listening in on the women's sparring.

"You forget you cannot marry her," Gerald scolded, wiping a grin off of Calem's face.

"I cannot forget," Calem groaned quietly, hanging his head. Then he glanced back at Miss Lia, who had just scored another point against Miss Genevieve. How the latter still had enough ego to keep producing barbs for Miss Lia, when each one was inevitably directed back at her, he didn't know. Turning back to Gerald, Calem quietly added. "All I am doing is enjoying her wit. It's not as though I'm trying to get her to love me."

Gerald raised an eyebrow. "But *you* are falling more and more in love with *her*."

Calem slumped. "That would be happening whether or not I listened to her. It isn't something I can just halt, Gerald. Surely, you can understand that."

Gerald looked over at Miss Gloria, then, and his besotted smile surfaced. "I do understand that, my friend," he acknowledged. "What I still don't understand is why you cannot break out of your betrothal. When can you explain it to me?"

Calem sighed. "All will be made clear once we reach the capital."

Gerald grunted. "If you say so." He took a bite of his food before continuing, his tone more jovial now. "So, to keep me busy, I've been trying to figure out whom to pair Miss Genevieve with. It is proving rather difficult. For Miss Lia, though, I could name a dozen, provided her skill doesn't scare them off."

Calem ignored the latter comment, already knowing Miss

Lia's destined partner, and thought for a moment. "How about Sir Rupert for Miss Genevieve?"

Gerald laughed. "Of course! Why did I not think of him before? He would never put up with her childish behavior, which may be what she is waiting for, to be honest. You might be on to something there…"

Suddenly, the hair on Calem's neck rose, and he stiffened. "Something is wrong," he told Gerald quietly, setting the other man on alert as well. Calem looked toward the door. He saw a pair of men. They were heading straight for the women's table. "Gerald." He nodded in the men's direction. "Our old friends are here."

Gerald looked over. He seemed to immediately recognize the pair as well. They had given the two knights trouble the last time they'd been in the town. Both men were larger than Gerald, which was saying something. Calem had been laid up for a few days as he recovered from having his arm sliced open. He suspected they may have stolen his armor, as well. He had no proof, but there were few people who would dare to mess with knights.

Calem stood and approached the ladies' table. "Excuse me, ladies, but we had best be on our way.

"Well, if it ain't the little knight," one of the men sneered. The hair on Calem's neck stood up again as fear entered the expressions of two of the ladies.

Miss Lia, however, just looked bored. "Why don't ya pick on someone yer own size, Ned?"

The larger of the two men, who was apparently Ned, went white as a sheet. "M-miss Lia!" he stammered.

Suddenly, Miss Lia was on her feet, a knife in her hand. "In the flesh," she replied, a malicious smile creeping onto her face.

Ned took a step backwards. Then another. He stumbled against a chair with his third step, and lost his nerve completely. He turned and fled the tavern entirely.

Unfortunately, his companion had no such fear. "I 'eard o' you, Miss Lia. You bloodied up me buddy Ned real bad, so's I reckon I oughtta take care of ya for 'im. 'Sides, I been lookin' for ya ta bring ya to me brother, anyhow."

Miss Lia thumbed the sharp edge of her blade. "I'd be more'n 'appy ta show ya what comes from messin' with me."

The man grinned evilly. "Shall we take this outside, miss?"

Miss Lia returned the grin. "Ladies first."

Without turning away from Miss Lia, or the knights, the man backed out the door. Calem followed Miss Lia, while Gerald remained inside with the other two ladies. Checking back, Calem saw all three watching from the windows.

The sharp sound of ringing steel made Calem whip his head back around. The man had drawn a sword, while Miss Lia still had nothing but her knife.

Calem put his hand on his own sword, ready to either offer it to her or step in if it looked like she needed help. However, he soon saw that there wouldn't be a need. In this street brawl, Miss Lia fought like a different person. She threw her whole body into her dodges, crouching low or leaping to the side, and went for any dirty moves she could. Even so, the large man seemed to constantly have the upper hand, as he was always on the attack. To Calem's trained eye, however, he could tell she was in complete control of the situation.

Until she wasn't. The man feinted a downward swing, then pivoted sharply, striking the side of her head with his pommel. Miss Lia crumpled to the ground. Calem stood frozen in shock, pain exploding through the left side of his chest as he took in what happened. A moment of dreadful silence followed, broken by the man's malicious laughter. Calem started forward as the man used his boot to roll her onto her back, but froze as he held his sword to her throat. One wrong move on Calem's part, and the villain could kill her before the knight could touch him.

The man crouched next to Miss Lia's motionless form. "I've orders ta take ye back to me brother, Bob," he said as he pressed his blade closer to her skin

Calem seethed. Of *course* Bob was desperate enough to send someone after her.

"Shall we be goin?" He moved his free hand to grab her by the hair, likely to force her to her feet.

Calem saw what would happen next a moment before it happened. With her attacker's attention split between her face and the threat Calem posed, Miss Lia tensed her arms and legs. First she used her free hand to throw dust from the road into his face. Then she spun, propelled by her feet and other arm. Her head and neck moved away from his blade, and her legs swept his out from under him as he fought the blinding sand. She then rolled and came up in a crouch, then darted forward, grabbing his sword from the ground and holding it to his throat as he lay face up on the ground.

"Never let your guard down," she said through gritted teeth. She stepped back, keeping his sword pointed at him. "Get out of here. I never want to see your face again."

Bob's brother scrambled to his feet and ran away as fast as his feet could carry him.

With the man gone and the danger passed, Miss Lia stuck the point of the sword in the dirt and sank to the ground in obvious exhaustion. Calem flew to her side, catching her as she fell from her crouch next to the sword. "Miss Lia?" He was certain she could hear his panicked whisper, but she didn't respond. She simply trembled in his arms. "Princess," he whispered more forcefully, "are you alright?"

She managed a nod this time, and tried to push him away. She barely managed to take a step before falling again. He caught her and carried her to the carriage. Gerald, Miss Gloria, and Miss Genevieve reached them in the next moment. Gerald opened the carriage door as the young women fretted over Miss Lia, though they backed away as Calem moved to put her into the carriage.

Once he had settled her into her usual spot, he backed away. Miss Genevieve entered next, taking her usual seat across from Miss Lia. Miss Gloria entered last. As she moved to sit next to her friend, Miss Genevieve pulled the startled young woman to the seat next to her, instead. "She needs some space," Miss Genevieve said to Miss Gloria, who nodded in surprised agreement. To Miss Lia, she said, "Lia, lie down."

It caused Calem a great deal of concern when Miss Lia obeyed Miss Genevieve's command without a single witty return. In truth, she didn't utter anything. This lack of response also seem to concern Miss Genevieve, for she turned to him and said, "Sir Calem, get us out of here."

Calem acknowledged her first sincere words to him with a nod. He swiftly climbed into the driver's seat. Gerald, who had also retrieved the other man's sword, quickly mounted, and once he had both riding horses under control, Calem set the carriage into motion.

∽

It took about three hours to reach the next town, where they had already planned to spend the night. As soon as they stopped, Miss Genevieve ordered Calem into the carriage. He opened the door and poked his head inside. "She's burning up," Miss Genevieve said from where she knelt on the floor, dabbing damp fabric on Miss Lia's brow. Miss Gloria was kneeling as well, dabbing along Miss Lia's arms. Both young women moved aside to give him room.

The one relief Calem had in that moment was that they were only a day out from the capital by carriage. If no help could be found here, he could ride Stoneheart to Katiera and bring someone back by morning to help.

Calem gathered the alarmingly warm female into his arms and carried her into the inn. As Calem stopped here every time he was in the area, the innkeeper recognized him on sight. He smiled, until he realized the knight was holding a person. He frowned and rushed over through the crowded common room. "What's wrong with her, Sir Calem?"

"Fever." Calem was surprise at how steady his voice sounded, as if his nerves recognized he needed to get the words out quickly and clearly to get Miss Lia the help she needed. "Do you have anyone nearby who can help her?"

The other man nodded. "We do." He then poked his head back out the door. "Charlie! The horses can wait! Go get the apothecary at once!"

The stable boy, who was about to take the reins from Gerald, nodded and darted down the street. About five minutes later, he returned, along with an out of breath man. The man took a few moments to catch his breath, then asked, "What's wrong, Seamus?"

The innkeeper pointed to Miss Lia. "Fever, Sean."

The apothecary frowned. "Set her down, I need to look at her." Seeing nowhere else to do so, Calem gently laid her on the floor and rested her head in his lap. The apothecary opened his large bag and began pulling out tools and herb onto the nearest table. He then placed a hand to her forehead, then her cheek. "Not terribly high, but high enough," he said. "I need some tea water!" he ordered.

The innkeeper disappeared instantly. The apothecary, meanwhile, began grinding some herbs. When the innkeeper returned a few moments later with a cup and a steaming pot of tea, the apothecary put the first of the herbs into the hot water to steep. He then started working on different herbs.

After several long, tense minutes, the concoction was ready. "Sit her up," the apothecary instructed. Calem did so, holding her upright while the other man helped the still-steaming liquid to slide down her throat. She began to shiver. "We need to get her off of this cold floor," the apothecary stated.

"It's a good thing you wrote ahead to let me know you were coming, Sir Calem," the innkeeper said as he laid a blanket over Miss Lia. "Otherwise, I'd not have a room for you. As it is, I only have the two you requested. This young woman really ought to have one to herself."

"I agree," Calem replied, now even more grateful to have sent word ahead the night before. He shifted to pick Miss Lia up again. "Sir Gerald and I will sleep in the stables. The other two young ladies can have the other room." Calem then followed the innkeeper toward the stairs.

"As if any of us will be able to sleep," Miss Genevieve added, falling into step behind Calem. "Gloria and I have already agreed that we will assist the apothecary through the night if it is needed." Gerald and Miss Gloria followed behind her. Calem was slightly confused Miss Genevieve was the one speaking on their behalf, as if Miss Lia was *her* dearest friend.

Climbing the stairs behind the innkeeper, Calem took some comfort in how easily Miss Lia was breathing. Hopefully the fact that the fever wasn't causing coughing or congestion was a good sign.

On the first floor up, the innkeeper led them down the hall and opened a door. Calem followed him inside. Miss Genevieve hurried past him and pulled down the covers on the bed, so that once Calem set Miss Lia down, they could cover her in the blankets.

The innkeeper opened the door across the hall, as well, telling them it was their second room for whomever would use it. He then returned downstairs. A moment later, the apothecary entered the room.

The next few hours were tense for the traveling party. Miss Gloria and Miss Genevieve would take turns bathing Miss Lia's head with cool water, and Calem and Gerald would fetch more of it, or more hot water when the apothecary needed to make more tea for her. The apothecary was calm throughout, reassuring all of them that Miss Lia was not in any apparent danger. This did little to settle Calem's mind as he paced at the end of her bed while he waited for his next task.

Sure enough, sometime before midnight, judging by the moon, Miss Lia began to sweat. Calem finally felt able to take a full breath, then. He'd seen enough fever to recognize one breaking.

The apothecary agreed. "She's pulling through it now," he said as he packed his bag. He then looked at each of them in turn. "Have any of you some idea of where the fever came from?"

Miss Gloria, unsurprisingly, was the one to answer. "On occasion she will get a fever when no one else around her will. None of the rest of us has been ill."

"Well, keep an eye on each other anyway. Consult me if you're still here, or another apothecary immediately if any of you catch it." He placed the last of his supplied back into his bag. "Where are you bound from here?" he asked Calem.

"The capital, sir," Calem replied.

"Perfect. I have a colleague there who would be worth contacting if you need aid while you are there. Come with me and I'll write his direction for you."

Although loathe to leave Miss Lia, Calem followed the man out of the room. They passed Gerald, who paced in the hallway, unable to stomach much time in the sickroom. The larger knight joined them as they descended to the common room, now all but empty.

The innkeeper was there, tidying up for the night. He was able to provide quill and parchment for the apothecary to write the information on. "Here's the direction. My friend, a Mr. Grant, is a very good physician, and you would be in good hands should you need his services

"Thank you again, sir," Calem replied with a nod. "What do we owe you?"

The apothecary looked at the innkeeper, who nodded. "I'll have Seamus put it on your tab."

"Very well, then," Calem replied with a nod. "Safe travels."

The apothecary returned the farewell, then left. Once he was gone, the innkeeper addressed Calem. "Sir Calem, before you retire, I'd like to say that, aside from your ill traveling companion, it's been a pleasure to see you again. I wonder, are you returning because you've heard the news from the capital?"

Calem blinked in confusion."What news?" he asked.

The innkeeper frowned. "Well, if you don't know what I'm talking about, I had best let your mother tell you. She passed through a few days ago."

Calem wondered how bad the news was if the innkeeper was unwilling to tell him personally. He hoped his wedding day hadn't been moved up. "Then, she is at the capital?

The innkeeper nodded. "Yes, along with most of your family, and scores of others waiting for word of the lost princess."

Calem's eyes widened. That almost certainly meant his mother had brought his sisters along. Suddenly, he found himself desperate to reach the capital. However, he was exhausted. Even if he was not exhausted, he wasn't about to leave Miss Lia here, ill. At least, not tonight. Instead, he excused himself and made his way out to the stables. He crashed onto a bed of hay, emotionally and physically drained.

Gerald, having followed him out, looked down at him. "I guess I'll take the first watch," he said with a grin.

He turned and was about to leave when Calem called out. "Gerald."

"Yes?" he replied, turning back.

Calem took a breath before continuing. "Once we reach the capital, and drop the ladies off with His Grace's sister, I want you to come to the castle with me."

Gerald raised an eyebrow in confusion, but nodded. "Of course, if that is your wish."

Calem nodded. "I believe it's time for you to meet my mother, and learn why my betrothal is so important."

Fourteen

Late in the night, Lilia slept fitfully. It seemed as though every few minutes, her dreams would frighten her awake again. The same scene played out over and over. Ned and another large man entered the room, but Ned fled when he recognized her. After that, she only saw flashes, as if the memory was scattered and her mind was trying to piece it together again.

Then came the memory of the man holding a sword to her throat, but she was unable to move. Suddenly, she was very awake. The room was dark, however, and it was still quite difficult to move. Not knowing where she was, she started to panic as terrifying scenarios came to mind. Had she been captured by the man with the sword? Where were Gloria and Genevieve? Sir Calem and Sir Gerald?

Her breaths became shallow and rapid. Her breathing became easier, however, when she recognized Gloria sleeping on one side of her atop the blankets. Genevieve was on her other side, sitting in a chair, but slumped onto the bed. Between the two, they had her pinned beneath the blankets. Both were beginning to stir, having either felt or heard her struggling.

"What happened?" Lilia asked

Genevieve was the first to shake her sleep away enough to reply. "Oh, Lia!" she cried. "You were so brave! There was this bad man threatening us, but you took care of him! You fought and we saw you fall to the ground! We thought he had killed you!" She sniffed, and Lilia realized that she was actually crying. "Suddenly, however, you were holding a sword to his throat and sending him scurrying away!"

Gloria, who had finally rubbed the sleep form her eyes, continued the story. "Once he was gone, you collapsed to the ground. Suddenly, Sir Calem flew to your side. You tried to push him away, but barely managed a step before you fell. He caught you and carried you to the carriage. As we rode, you came down with a horrible fever. Genevieve and I used a water skin to cool you down until we arrived at this inn, where we could get some better help."

Lilia, who had managed to sit up, was silent, overwhelmed by their tale. A moment later, there was a soft knock on the door. Gloria and Genevieve looked at each other and grinned, which made Lilia wonder if she was still dreaming. "That will be Sir Calem," Gloria giggled, "wondering if you're alright."

Lilia raised an eyebrow in confusion. "How are you so sure?"

It was Genevieve's turn to giggle. It was the most sincere version of the sound Lilia had ever heard from the young woman. "Because he has done it every half hour since his watch started," she replied. She then turned to the door and called, "Come in!"

The door creaked open and, as the others had predicted, Sir

Calem peered inside. The worry that lined his face, visible in the light of a candle in the hall, faded to a relieved smile when he saw that she was sitting up. "Miss Lia," he breathed.

The way he said her name made her tingle. "Sir Calem," she replied with a nod and a small smile of her own.

"I'm relieved to see you awake," he said, sounding like he was holding back from saying much more.

She was grateful it was so dark, as it meant he couldn't see the blush his words had brought to her cheeks. "Thank you, sir."

He nodded. "Well, I shall leave you to rest." He nodded to each of them, his gaze lingering the longest on Lilia. "Good night, ladies."

"Good night, Sir Calem," Genevieve and Gloria said in unison. They wore matching grins as they said it.

He looked down in embarrassment. Lilia couldn't blame him, for she, too, felt embarrassed by her friends' behavior. "Good night, Sir Knight."

He gave her a small smile before shutting the door. As soon as it was closed, Genevieve and Gloria burst out giggling. "He is *definitely* in love with you," Genevieve said.

Lilia let out a sigh and laid back down. "Even if that were true, he is betrothed to someone else."

The giggling died on the instant. "Really?" Gloria asked, not bothering to hide her disappointment.

Lilia swallowed past the lump in her throat. "Yes. So, please, stop embarrassing him."

"Oh, Lia," Genevieve said sadly. She put a hand on Lilia's arm. "I'm so sorry."

Lilia frowned and looked Genevieve in the eye. "Genevieve, did I miss something? I thought you *hated* me."

Genevieve hung her head. "I'm so sorry for all of that, Lia.

You saved us yesterday." Tears pooled in her eyes, and she furiously wiped them away. "While I know I've never done anything to deserve it, I realized that had only I been threatened by those men, you still would have done what you did." She looked up at Lilia. "You have a heart of gold. I've heard that for years, usually from people comparing you and me, but I finally saw what that means yesterday."

Lilia squeezed the girl's hand. "Everyone deserves to be saved, Genevieve. Now, get into bed, both of you. You'll both be stiff sleeping as you were."

In a flurry of movement and blankets, the other girls climbed into bed. A few minutes later, Lilia heard the steady breathing of both of the other girls. She was afraid to sleep, however, after her dreams earlier. What helped her get to sleep was imagining Sir Calem carrying her in the safety of his arms.

When Lilia awoke next, she felt amazingly rested. She looked out a nearby window to see that the sun just peeking over the horizon. As the others were still sleeping, obviously worn out from tending to her the evening before, she quietly crawled out of bed, found her trunk, and changed into clean clothes. Then she tiptoed from the room and down the stairs. She looked around the common room for Sir Calem, but saw neither him nor Sir Gerald. She decided to check the stables. She found Sir Calem doing some exercises next to his horse's stall, his back to the inn. "Good morning," she said quietly.

He froze mid stretch at the sound of her voice, then suddenly stood straight. "Miss Lia! What are you doing up and about?"

She nodded towards the sun. "I have a hard time sleeping when the sun is up."

He nodded. "I just thought you would be exhausted, if not still unwell, after your...day." He approached her and felt her forehead. His touch made her skin tingle. He sighed in relief. "Your fever seems to have completely vanished. That is a good sign."

"Thank you," she blurted unexpectedly.

He frowned in confusion. "For what?"

She blushed. "The girls told me what happened. Thank you for taking such good care of me yesterday."

Their eyes met for a moment, then he suddenly turned away, bracing himself on the beam of his horse's stall. She watched as he took several deep breaths, wondering why he suddenly seemed so panicked. After a moment, he had calmed visibly, but he spoke to her in a quiet voice. "Miss Lia, I'm not a man that scares easily. I may only have a few years on you, but I've spent the last several years fighting alongside the soldiers of your father, the king. I defended lands both here in Katniona, and in Callarda. I even went into Malanna during the final press that convinced them to cease hostilities, leading to the peace treaty that holds now. I saw many things on the battlefield that still haunt me." He slowly turned to her. "Yet, I have never been more scared than I was yesterday, when you crumpled to the ground. For a moment I was too shocked to move. When I *could* move, he put a sword to your throat, threatening to kill you if I took another step." He shuddered and looked away. "It was like the man had ripped out my heart and stabbed it, and then continued stabbing it just for his own amusement."

Lilia took a sharp breath. *Does he love me in return?*

He wasn't done, however. He looked back at her. "Then,

suddenly, miraculously, you were standing over him, holding him at the point of his own sword. He was at your mercy. You truly astonished me then, because you *showed* him mercy." He turned away again. "I fear that, had I been in your position, I wouldn't have been able to do that. I would have disposed of him without a second thought." He turned to her once again. "How do you do it?"

She frowned in confusion. "Do what, exactly?"

"How do you stay so strong? So kind?"

She gave him a gentle smile. "Sometimes we become strong when it's the only choice we have. Also, I've learned that everyone deserves a second chance."

He studied her for a moment, as if searching for something. "Is that why you forgave me so easily? When I had told you of what I had done?"

She nodded. "Yes. Also, the strength I've gained from having to be strong helped me to decide to accept what I am. I might not like it, but this country needs me."

He gave her a sad nod. "That it does."

Their gazes met once again. There was no denying the connection between them. She also couldn't deny that it seemed impossible. It was no longer just *his* betrothal keeping them apart. Lilia took a deep breath and changed the subject, needing to focus on something less painful. "Shall we be off? I'm going to wake the ladies. If you would be so kind as to wake Sir Gerald?"

Sir Calem resumed his formal stance at her formal tone, and gave a polite nod. "Your wish is my command, my lady."

Once everyone was awake and had their belongings packed and downstairs, they ate a quick breakfast before loading into the carriage. Everyone, it seemed, was eager to reach the capital that afternoon, or, at least, no one felt the need to say anything over the morning meal. Once they were ready, Sir Calem settled their tab with the innkeeper while Sir Gerald helped the ladies into the carriage. As they climbed in, Genevieve insisted that Gloria sit next to her. She wanted their 'protector' to have an entire side to herself. Gloria readily agreed.

Lilia never thought she'd feel less comfortable being the rider with more space, but it wasn't the extra space making her uncomfortable. Neither Gloria nor Genevieve said more than a handful of words during the first hour of their journey. At least, not to her. Most of that time was spent with them staring — awestruck — at their 'protector' with occasional whispered conversations between them. Lilia wasn't sure if the exclusion or the attention was more embarrassing, but both were quite uncomfortable.

As the pair looked to be starting another whispered conversation, Lilia put her foot down. "Gloria, sit next to me. Right now." Gloria immediately moved across to sit next to her, "And Genevieve, say something rude or entitled."

Genevieve's eyes widened. "Er..."

"Really?" Lilia asked. "Nothing? Neither of you can think of anything to say to me, polite or otherwise?" A moment of stunned silence floated between them. Then Lilia threw up her hands in disgust. She opened the window and yelled, "Stop!"

As soon as the carriage rolled to a halt, she hopped out of the conveyance, rushing past a surprised Sir Gerald, who had descended to see what was needed. She mounted the now-empty driver's box. "Give me the reins," she ordered.

Sir Gerald's eyes widened. "Miss Lia, what is wrong?"

She clenched her jaw. "I can't stand the blasted silence! I have an entire side all to myself. Genevieve hasn't said a rude thing to me all morning. Why, neither she nor Gloria has said much of anything to me at all! I'm so unnerved by it all that I can't think of anything to say either!"

The men chuckled as Sir Gerald handed her the reins. "I'm sorry the situation is so...distressing," he said, chuckling again.

She rolled her eyes and, once Sir Gerald had secured the door and stepped clear of the wheels, she flicked the reins. She was not about to wait for him to mount, as she knew the knights would catch up easily. The carriage lurched forward, and she began to feel a light breeze on her face, which built as the horses increased their speed. She closed her eyes momentarily as she enjoyed the sensation, and she wondered why she hadn't asked to drive sooner.

Lilia was still driving when they reached the city walls that afternoon. The city streets were packed, and it seemed as if everyone was waiting on bated breath for news of Princess Kalysta's return. Lilia couldn't dwell on it at the moment, however, for the crowded streets demanded her focus so as not to run over or collide with anything or anyone. Even so, she expertly maneuvered the conveyance through the streets, following Sir Gerald to the home of the duke's sister, Lady Garnet. If Lilia remembered correctly, the lady was a countess, and, according to His Grace, she had been blessed with a match of both advantage and love.

The lady herself came out to meet them as Lilia pulled the horses to a stop. "You can be none other than Miss Lia," she said confidently as Lilia descended from the box.

"You are correct," Lilia replied as she dipped into a perfect curtsy.

The countess grinned. "I am Lady Garnet. It is a pleasure to finally meet you."

"The pleasure is mine, Lady Garnet," Lilia said. Gloria had

overflowed with praise for the countess and all the lady had done for her during her prior visit.

When the lady continued to grin, Lilia began to wonder what she found so amusing. Her puzzlement must have shown on her face, for Lady Garnet told her, "My brother has spoken very highly of you."

Lilia narrowed her eyes, suddenly wary. According to Sir Calem, His Grace was one of only five people who knew her true identity, but there were also any number of childhood scrapes he could have told his sister about as well. "What has he said?"

Lady Garnet chuckled. "He tells me everything, dear, including your level of skill with that." She motioned to the sword Lilia had made sure to belt on that morning. She promised herself to never be without it after the Bob fiasco, when it would have come in handy. "I did grow up in Farreden, you know, and I'm still familiar with many of the adults there, at least. Of note, however, he did mention that you may be able to tell me more about you, especially about how you are to be outfitted. However, that can wait until you have rested from your travels. I have some refreshments waiting in the drawing room, if you are hungry."

"I don't know about Miss Lia, but I am famished," Genevieve said from behind Lilia, who turned to see Sir Gerald assisting Gloria out of the carriage as well.

Lady Garnet's grin fell. "Ah, you must be Genevieve."

Genevieve nodded and gave a graceful curtsy. "Lady Garnet, thank you for having us."

The countess's grin returned, though not as wide as it had been. "You, on the other hand, are not quite as my brother described, though that is not in the least a bad thing." She then turned to the third young lady. "Miss Gloria." She greeted the young woman with a great deal of warmth. "I am ever so happy to see you again, and with your knight in tow, even! Are you both excited for your wedding?"

Gloria blushed and smiled, casting a lovesick glance a the knight. He returned her look with a foolish grin. "Indeed we are, Lady Garnet," he replied. Then he offered the countess a bow. "Now, I beg you to excuse my companion and myself. We are needed elsewhere at present." Sir Calem, who was still astride his horse, bowed to her as well.

The countess nodded regally and waved them away. "Of course. The girls are safe with me, as I'm sure you know. I do expect you to return soon, however."

Sir Gerald mounted, then bowed to her again from his saddle. "As you wish, my lady." He then turned his horse and left the courtyard. Sir Calem followed close behind, but turned back at the entrance, casting Lilia one last glance before turning onto the crowded streets and out of sight.

Lilia turned to find that all three other women had watched the exchange closely. She blushed furiously. "If you would excuse me, Lady Garnet, I wish to retire. I am quite exhausted, and not particularly hungry."

The countess nodded. "Of course, my dear." She then led the way inside. Once she directed Genevieve and Gloria to the drawing room, she led Lilia upstairs. "I have a room ready for you, of course. His Grace wasn't sure how long you would be staying, saying that you may be obtaining other lodgings soon, but I insist you stay with me for a few days. At least stay until we can get you dressed well enough to go about town. Perhaps we can get you some dance instruction as well?" Lady Garnet led Lilia to a room at the end of the hallway. "I hope it is to your liking," she said as she opened the door.

Lilia stepped inside and couldn't help but turn around in awe. Many different kinds of birds were painted as if flying through the sky blue colored walls. Looking up, she saw more birds and scattered clouds on the ceiling. She couldn't keep the grin from her face. "I love it."

The countess smiled. "My brother insisted you take this room." She entered the room and shut the door. "The one thing he did not tell me is why you are to have this room, which I sense is tied to why you may not stay long. Now, I don't wish to pry if this is a secret you don't trust me with yet, but I would like to know so I can help you as best I can."

Lilia pondered for a moment. True, she hadn't known Lady Garnet long, but both Gloria and Sir Gerald were well acquainted with her and seemed to trust her greatly. She also agreed that it would be helpful if the lady knew just who she was dressing, and potentially helping protect. Sir Calem had told her she looked just like the queen, so if anyone were to be hunting for the princess, she could be easy to spot.

Her decision made, Lilia used the necklace chain to retrieve the crest from her under her dress, displaying it for the countess. The lady looked at it and gasped. "Princess Kalsyta!"

Fifteen

Calem's initial plan had been to hurry straight to
the castle from Lady Garnet's house. However, he had heard
something on the way to her house that made him change his
mind about that. A quick word to Gerald on the street corner,
and they changed their route, weaving their way through the
capital city, keeping their ears open.

As they passed through a part of the city that wasn't quite
slums, but wasn't exactly well-off either, they caught wind of
another, similar conversation. A group of men had gathered at
the mouth of an alley to chat and smoke. With the noise of the
rest of the crowd, they were talking rather loudly.

"Wot's this about the princess?" one of the men asked as
Calem rode near the group. This caught his ear, so he came to a
stop just beyond them. Gerald stopped near him.

"I says it may not be good fer the princess ta be found,"
another man replied. "'Specially not fer her."

"Yeah, coz it'd be upsettin' ta learn you was really royal," a
third replied. This got a laugh from several of the others.

"Naw, I mean coz it might be dangerous fer her t'come back," the second man, who appeared to be taller than the other, snapped.

"An' why's that?" the first man challenged. "I didn't think you had anythin' against the royal fam'ly."

"Not me," the tall man replied quickly, throwing his hands up in a show of innocence. "Not that I owe 'em any favors, but I don' hate 'em."

"Then what you spoutin' 'bout?" a fourth man grumbled.

"That some'n else does, and that some'ns been lookin' fer others who ain't happy with 'em either."

"An' you think they mean ta stop the princess comin' back?" the third man asked.

"What kind o' fool idea is that?" the first man spat. "They tryin' ta start the war again?"

"Maybe," was all the tall man said in reply.

Having heard enough, Calem rode on, Gerald on his tail. Calem was very concerned. People voicing their complaints about their leaders, or wishing them ill, was nothing new. However, to be voicing things like that on the side of the road was bold indeed. The man was likely sounding out his pals to see if they were for or against the idea of preventing the princess's return, because if he was just repeating such a treasonous rumor, he'd not have done it so publicly.

They started a more direct route towards the castle, but hunting down the rumor had taken them further away from the structure than where they had started, so it took them a good half hour to reach the castle gates. Once they were in the castle courtyard, they moved to the stables. A stable boy met them as they approached. "Welcome back, Sir Calem!"

Calem grinned. "Thank you, Johnny."

The lad's eyes went wide. "You remember me name?"

Calem grinned and nodded. "Of course. You were very helpful to me the last time I was here."

Johnny grinned. "I'll take good care o' yer horses, sirs!"

Calem ruffled the lad's hair. "I know you will." He then led Gerald into the palace that was the center of the castle complex.

Gerald seem to soon realize that Calem knew exactly where he was going, and was obviously confused. "How do you know your way around?"

Calem took a deep breath as he decided how to answer. "I spent a few days here right after the war ended," he replied over his shoulder. "Well, more like a month. I had done the king a great service, and lodging in the castle was my reward."

Gerald furrowed his brow in confusion. "What did you do to earn such a privilege?"

Calem sighed. He generally kept his exploits secret, for various reasons, but he knew Gerald to be a good friend and worthy of his trust. He took another deep breath, and said, "I was in charge of the mission to locate the crown prince."

Gerald's eyes widened. "I heard about that. Everyone was sure the princes had been killed early in the war, but you managed to track them down somehow." Gerald chuckled. "To think...all this time I've been traveling with a legend." He laughed at his facetious comment, then grew more serious. "Too bad you didn't come through this time, eh?"

To hide the smile that was threatening after that comment, Calem turned to face forward again.

A few minutes later, as they were reaching the guest chambers, which Calem didn't know as well, they crossed paths with a familiar looking servant. It was one of the apprentice scribes.

"You are back, sir!" the lad enthused. "We have been waiting for you! Shall I lead you to your mother?"

Calem smiled and nodded at the young man of twelve or so. "I would be most grateful, James. Thank you."

The servant's eyes widened, and Calem wondered why it was such an odd thing here for someone like him to remember a servant's name. The lad recovered, and bowed before leading them deeper into the guest wing. He stopped a short time later before a large double door. He knocked twice, indicating visitors were coming in, and then opened the door. "Sir Calem and Sir Gerald to see you, Your Majesty," James said. He then bowed and stepped aside to let the knights enter.

Calem's mother was the sole occupant of the sitting room of the exquisite guest suite. She was marking her place in a book as they entered. When she looked up at him, she smiled. The size of her smile, as always, warmed Calem's soul. "My son!"

Out of the corner of his eye, Calem saw his friend's mouth drop open in astonishment. He didn't blame Gerald in the least for his reaction, as he'd not warned the man they were meeting a foreign queen that day. Calem chuckled as he crossed the room to where his mother was rising from her armchair. Her black hair cascaded down her back, and her green eyes sparkled. He kissed her cheek without needing to bend, as she was nearly his height. "Hello, Mother dear."

She pulled him into an embrace. "I have missed you so! Your sisters have, as well! They will be so glad to see you are here."

Calem smiled broadly. He returned her embrace, then gently pulled free, keeping one of her hands in his. "I'm glad someone missed me, at least. I will see the girls shortly, but first allow me to introduce my friend."

He turned to find his 'friend' glaring at him. "*Prince Calem?!*" the larger knight bellowed. Calem felt his mother flinch. Gerald must have seen it as well, for he said, "My apologies, Your Majesty. I was just distressed that your son kept his full identity from me for the many months of our acquaintance, but my outburst was inappropriate."

"Oh, it's no bother," she replied, waving a dismissive hand. "You merely caught me by surprise."

Calem, however, shrugged as he held the other man's gaze. "Is there a problem?"

"Of course there's..." Gerald started, then stopped as he thought about it more. "I mean...I thought..." He took a deep breath. "Actually, it makes sense. This explains quite a bit, to tell you the truth." His eyes widened. "Your betrothal... It's not just a couple of mothers trying to expand the family wealth or standing."

Calem shook his head and looked down, his smile fading completely. "No. It is two kingdoms trying to more permanently end the war. I am engaged to the princess of Malanna."

"About that..." his mother interjected. He drew in a sharp breath and his eyes flew to her face. "There has been a change in plans..."

Calem had worried that the terms of the arrangement had changed since the innkeeper's comment the night before. He had no idea if the change was good or bad. He frowned. "What kind of change?"

His mother started to wring her hands. "Well, I know that we discussed your brother having no desire to marry Princess Catalina — indeed, I have no wish to see her on my throne — and he asked to wait and see if he would get along better with

Princess Kalysta, if she were found, and that you would have to marry Princess Catalina instead if that happened..."

Calem's brow creased, and he narrowed his eyes. Mother was rambling. She *never* rambled. This was quite worrying. "What has changed, Mother?" he asked in a commanding tone.

She took a deep breath, likely to steady her nerves, before trying again. "I don't know if she arrived before or after you left, but Princess Catalina has been here in Katiera for the last few months. In the time, she has grown close to the princes here. She has developed a tendresse with the oldest, Kenneth. Considering their feelings, and knowing you were not enthusiastic with the match as it was, the treaty was amended, and now they are engaged."

Calem's head began to spin, and he put a hand out to steady himself. Gerald rushed to his side and helped him to a chair. Unsure if he could believe his ears, he looked up to see Gerald grinning from ear to ear.

Free. He was actually free of that dreaded arrangement. He took a deep breath, then another, feeling like he was breathing more easily than he had in months.

Once he was sufficiently recovered, his mother continued. "As you have apparently realized, you can now marry whomever you wish, as your brother will now be the one to marry Princess Kalysta."

Just like that, the bubble burst. Calem's expression hardened as the warmth from a moment before turned cold again. Gerald, however, was still grinning. "That is great news, Calem! What are you waiting for? Go get her!"

The queen's eyes widened. "Get who?"

Gerald grinned and shook Calem's shoulder. "Your son here

fell in love with a fiery young woman who is as good with a sword as he is, maybe better."

The queen smiled. "Oh, how wonderful! When can I meet her?" She turned to Calem, who was getting to his feet. Seeing his expression, she frowned. "What is wrong, dear?"

"Mother, Gerald, if you would come with me, I have some urgent business with the king of Katniona. Gerald, be prepared to learn another secret I have not yet told you."

His mother's and Gerald's eyes widened, but they nodded and followed Calem silently from the room. Encountering James in the halls again, Calem sent him ahead to find out where the king was. He returned shortly to inform them that His Majesty was in his private chambers. Calem changed course and followed the servant to the family wing of the palace.

When they arrived at an even grander set doors than those of the royal guest suite, the servant knocked properly, then waited for a reply from within. At the moment, however, Calem was unable to wait. He pounded on the door. King Kelvin opened the door with an annoyed look on his face. The look quickly became hopeful surprise. "Calem! You've returned!"

Jaw tight, Calem nodded. "I...we need to speak with you privately, sir."

The king stepped back, allowing all of them to enter his sitting room. James, though, was dismissed to attend to his other duties.

Gerald led Calem's mother to a couch while Calem paced in front of the windows. The king shut the door behind them then approached the young prince. "Calem, what is this about?"

Calem took a deep breath. "Sir, I found your daughter." He

faced the others to see how they would react at his pronouncement.

His mother gasped. She covered her shocked look with her hand.

Gerald's eyes widened. "Who? When?"

The king's eyes widened even more than the knight's had. He staggered to his large armchair, even more off balance than Calem had been upon hearing his mother's news. "My daughter…" The shock was as apparent in his voice as on his face. "Where is she?"

Calem focused on the king, knowing his friend would get his answers as well. "She is here, in the city," he replied. "We have left her with a lady of impeccable reputation."

Annoyance joined the shock still written on the king's face. "Don't toy with me, boy, who? Which *lady* did you leave my daughter with?"

"Lady Garnet, sir."

The king nodded his approval, but Calem's attention was grabbed by Gerald's sharp gasp. The knight had put the pieces together. "Miss Lia…"

The sound of her name made Calem's heart skip a beat, but his jaw tighten. He nodded. "Yes. She has been living in Farreden, in the far north, as the daughter of the local blacksmith and his wife."

The king looked near to fainting. "Calem, you had best be completely certain this girl is my daughter, for I don't think I could bear losing her again."

Calem held the man's gaze. "Not only is she the spitting image of Her Majesty, but I confronted her parents. They confirmed that she is the princess. As proof, they offered a necklace bearing your crest that was given to them by the man who brought her to them. They also gave me the man's name."

Hope and pain warred in the king's expression. Calem was certain the hope was for his daughter and the pain was for the man who had protected her. "What name did they give you?"

"It was your old friend and scribe, Marcus."

The king bowed his head and was silent for a moment as he mourned his friend and processed the news. When he looked up, tears were running down his face. "My daughter is alive!" he cried. He jumped to his feet and headed for the door. "I must see her."

Calem put a hand on the king's arm to stop him as he passed. "That may not be the wisest course of action, sir."

The king glared at him. "Explain."

"For now, she is anonymous. Safe. However, on the way to the castle, not even an hour ago, I heard rumors of a plot to do her harm. Earlier, as we rode into town, I heard whispers of a plot to thwart the formation of the alliance you are attempting to create."

The king scowled and turned to Gerald. "You heard these rumors?"

Calem saw his friend swallow before nodding. "Yes, sire."

The king started pacing, obviously trying to find a way to get what he wanted without endangering his child. When he stopped he turned to Calem. "What do you suggest?"

Calem had already been asking himself the same question, but it still took a long moment for him to come up with something. "She is just getting used to the idea of who she really is. Even without the threat, it may be best for her to have time to come to terms with her identity. She also needs to learn how to behave; how to act, how to dance, how to *be* a princess. She will be getting that education soon, anyway, as that is apparently how Lady Garnet has always prepared the young women her brother sends down from Farreden for her to bring out. I imagine the dancing lessons will start as soon as your daughter is measured for a wardrobe."

"So, I can't see my daughter yet? Is that what you're saying?" The king looked ready to explode with anger.

Unafraid of the king's rage, Calem stared the taller man down. "If you want her to remain safe, then yes!"

Deflated, but still angry, the king stormed back to his chair. He then slumped into it. The anger drained and he put his head in his hands. "How do you suggest I see her, then? I'm desperate, Calem. It's been seventeen years…" He trailed off for a moment before looking up at Calem, who had moved to his side. "Do you have something in mind?"

Calem frowned in concentration, trying to come up with a solution. He had an idea a moment later, but he was uncertain, at best. "How many other knights have returned? Are we among the last?"

The king gave him a confused frown, but shook his head. "No, you are among the first. That's why I was so surprised to see you back."

Calem smiled. "That is perfect. When we set out, you suggested that we bring back any young woman whose identity could not be confirmed that was of the right age. I imagine some of the other search parties will be bringing back candidates. If they do, then we could start a rumor that the princess has been found by some of the recently returned knights. If we wait long enough, our return will not be thought of as recent, casting suspicion elsewhere. This will also give Miss Lia time to learn what she needs to know."

The king nodded. "That is all well and good, but when will I see my daughter?"

"Then, you will announce that a ball is to be held in her honor. Sir Gerald and I will make sure she is there. That is when you will finally get to meet her."

"And you may see her before then," Gerald added. "Miss Lia will likely attend many society events as part of her training under Lady Garnet."

Calem's mother spoke up. "Miss Lia... Is that the name Princess Kalysta has been known by all these years?"

Gerald nodded. "Yes, Your Majesty."

The king looked up at Calem. His brow was still creased with worry, but overall, he looked quite relieved. "Once again, Prince Calem, you have come through for me. How can I ever repay you?"

Calem looked over the top of King Kelvin's chair for a moment, rubbing his chin with his thumb as he thought. *Dare I ask for her hand? Surely he would consent. Mother would likely understand, as well. And yet...no, it doesn't feel right. Now isn't the time for this.* He turned his gaze back to the king. "Stick to my plan, and we'll call it even, for now. Also, please continue to call me Sir Calem for the time being. Until the ball, at least, I intend to continue serving as your Knight to make sure this plan comes together."

"Very well," the king replied, sounding unconvinced. He narrowed his eyes and studied Calem. "What has you so concerned for my daughter's safety?" Calem schooled his face to reveal nothing. After a moment, the king came to his own conclusion. "You are keeping her safe for your brother, no doubt. Your concern for others, and for this alliance, does you credit, Sir Calem. You are a good man." With a nod, the king rose from his chair. "Now," he said as he strode toward the door. "I have some reports to review before meeting with my advisors later. Plus, I need to tell my wife what we have discussed."

"How does Her Majesty fare?" Calem asked as he helped his mother to her feet.

"As poorly as when you departed," the king replied. "She still keeps to our chambers or her garden almost exclusively."

"Which may work to our advantage," Calem said. "The princess looks a lot like the queen, but because even I have seen her so rarely, it took me a full day to see the resemblance."

"We will leave you to speak with her alone," his mother added. She curtsied as Calem and Gerald bowed. The king nodded in reply and opened the door.

"Thank you for your time, Your Majesty," Calem said as the three of them reached the door. Then they departed and the king shut the door behind them.

Calem walked slowly beside his mother as they returned to her quarters. "Oh, Calem. Your duties have been making you miserable, haven't they?"

He looked down and nodded. Of course she realized his dilemma. With all that she had seen and heard the past hour, it was likely very easy to recognize he had feelings for Miss Lia. "It would seem that love, or at least romance, is not to be part of my life."

His mother turned to him. "Are you certain you love her?"

Calem held her gaze. "I've never been more certain of anything in my entire life."

Her eyes went wide. "I see." She furrowed her eyebrows in thought. "Well, I will speak with your brother and see what I can do."

Calem grimaced. "Mother, please, don't say anything. Her

safety depends on discretion. While Collin is good at many things, keeping a secret is not always one of them."

She sighed and nodded, worry still creasing her brow. "I suppose you are correct." She stopped a moment later. Calem looked around and realized they had reached the wing where his family was staying. "Now, I had best get some rest. Make sure you greet your sisters soon."

Calem nodded. "I will."

She kissed his cheek and entered her rooms. Once she was inside, he turned to find Gerald standing at a respectable distance, looking pensive. Calem approached him. "What is on your mind, my friend?"

"I was thinking about how much more pleasant the king is when he's not standing on ceremony," Gerald said, cracking half a grin to show he was joking. "Actually, I was thinking that I should go inform Lady Garnet and her guests of the plan. we are expecting them to play a rather significant role, after all." Then he grinned. "I'll likely spend most of my time there, or thereabouts, so if you need me for anything, begin there. I'm sure Lady Garnet or her guests will be able to tell you where I am."

Calem tried, hard, to be happy for his friend, but he couldn't manage a smile in that moment. The best he could manage was a curt nod and a neutral tone. "Go to your lady, Gerald, and yes, tell the countess what we have discussed." Well, his tone was *mostly* neutral.

Gerald frowned at him, hearing the bitterness in Calem's voice and quickly realizing why it was there. "I'm sorry, Calem. I really am. Life has not been kind to you lately." A second later, the knight's eyes lit up, and a grin spread on his face again. "If you want the girl, why not challenge your brother to a duel? Everyone knows you're the best."

Calem slumped, leaning against the wall. "I'm only the best in Katniona. Unfortunately, even I have a hard time besting my brother. It only ever happens on rare occasions, and it has been a long time since I last did so." He looked away in agony. "Aside from that, since our bout with Miss Lia, I'm not as confident as I had been. Also, my brother has always been good at getting under my skin, making me doubt myself, shaking my confidence even further. He fights dirty, not with technique, but with words. I don't trust myself to be able to win her that way."

Calem looked up to see his friend scowling at him. "Well, you've got to think of something. Why didn't you say anything when we were speaking with the king? Surely he would have agreed to you taking your brother's place, after how much you've done for him and this country."

Calem nodded. "Perhaps, but I felt like the time wasn't right."

Gerald's frown grew troubled. "Just...make sure the right time is *before* she is married."

Calem heaved a heavy sigh and nodded. "I know. Don't worry. I'm sure I'll think of something."

Sixteen

"YOUR HIGHNESS..." LADY GARNET WAS OBVIOUSLY IN shock as she sank into a curtsy.

Lilia scowled at the lady's head. "Don't *do* that! I've only known of my true identity for a few days and I'm not used to people curtsying to me." She almost sighed with relief when Lady Garnet stood straight again. "Thank you." She then took a deep breath. "Now, there is something that has been bothering me for quite a while. I'm hoping you have an answer."

Lady Garnet nodded. "I will do my best. What has been bothering you?"

"Who *exactly* is Sir Calem? Surely only a prince would have a betrothal he absolutely could not get out of."

Lady Garnet cast her an amused grin. "You have just answered your own question."

Lilia's eyes widened. Yes, she had guessed he may be a prince, but it was still shocking to hear that he actually was. "He's a prince..." She suddenly remembered all of the things she had said to him and couldn't help but feel a little chagrined.

Lady Garnet let out a chuckle as she nodded. "Yes, he is. The second prince of Callarda, to be specific." She then studied Lilia closely before asking. "Is there an understanding between the two of you? It certainly looked like there may be."

Not caring that princesses were supposed to sit properly, Lilia slumped into the nearest chair. "No. He is determined not to back out of his marriage arrangement. I can't say I blame him." She sighed. "Part of why I'm drawn to him is that he is such an honorable man."

Lady Garnet looked at her with confusion. "Have you not heard?"

Lilia looked at her askance. "Heard what?"

"My letter to my brother must have arrived in Farreden after your departure. Princess Catalina of Malanna, who was to marry Calem, has fallen in love with your oldest brother. The treaty has been rewritten and she is to marry him instead. Calem is a free man."

Lilia's heart and mind raced at the news, and hope filled her chest. "He said something about me having to marry a prince. Would, or could, that be him?"

Lady Garnet sighed, casting her a look full of sadness. This put a stopper on the surge of hope Lilia felt. "Unfortunately, no. It is his older brother you are to wed."

Lilia scowled in thought as she stood and began pacing. "There must be some way around this. Surely I need not marry the brother if I am in love with Calem."

Lady Garnet' sigh revealed her pity. "I'm sorry, Your Highness, but it is not that simple. By refusing to marry the crown prince, and thus refusing to become queen of Callarda, you risk offending the future king, which could spark a new war."

Lilia's scowl deepened. She was about to reply when there was a knock on the door. "Who is it?" Lady Garnet called out.

"Gloria and Genevieve," came the muffled reply. Lilia was fairly certain it was the latter who had spoken, but the sound did not penetrate well enough to be sure. "May we come in?"

"Just a moment," Lady Garnet called back. She turned back to Lilia. "Do you wish for them to know who you really are?" she asked quietly.

Lilia wrung her hands. "I'm uncertain. What do you think?" She asked in the same quiet tone.

The countess thought for a moment. "Well, I would trust Gloria with anything, but I don't know Genevieve very well at all. From what I've heard from my brother, I wouldn't tell her about this. She seems to be different from my brother's reports, however, so I am no longer certain about that. I will leave it to you to decide."

Still unsure of what to do, Lilia dropped the pendant back into her dress and nodded for Lady Garnet to call them in. The countess nodded in reply and, in a raised voice, called, "Come in!"

Gloria and Genevieve entered the room and looked around in awe. Gloria smiled at Lilia. "Of course His Grace would insist you get the best room in the house."

Lady Garnet let out and amused chuckle. "I suspect you all know who his favorite person is."

Genevieve let out a sigh. "Yes. I've known it for years. That is part if why I would treat Lia so abominably. I was jealous that my guardian cared more for her than for me. Unfortunately, the jealousy didn't inspire me to try to be better so he would approve of me as well, or to change my attitude." She cast Lilia a look of sorrow. "I had to have her save me before I could look past her favored status."

The countess frowned, obviously confused. "Save you? What are you talking of?"

The three girls exchanged a look, unsure how to tell the countess of the event. Genevieve gave them a small nod and took up the tale. "It happened only yesterday, and oh! It was horrible! There were these two men that entered a tavern we stopped at for a meal. They came straight to our table intent on some form of mischief with us three young ladies, as the knights sat at their own table nearby. One of them recognized Lia and ran off, terrified. The other, however, wanted to beat her up to avenge his friend. So, he and Lia went outside, with Sir Calem close behind. Suddenly he pulled a sword on her!"

Lady Garnet gasped and her eyes flew to Lilia's face. "Is that true?"

Lilia frowned in concentration, trying to recall the events that Genevieve was recounting. "Maybe," she replied hesitantly. "It sounds familiar, but I had a fever that evening. I don't really remember what happened after the first man fled."

"Well, we do," Genevieve told them, indicating herself and Gloria. "So, all Lia had was her throwing knife, which looked minuscule compared to his sword. However, she used it to parry every blow! But then, the man used a dirty trick and hit her in the head with the hilt of his sword. She crumpled to the ground!"

Lilia clapped her hands, suddenly remembering the fight in vivid detail. She couldn't help but grin. "Actually, he mostly missed. I ducked away enough that he only got me with his wrist, then fell so that he thought he'd hit me harder."

Gloria gasped. "You remember?"

Lilia nodded as the scene unfolded in her mind's eye. "Now I do, yes. I let him think I was unconscious. Then he came and stood over me and rolled me onto my back with his boot. He put his sword to my throat for a moment, then crouched down and told me he had come to collet me for his brother..." She frowned as she tried to remember who the man's brother was. "Bob!" she suddenly said, her eyes flying wide open. "Bob sent him to collect me!" She scowled. "Why, that dirty, rotten—"

"Ahem," Gloria interrupted, obviously worried that Lilia may say something not fit for a lady's ears. "So, he was over you, then suddenly he was on the ground and *you* were holding his sword at *his* throat. Then you let him run off."

Genevieve picked up the story again. "Then, Lia collapsed from exhaustion. Sir Calem had to carry her to the carriage." She heaved a dramatic sigh. "It really is too bad that he's betrothed. You two are perfect for each other."

Lady Garnet looked at Lilia with a questioning glance. Lilia took a deep breath, turned to her friends — she was pleasantly surprised that it had become so natural to think of Genevieve as a friend — and said, "Actually, he has been freed from his marriage arrangement."

Both girls squealed with joy. "That is the best news!" Gloria cried.

"Oh, I'm so happy for you!" Genevieve exclaimed as she embraced Lilia. Lilia did her best to return it, though her thoughts were already heavy with the next thing she needed to tell them.

"Oh, we need to design your wedding gown!" Gloria said excitedly.

"May I...be one of your bridesmaids?" Genevieve asked hesitantly.

It was then the girls realized Lilia hadn't joined them in their excitement. "What's wrong, Lilia?" Gloria asked with a confused frown. "We thought you would be happy with the news."

Lilia fingered the chain of her necklace, which suddenly felt extremely heavy, then turned and walked to the window. The bright blue sky was in stark contrast to her sullen mood. "It would be wonderful news...were he the only one who was betrothed."

Gloria and Genevieve gasped. "Lia, what are you saying?" the latter asked.

Lilia took a deep breath before turning around and nodding to Lady Garnet. The countess turned to the girls and motioned to Lilia. "Miss Gloria, Miss Genevieve, I would like to introduce to you Her Royal Highness, Princess Kalysta."

Both girls' faces filled with shock as they gaped at Lilia. Genevieve was the first to recover. "Your Highness..." Lilia watched, wide eyed, as Genevieve sank into a curtsy. Her shock made her wobbly. Somehow, she managed to elbow Gloria from that pose. The nudge helped Gloria to recover from her shock, and she followed the other girl's example.

Lilia glared at them, feeling a little hurt by their reaction. "Girls! Honestly!" she snapped. "You should know me better than almost anyone! Do you really think I enjoy seeing the tops of your heads like this?! This is ridiculous! Stand up!" That the girls only stood once she commanded them to did nothing to relieve Lilia's disgust. "Please, I need you to be your normal selves right now. I only learned about this after we left Farreden. It's hard enough to handle without you two bending and scraping." She stepped closer to them, hoping she could close the emotional distance as well. "Do you want to know why I left you this morning and drove the carriage?"

They both nodded simultaneously.

"Because you were acting like this! That was just for me being 'your hero' after yesterday! If I'd known you were going to act like this, I wouldn't have told you! So, please! Don't treat me any differently!" She was almost frantic, needing them to understand how much she was going to depend on them treating her normally.

Genevieve's eyes widened in shock. "You mean, you really want me to go to back to saying mean things as I was before yesterday? To a *princess?*"

Feeling somewhat more at ease, Lilia let out a grin. "When she has asked you to, then yes." She then arched an eyebrow. "Besides, you were never able to best the princess in a battle of wits. Who's to say she didn't enjoy responding to the barbs?"

Genevieve's eyes widened further. "Are you really telling me that you enjoy our sparring?"

Lilia smiled and nodded. "Yes. Now that I'm no longer worried about responding in kind, I find it quite enjoyable."

To Lilia's surprise, Genevieve grinned. "I'm so glad! You don't know how many years I've been waiting for you to snap back at me. It was so refreshing when you began to do so."

It was Lilia's turn to stare. "You mean, all these years, you've been trying to provoke me into sparring with you?"

Genevieve's grin faded, and she hung her head, shaking it. "Not all of them. In the beginning, especially after you cut my hair with your knife, I meant every insult I threw at you." She looked up and gave a hesitant smile. "I got you to snap once, when we were twelve, and after that I made it my mission to break your silence.

I'm not sure if you noticed, but I did try to keep us from drifting *too* far apart after that. I have fond memories from when we were friends as little girls, before whatever started our rivalry. However, I couldn't see a way to get around my pride to actually fix things before now. You have no idea how rewarding this trip has been for me, Lia. You also have no idea how good you are at the game."

Lilia struggled to find a response. It was true, she also remembered those time when they were little girls fondly, but their rivalry had always seemed impossible to bridge. Maybe it wasn't just Genevieve's pride that had gotten in the way. Maybe that was why it was so easy to think of her as a friend again now.

Lilia was saved from trying to put her thoughts into words by the sound of hooves on the cobblestone of the courtyard. All four women hurried to the window to find Sir Gerald dismounting below. Gloria ran to the bedroom door and flung it open. The others rushed after her.

Lilia was the first behind Gloria, and was able to watch her rush into the knight's arms. She smiled at the sight. "Sir Gerald!" Lady Garnet sounded a little out of breath. "We are pleased to see you again!" she said as she reached the bottom of the stairs. She ushered everyone into the drawing room and rang for tea. "I know I told you that I expected you back soon, but you are here earlier than I anticipated."

Sir Gerald nodded. "That is because I come bearing news, good lady. Sir Calem sends instructions regarding a certain young lady's...safety and schedule." He cast a quick glance at Gloria and Genevieve. "Is present company aware of the situation?"

The countess nodded. "Yes, we all know."

He nodded back, then looked at the door and frowned.

"Might you know if this room is a secure one for discussing a sensitive topic?"

She frowned. "While I am fairly certain it is, I'm not positive. The bedrooms would be better, as the walls are thicker, but that isn't an option at the moment."

"Agreed," Sir Gerald replied. "Well, then I shan't be direct. Let me put a scenario to you, if you don't mind."

"Not at all," the countess said, shaking her head. "What is this scenario you have for us to ponder?"

Gerald glanced at all of them, then continued directing his comments primarily to the countess. "As you are, no doubt, aware, the knighthood has been sent on a quest to find the missing princess. Should the princess be found, we are wondering if you would see to it that she knows how she is expected to behave in polite society; addressing everyone, dancing, dining etiquette...everything. Once the knights have all returned, a ball will be held in her honor. She needs to be ready for it."

The countess nodded. "I see. Yes, I would be willing to oversee her education. You undoubtedly recall that I provided such instruction for Miss Gloria when she was last here. Other than her education, what would you have me do with her once she arrives?"

"Well, as she has mostly likely grown up using a different name, let her keep using it until her presentation. This may not be news normally shared with ladies, but I should warn you there are whispers of those in the city who may wish her harm."

Lady Garnet nodded gravely. "Not everyone is thrilled about becoming allies with Malanna after their actions during the war. Also, those from Malanna may not wish for an alliance between Katniona and Callarda, which is the alliance the princess would be creating, for it would mean a stronger army should they attack again." She sighed. "Now, have you any idea when I should expect her?"

"I imagine she will be coming any day now. When we set out, His Majesty requested that we return by summer's end. Sir Calem and I are among the first to return, but we expect the others to return over the coming weeks, sooner if they found her. Or, heaven forbid, learned of her passing."

The countess nodded. "Indeed, let us hope that has not happened. Well, if any of the other knights bring back ladies, either ladies who may be the princess or ladies who have captured their hearts, as Miss Gloria has yours, I would be more than happy to put them up as well." She grinned. "It will be a grand undertaking to see that these ladies are prepare for whatever awaits them during their time in Katiera."

Lilia smiled at Lady Garnet's intelligence. If all of the girls were together, anyone trying to harm the princess would have a difficult time figuring out which it might be, making things even safer for her. Not that she was overly concerned for her own safety, but she didn't want anyone else getting hurt for her sake.

Sir Gerald's eyes widened as he, too, recognized the importance of Lady Garnet's suggestion. "A very wise idea, my lady. You are most generous." The tea then arrived, and they spent the next half hour chatting about other topics as they partook of the offering. Lady Garnet showed she was already serious about her task of educating the girls, as she gave Lilia and Genevieve pointers on how to handle tea time in polite society.

Once the tea was finished, Sir Gerald stood. "If you would excuse me, ladies, I need to report back to the castle. It seems that I will be serving as a go-between from here to there."

Lady Garnet nodded. "Thank you for coming, Sir Gerald. I will prepare my servants for the coming storm."

Sir Gerald bowed, then turned to Gloria and took her hand. Lilia watched with a grin as Gloria blushed when the knight kissed the back of the hand he held. "Until later, my dear," he said softly.

She smiled up at him. "Farewell, my love."

The knight offered them all one more bow before leaving to deliver the news. Once he departed, Lady Garnet turned to the girls. "Well, we had best prepare for these ladies that might be coming." She frowned in thought. "Although, if there are too many, I will not have enough rooms for everyone to have their own. Do you girls mind sharing a room, if it becomes necessary?"

The three young women looked at each other and grinned.

Seventeen

CALEM COULDN'T HELP BUT BE AMAZED. HIS PLAN FOR the princess's safety was working far better than he had antici-pated. It had been a month and a half since he had left her with Lady Garnet, and the lady now had twenty or so girls at her house. And, if Gerald was to be believed, Lady Garnet was enjoying every minute of the strange experience. As if running a school, the woman had all the girls on a schedule with some of the best tutors in the city seeing to their aristocratic education.

Better yet, the terrorists were, as yet, unable to decide if any of the girls was actually the princess. Calem and Gerald were taking turns walking the city every day, listening to the crowds, hoping to prevent the threatened treachery. They would do so in disguise, including taking a page from Miss Lia's book and adopting rough accents similar to the one she used in Farreden. From what they heard, they were convinced that, while the villains were sure the real princess was among Lady Garnet's guests, they were uncertain which of them she was and were unwilling to slaughter the whole lot of them.

There were two reasons for this. The first was that the other knights who had brought in young women were taking turns standing guard around the manor. However the second and more significant reason was Miss Lia herself. Calem had seen her out among the people, finding small ways that she could help them. The torture of having her so close, yet out of reach, was painful, to say the least, and he'd avoided speaking to her and making that pain worse.

During her trips among the people, she was especially attentive to the wounded, and she always took a pouch with poultice and bandages with her, binding the wounds of people who had no money to pay a doctor to do so. People started calling her the "chestnut-haired warrior angel," as she would keep her sword on her as she undertook these journeys. He knew she'd had to use it, too. She had been the talk of the taverns a few weeks back after taking down a man who had tried to rob her. Not only had she quickly disabled the man by cutting a gash into his arm that left him unable to hold his club, but she had insisted on binding his wounds before sending him away. Hearing stories like this, Calem was unsurprised that the main reason the terrorists were unwilling to storm Lady Garnet's house was Miss Lia's kindness.

While her safety seemed fairly sure, her affection for him did not. This doubt made him irritable, and his irritation increased each time Gerald reported to him on the state of the countess's manor. Lately, he was bringing back word of her flirting with more and more of the men she interacted with, and she had an ever-increasing crowd of admirers. The mean-spirited part of him would rejoice when they realized that she was unable to marry them, for they would feel what he had been feeling for the last several weeks: her unavailability. However, he had to prepare for when his brother would step forward to claim Miss Lia's hand.

It was this thought that led him to punching the wall of his room in the palace. When he looked down at his hand, he was disappointed to see that it wasn't bleeding. He was about to repeat the action, hoping for a different result, when there came a knock on his door. He heaved a sigh, then turned to the door. "Come in."

When the door opened, Calem seriously considered replacing the wall with his visitors face for his next punch. "Calem! You should have been there!" cried his brother. "There was a beautiful young woman there that is just perfect!"

Calem rolled his eyes and affected his bored tone, which he had perfected for the purpose of listening in court, as his brother recounted the events of the parties he had attended. "I'm listening."

His brother rolled his eyes in reply, recognizing the tone for what it was, but continued to gush praise over whatever young woman had caught his attention that evening. "She had these mesmerizing hazel eyes, and long, chestnut-brown hair." He shook his head as if in disbelief that someone could be so beautiful. "I've never seen her equal."

Calem knew of only one young woman that fit his brother's description, and he nearly flinched. He recovered quickly, and continued the conversation before his brother would suspect anything. "You've said that before, Collin, about other beauties you've met."

Collin gave an exasperated huff. "I know, I know...but this one is different. And she's the most wonderful dancer, too."

The sudden image of Calem holding the woman he loved in his arms made him pause, and his heart ached —not for the first, nor, likely, the last time — at what could never be. He forced an annoyed sigh and another eye roll. "What is her name?"

"Miss Lia. Although I've heard that it is short for Lilia."

Calem grunted to cover the painfully sharp gasp caused by hearing his love's name on his brother's lips. Hoping to change the subject, and unable to keep all of his irritation out of his voice, he asked, "Why do you meet all of these young ladies, Collin? Do you forget you are a betrothed man?"

Collin scowled at the reminder. "No, but there have been so many knights who have returned with no solid news of the princess. They have only returned with two dozen girl who *could* be her. What if no one ever finds her? She may not have survived childhood."

Calem raised an eyebrow. "Is that what you're hoping for? That the princess was killed so you may marry whomever you wish?"

Collin's face flushed at the accusation. "No, of course not. I do hope she was found..." he looked out the window, as if he was one of the birds on Calem's wall, only caged. "I just wish I was free. I envy you that, Calem," he finished quietly.

Calem felt a surge of pity for his brother. He himself had felt like that not so long ago. He considered offering to trade with Collin, but knew the idea carried its own risks. Not inclined to show his brother his current feelings, he went and laid on his bed, looking up at the ceiling. "If you were to be freed, who would you court right now?"

Collin's grin returned. "Probably Miss Lia. Not only is she beautiful, she is also witty, and as sharp as they come. I've never met someone who can best me in a battle of wills before. It is quite refreshing."

Of course, Calem thought as he counted the number of

birds painted on his ceiling. There were seventeen. All thoughts of offering to trade with his brother fled. Collin would know he had been played the moment Miss Lia's identity was announced, and he'd be furious over it. Offering to trade now would make things even worse in the long run, he was sure of it. He sighed his momentary hopes draining once more. "Are you the only man who desires her attention?

Collin's grin turned into a smirk. "No, there are many, however, I have something none of the others have."

Calem barely refrained from rolling his eyes again. *Here we go...* "And what would that be?"

"I'm next in line for a throne! I could offer her an entire kingdom!" Collin's smirk grew even cockier.

It took everything Calem had to not grind his teeth and to keep his face expressionless. He was determined to give nothing away. "You're probably right," he replied once he was sure he could trust his voice. "Who could resist becoming queen? However, are you certain that you want your bride to feel that way? Being betrothed is hard enough on you. Marrying someone who just wants your title would be even worse."

The corner of Collin's mouth dropped dramatically at his brother's words, which brought out a frown of disappointment. "I suppose you are right." He looked out the window once more. "Do you think she already feels that way about me? That she sees my title and nothing more?"

Calem raised an eyebrow. "Well, considering you prefer to attend these events incognito, she *probably* doesn't know you have a title at all, let alone such a prestigious one." *Of course, since she already knows me, Miss Lia might actually recognize you as my brother.* The brothers looked a great deal alike, despite the older being half a head taller than the younger.

Calem's words drew a grin from his older brother at their shared habit of dressing in disguise, even if Calem wore his for a more important reason than Collin did. "Probably not, brother, thank you for reminding me of that." He grinned at Calem again, but it was more sincere this time. "Thanks, Calem. I love these talks. You keep my feet on the ground, but you always make sure I leave with my confidence intact. You really are a good brother."

The two of them exchanged farewells, then Collin departed, leaving the younger son to resent his brother in peace. Calem groaned as soon as the door was shut. Alone with his thoughts, he agonized over what he had learned.

Even with the reports he received from Gerald, it was hard to believe that the woman he loved was flirting with all and sundry. However, he couldn't ignore the fact that his brother was witness to the change and had fallen under her spell like all the other men. Collin's behavior now reminded Calem of all the women whose hearts Gerald had broken.

That thought made Calem sit up straight. Was Miss Lia taking a page out of Gerald's book? Gerald had claimed many a woman's heart, true, but he had generally been flirting with them to get information. Could Miss Lia be doing something similar? *Is she also pretending? Leading many men on just a little bit, rather than letting any of them get too close?*

His hope renewed and his faith in Miss Lia strengthened, Calem got to his feet and went in search of his friend. He found the larger knight just a few minutes later searching for *him*. "Calem, there you are." Gerald said, obviously relieved he had tracked the younger man down quickly. "To your chambers, I have news."

Calem nodded and turned around, returning the way he

had just come. As soon as they were inside, and the door was closed, he turned to his friend. "What is this about, Gerald?"

"I've been wandering the city again." The remark was unnecessary, as the man was still dressed as a workman. However, Calem chose not to point out his friend's gaffe. "The rumors that the princess has been found and staying with Lady Garnet have begun spreading in the middle-class. While Lady Garnet hasn't heard any directly, she said the girls with her have been receiving more analytical looks over the past few days. She suspects the elite have heard these rumors, as well."

Calem's eyes widened in alarm at the news. "Any word of the terrorists?"

"I believe they are responsible for the rumor jumping up to the middle class, perhaps to force her out of hiding, I *am* certain they do not yet know of her identity. However, it sounds like they are trying to find a way to get into the ball they are certain will be held in her honor."

Calem started pacing. "That sounds reasonable, especially considering I haven't heard anything from the king indicating he is spreading the rumor yet."

Calem could feel his friends eyes following him as he pace. "What should we do, Calem?"

Calem stopped mid-stride as the best course of action came to him. "We spread the rumor. We were planning on doing so anyway." He strode to the door and pulled it open.

He heard Gerald following along behind. "Where are we going?"

Calem answered his friend without stopping or looking back. "To tell the king. This was the plan all along. Now it is time to put it into action." They reached the throne rom a moment later. The king wasn't there, which wasn't surprising, but the footmen standing guard were able to direct them to His Majesty's study. Calem thanked them and led the way there. Once they reached it, he pounded on the door, pounding a little harder than he intended.

A moment later, the door opened, revealing one of the king's advisors. The man's eyes widened when he saw who was interrupting his meeting with the king. "Your Highness!" The man bowed quite properly. "What brings you here?"

"I need to speak with His Majesty, immediately. Privately." Calem almost cringed at how princely his voice sounded in that moment, but the matter was too urgent not to use his most formal tones.

The advisor nodded and allowed them entry before leaving, closing the door behind him. King Kelvin, seated behind his work desk, narrowed his piercing blue eyes at the intruders, who both bowed to him. "Sir Calem. Sir Gerald." There was no warmth in his tone, nor did he looked thrilled to see them. "The last time you were here together, you told me I couldn't meet my daughter yet."

Calem ignored the king's bitter comment. "Sir, rumors are spreading, saying that the princess has been found. They have spread beyond the lower class, and speculate on where she is residing."

King Kelvin's eyes widened. "Why wasn't I informed?"

"Because we weren't the ones who started it," Calem replied.

The king frowned. "Then, who was it?"

"We don't know yet," Calem admitted.

King Kelvin let out and exasperated sigh and ran a hand through his hair. Then he began pacing, a sign he was truly troubled. "So, what are we going to do now?"

Calem watched the king and felt no small degree of pity for him. "I believe the time has come to move to the next stage of our plan, Your Majesty," Calem said. "The rumor has already started, so we merely need to fan the flames, rather than spreading one of our own."

The king's eyes lit up. "Yes, a very good idea."

Calem nodded. "When would you like to hold the ball?"

A smile tugged at the corner's of the king's mouth. "In two weeks, under the Harvest Moon. I don't think I could handle more than that."

Calem nodded, "Manageable, but in that case, rather than fanning the rumors, we need to announce the event, correct?" The king nodded in agreement, obviously realizing his people would need time to prepare for a royal ball. Calem turned and opened the door, intent on finding someone to take a message to the herald. To his relief, James was standing nearby, likely waiting for any message the king might have. "James, take this down."

The lad drew a clean piece of parchment, his writing board, and a charcoal pencil from his satchel. "Ready, sir."

"Let it be known that His Majesty, the King, having heard reports that his daughter has been found, will hold a ball in her honor on the night of the Harvest Moon, two weeks hence. She is to present herself to His Majesty, the King and Her Majesty, the Queen, on this occasion."

"And if she doesn't present herself?" the observant servant asked once he finished writing.

Calem racked his brain for an answer to the question. What he came up with was a scenario he had already pondered before, the day he gave Miss Lia her necklace. "If she does not present herself, the King will pronounce her dead and enter a period of mourning for her. He will also release the Crown Prince of Callarda from his marriage agreement."

Once James was finished, he skipped off to deliver the news to the herald. Calem shut the door, then turned to find the king standing close at hand, his arms folded, glaring at him. "You make decisions for me now, do you?"

Calem returned the king's glare. "Had it been about something I wasn't certain would happen, I would have consulted you, but I had to think fast. You know as well as I do, Your Majesty, that hesitation is a sign of weakness, something a ruler should never show. Besides, is that not what would have happened had none of us found her? It's not like you have another daughter for my brother to marry."

The king heaved a heavy, burdened sigh that made Calem feel a little guilty for his angry tone. "No, I do not. I suppose I would have done exactly as you said." The king took a deep breath. "I suppose this is part of why you have been such a skilled battlefield leader; you are able to see how things are changing and make quick decisions to react to them."

Calem let out a breath, relieved the king's anger seemed to have dissipated. He turned to Gerald, who was still waiting silently where he had been since entering the king's study. "Hurry and warn Lady Garnet."

Gerald gave a nod and hurried from the room.

Eighteen

LILIA YAWNED AND STRETCHED AS SHE SAT UP IN BED. SHE had been in the city for roughly six weeks now, and was having the most wonderful time. Just like Gloria had predicted, Lady Garnet had taken them first to a small assembly, during the third week of their stay. To Lilia's dismay at the time, she had been a rousing success. She felt sorry for all of the men that had taken a fancy to her, since she was unavailable twice over yet unable to tell them so.

She was relieved she was not the only one enjoying popularity at the assembly. Gloria, of course danced almost exclusively with Sir Gerald, though he had also spared a dance apiece for Genevieve and Lilia. Genevieve and Diana, the first girl to have "enrolled" with Lady Garnet after Lilia and her friends, and the only other girl that Lady Garnet had deemed ready for that night, had also stood for more dances than not.

Since the girls had enjoyed such success, Lady Garnet began taking them to larger parties. They had attended so many in the month since then that Lilia had long lost count. Even though the thought of attending such large balls and parties had, initially, made her nervous, she came to enjoy, even appreciate, those times, as then she was not being taught things she already knew.

This wasn't to say that she hadn't learned new things from her time with Lady Garnet. One of the first things she learned was how to hide her feelings. Remembering the persona Sir Gerald had displayed when she'd first met him, Lilia had adopted a similarly flirtatious mask to keep the gentlemen entertained, yet uncertain. So far, it had worked well, keeping the men off balance so that none of them was really willing to wholeheartedly pursue her because they couldn't be sure of her feelings. She didn't know how else to keep them from being hurt when they finally learned she had never been in their reach.

The worst part of this new persona was that she knew Sir Gerald was reporting to Sir Calem regularly on her progress. The thought of the younger knight knowing all her flirtations made her cringe. She fervently hoped he would be able to see through her performance. Not for the first time, she considered asking Sir Gerald to take him a message from her, explaining what was happening in her own words to him.

While pondering these things, and waiting for the other girls to awaken, she climbed out of bed and sat at the dressing table to brush her hair. Once she was certain it was free of tangles, she gathered her hair up into a loose braid. She had just finished when her roommates began to stir.

Gloria was the first to awaken, and unbeknownst to her, she copied her friend as she yawned and stretched upon sitting up. When she was awake enough to see clearly, she looked around.

Upon spotting Lilia, she grinned. "How did you enjoy the party last night?" she asked. "I daresay you were a success, as usual."

Lilia sighed and nodded. "I at least felt like I was, which is a little frustrating. I did enjoy it, though. It was great fun, but I was also grateful to see my bed when we arrived home." She sighed again. "I will be relieved when I no longer have to play with hearts I know I cannot keep. Not that I want any of them anyway..."

Gloria nodded then raised an eyebrow. "And what did you think of the new fellow? Collin, I believe?"

The image of the handsome man's face flashed across her mind, eliciting a frown. "He looked oddly familiar, but..." She trailed off as an image of Sir Calem's face flashed as well, and she realized who her new admirer must be. "The devil! He's Sir Calem's brother!"

Gloria's eyes widened and her mouth formed an "o", and Lilia was sure she had seen the resemblance as well. "Your betrothed!"

Lilia scowled. "Yes."

"From the severity of your scowl," a sleepy voice added, "I'm going to assume that you are still in love with his brother." Lilia looked over to see Genevieve watching her as she stretched.

Lilia nodded miserably. "What am I to do?"

"Well," said Genevieve, "you could hope that your father, the king, will be understanding of the situation and let you choose which of the Callardan princes to marry, but I think that might be a little too much to hope for."

Lilia agreed as she began changing into one of her morning gowns. She knew they would soon be expected at breakfast, so she pushed the topic out of her mind and assisted her friends with their hair. They had fallen into this routine after realizing Lilia was an excellent hair dresser. Genevieve often joked that she had known all along, and that was one of the reasons she had asked Lilia to become her maid.

Of course, since this started before they were sharing a room, the other girls staying there noticed. Several of the other ladies expressed their desire for her to fix their hair, and she was in high demand every evening. After a couple of days of creating hairstyles for nearly ten girls, Lilia put her foot down. She would schedule three of the girls each night, and rotate which three she would style so everyone who wanted her to do their hair had the chance.

In the mornings, however, she always did Gloria and Genevieve's hair. It was her way of thanking them for being her friends and for keeping her secret. She knew they would keep it regardless, but she felt the need to show them her gratitude personally.

Once the three of them were ready, they headed down to breakfast. As was often the case, they were among the last to arrive. Lady Garnet had not yet descended, however, so they were not truly late. They took their usual seats, scattered among the other girls, and engaged in small talk as they waited for their hostess's arrival.

As soon as Lilia took her seat, Diana, who sat to her right, pounced on her. "Lia! Who *was* that dashing man you were dancing with last night?"

The girl to her left, Joy, snorted. Like Lilia, she was country grown and had a few less-fashionable habits to work on. "You are going to have to be more specific, Diana. She danced with fifty men last night."

The girl across from her, Anna, let out a quiet, refined chuckle. "There were not *that* many dances. Though, with how often someone would cut in, she may have danced with that many anyway."

Diana waved their comments away and returned to questioning Lilia. "You know who I mean. The new man. He was fearfully handsome."

"His name is Collin," was Lilia's simple reply. She wasn't certain of his identity and, if she was right, he was hiding his identity for a reason, like his brother did. So, she decided that it was likely for the best to keep the other girls in the dark about her suspicions about him.

Diana frowned. "Is that all you know of him?"

Lilia nodded. "He spoke a great deal, but I didn't learn much about him." Indeed, he had spoken quite a bit, a great deal of complimenting on her beauty, but none of his talk was about personal topics.

"Well," said Anna, "he was quite the most handsome man *I've* ever seen."

The other two nodded in infatuated agreement. "He really was!" Joy replied.

"I do hope he's available!" Diana commented. "And not so taken with Lia already that none of the rest of us have a chance."

While a part of Lilia wished she could set the record straight, she wasn't positive about who he was, and knew nothing of his thoughts or plans. So, she kept quiet. She was grateful that Lady Garnet walked in a moment later, soon enough that none of the girls would make anything of Lilia's silence.

Lady Garnet stood at the head of the table, which

succeeded in getting everyone's attention. She gave them all a wide smile. "Good morning, ladies."

All of the girls stood. "Good morning, Lady Garnet," they replied in unison.

Instead of taking her seat, as she usually did, Lady Garnet remained standing, though she motioned for them to sit. "I have some news this morning that is sure to excite you." Every girl sat straighter at that. Lilia's heart began racing, as she was certain she knew what the news was. "Some of you may have caught wind of the rumors that Princess Kalysta has been found."

That had, in fact, been a subject of discussion among the girls previously. They knew about the rumors, and that the rumors said she was likely staying in that very house. The girls had discussed which of them it might be. Genevieve had pointed out the other rumors they had heard, of people who wanted to make sure the princess *wasn't* found. All of the girls then acknowledged that it would be best for them not to know who she was yet, if she was even there.

Lilia's mind was brought back to the present as Lady Garnet continued. "This morning, there was a proclamation made saying that the king has also learned of this. He will be holding a ball, in her honor, in two weeks. At this grand event, she is to present herself to Their Majesties." Lilia's racing heart beat even faster upon learning her suspicions were correct.

Lady Garnet sat then, indicating her announcement was done. The table erupted with excited conversation. Diana turned to Lilia. "Oh! How amazing! I've been hoping she would be found! I'm certain she is beautiful!"

Joy rolled her eyes and snorted. "Of course she will be, Diana. She's a princess.'"

"Well," added Anna, "I heard she's betrothed to the Crown Prince of Callarda." She let out a dreamy sigh. "To think, one day she will be a queen! I wish it could be me!"

Joy snorted again. "Who wants to run a country?"

Lilia nodded her head in agreement. "I know I don't."

Diana frowned. "But either of you would be so good at it."

Joy shrugged and voiced Lilia's thoughts. "I'd be miserable. I'm glad they seem to know who she is, because that means I'm not her."

"If you want to talk about who is well suited to run a country," Anna added, "I'd have to say Genevieve." Lilia had to admit that could be true. Genevieve had been the one to suggest that Lilia do only three hairstyles a night and have the girls rotate, and she had also helped Lady Garnet organize the schedules. Lilia had never realized her former rival could be so organized when she put her mind to it.

Lilia was about to add her own comment, when everyone suddenly fell silent. She looked around to see what had caused the conversation to dissipate, and froze when her gaze landed on the disruption. Sir Calem stood in the doorway, looking directly at her. Had he not been haunting her dreams so often, she may not have recognized him. While he didn't dress to his true station, as a prince, neither did he look like a mere knight. He was, instead, dressed as a nobleman. He had on a well-cut shirt and a half cape that made him look a little taller.

Yet, his stormy blue eyes were still the same.

It had been so long since she had last seen him, as they had not spoken since he left her in Lady Garnet's care. Yet the distance and time apart had done nothing to temper the reaction his presence elicited. Her heart had raced nervously earlier, but now it beat at twice the speed and intensity as she stared back at the man she loved.

"Sir Calem!" the countess said with a smile. "What brings you here this morning?"

He looked away long enough to reply. "I need to have a private word with Miss Lia, Lady Garnet."

Lilia looked to the countess for permission to leave. When Lady Garnet nodded, Lilia stood and walked over to him. Gloria and Genevieve stood as well. As had become protocol for the household full of girls, whenever a gentleman wished to speak with a lady, that lady's roommates would accompany her to protect her reputation.

Calem led the ladies into the drawing room and shut the door. Turning back to them he said, "Miss Lia, I suspect you've heard about the ball." Lilia appreciated that he chose to dispense with formalities. She was finding that being in his presence was torturous. Getting to the heart of the matter quickly would help make the conversation shorter, along with the time spent so near him.

As she nodded in reply, she watched for some sign that her feelings were reciprocated. His expression gave nothing away, and his face was tightly schooled. A little *too* tightly, perhaps, which gave her reason to hope he still cared for her, as well. "Lady Garnet told us just right before you walked in."

"I have just come from speaking with the king." His tone was one of disinterest, but she found herself not trusting it. "At this ball, once you present yourself, he will announce your betrothal to the Crown Prince of Callarda. You will then dance with the prince." He paused and started pacing. "I realize you may have already figured out his identity on your own..."

Lilia nodded. "It is Collin, is it not?"

Sir Calem's jaw clenched, the first solid sign he wasn't as unaffected as he seemed. "Yes. I felt it was best if you were sure of who he was." She nodded, grateful that he had confirmed what she only suspected. "I also feel the need to warn you that he has fallen under your charms, and will be quite happy to marry you."

Her eyes narrowed, and she watched him closely. "Will you be happy for us?"

Pain flashed across his face, though he hid it quickly. "I will—"

"Because I will not."

The pain returned, lingering in his eyes as he searched her face. "If there was some way I could free you from this, Miss Lia, and allow you to marry whomever you wish, without sparking a new war, please know that I would do it in a heartbeat."

She clenched her hand as her heart thudded painfully. "I know," she whispered.

Genevieve, on the other hand, glowered. "The betrothal will be announced, and then that will be that?"

Sir Calem hung his head. "From my understanding, yes."

She scowled. "This is unacceptable! You've got to think of something!"

Sir Calem glared back at her. "You think I haven't tried, Genevieve?" He was truly upset if he was dropping the formal "Miss" before Genevieve's name. "I spent the entire time I was on my quest wishing my brother hadn't forced me into a betrothal with the enemy as part of the peace treaty. Upon my arrival here, I learn that I am a free man, but it comes too late. The woman I want to marry is the one I can never have, for she is to be married off to my brother. My brother! I have been looking at all of my options, trying my hardest to come up with a plan that isn't treasonous, but my hope is fading. I will continue to fight until the union is irreversible, but do you know what would happen if I were to voice my displeasure at the match? Wars have been fought over lesser offenses that a prince stealing his brother's promised bride. I cannot endanger thousands of lives just to be with the woman I love, no matter how much I want to!"

Lilia inhaled sharply. "You *do* love me?" she asked hesitantly, worried she had just imagined what he had said.

Calem reached towards her, but then pulled back as a pain so fierce she could almost feel it filled his eyes. "With all me heart," he replied quietly, but firmly.

Her heart pounded as she recalled when she had spoken those same words to him. That felt like an eternity ago, but wasn't even two months back, when they spoke in Gloria's sitting room.

The moment stretched and the anguish keeping them apart grew sharper, until Genevieve broke the spell. "Forgive me, Sir Calem," she said with her head bowed. "I cannot imagine what distress this must be causing you." She looked up at him. "Gloria and I will put our heads together. I'm certain we'll all be able to come up with something."

Sir Calem rubbed a weary hand across his face. "Forgive me for shouting, Miss Genevieve. I am just stressed. Extremely stressed. I know that this is no excuse to yell at a lady, however, so I beg your forgiveness."

Genevieve let out a sad grin as she nodded her acceptance of his apology. "I understand. I likely would have yelled at me, too."

Sir Calem managed a small, if sad, smile. "Thank you for

your understanding." He turned towards the door. "I had better leave. My brother likely knows I am here, and will become suspicious if I am gone for much longer." He nodded to Gloria and Genevieve. "Good day, ladies." He then turned to Lilia and bowed. "Your Highness." He stood straight and looked at her one last time before turning and walking out the door.

Nineteen

⁓

WHEN CALEM RETURNED TO HIS ROOMS, HIS BROTHER WAS waiting for him. "Where have you been?" Collin asked with a suspicious glare.

Certain his brother already knew, Calem didn't bother to invent a lie. "I had some business at Lady Garnet's house to take care of."

His brother nodded. "Ah. Who was it you went to speak with?"

"One of the ladies that accompanied me to the capital," Calem replied, hoping that would satisfy his brother.

He had no such luck. Collin raised an eyebrow and asked, "Which one?"

Calem barely refrained from letting out a frustrated breath. "Miss Lia."

Collin's eyes narrowed. "Why?"

Ready to let his frustration show, Calem turned to fully face his brother, "I have been charged with her safety and happiness. While Sir Gerald has been serving as a go between, it had been six weeks since I had last spoken to her. Especially with the announcement of the ball, I thought it would be wise to make sure she didn't need anything."

Collin scoffed in obvious disbelief. "Interesting. Who charged you?"

Calem was able to smile as he answered. "Her entire village."

Collin's eyes went wide. "Amazing. I suppose I cannot fault you with that hanging over your head. I wondered, for a moment, if you were interested in her, but duty has always been your motivation. You are a good man, Calem."

Calem raised an eyebrow. "What makes you believe I am not interested in Miss Lia?"

"Several things," Collin replied with a smile. He began counting off his points on his fingers. "One, you have neglected to visit her these past six weeks. Two, when you did, your visit was brief, almost to the point of rudeness. And three, you didn't wear your best shirt, choosing to go looking like a minor noble rather than yourself." Collin smiled smugly. "You really are only motivated by duty. Perhaps it isn't all bad, though. Had you not felt it your duty to locate Prince Kenneth, you would be marrying his bride soon."

Calem laid on his bed and looked up at the ceiling. Hoping to draw attention away from himself, he asked, "Why your obsession with Miss Lia? Did you not hear the rumor that the princess has been found?"

Collin scowled. "Don't remind me." He went and leaned against the window, the caged-bird look from the night before returning to his face. "I'm going to be miserable, aren't I?"

Calem sighed. "Not necessarily. You might be very happy, if you play your cards right. Whoever she is, she has most likely been raised in humble circumstances. So, if nothing else, she won't be anything like Princess Catalina, or any of the noblemen's daughters you generally dance with back home."

Collin turned back to his brother and studied him for a moment before grinning. "I suppose that, if I *don't* like her, I'll just have you marry her."

If only. "Perhaps you will like her, and perhaps not. We'll cross that bridge when we come to it." Calem climbed off of his bed and headed for the door. "Now I'm going to go for a walk. I promised the girls that I'd take them to visit the seamstress. Mother wishes for them to have new dresses, so that they look like the locals for the ball."

Collin stood straight. "I'll come with you." He grinned. "Two swords are better than one."

Calem smiled easily at that. He and his brother had trained with swords since they were able to hold one, and many of their childhood antics involved them teaming up to fight off make-believe villains. "If you wish."

Together, the bothers went to collect their sisters. All five of the girls were waiting impatiently for Calem to keep his promise. When they learned that both of their brothers would be escorting them, they squealed with delight. Once everyone was ready, Calem led them all out of the castle and into the town. Collin took his position at the back, making sure none of their sisters wandered off on her own. Fortunately, it was a short walk, as the shop was only a a couple of streets away.

As soon as the girls entered the shop, they began to "ooh" and "ahh" over the various fabrics and colors available. As they walked around, feeling the fabric and comparing colors, an elderly lady came out of a back room to see who had entered her shop. When she saw the girls, she gave a contented sigh. When she spotted Collin, who was already watching out the window, her looks grew curious at his being there. When she saw Calem, however, her eyes widened in recognition. "Your Highness," she said with a curtsy. "What brings you to my shop on this fine day?"

Calem gave the woman a smile and a nod. "Good day, Madame Jemima. It is a pleasure to see you again." He turned and gestured first to Collin. "I'd like you to meet my older brother, Collin." Collin gave a nod. Madame Jemima curtsied in return. Then Calem gestured to his sisters, who had mostly abandoned the fabric rolls to come meet the seamstress. "And these are my sisters: Cassandra, Cherise, Cecilia, Carissa, and Camilla." Each girl, from the oldest at thirteen to the youngest at four, curtsied in turn as Calem said their name.

Madame Jemima curtsied to each of them, as well. "Your Highnesses, it is a pleasure to meet all of you." She turned back to Calem as the girls returned to inspecting the fabric, except for Camilla, who clung to Calem's leg. "I can see the family resemblance. So, what brings you all here?"

Calem put a hand on his youngest sister's head, and said, "We are hoping to purchase fabric, and if you are able, have you make my sister's gowns for the ball. My mother is hoping for all of them to be dressed as locals for the event, even though most of them won't see any of it."

Normally, Madame Jemima would have been thrilled to make additions to the wardrobes of the neighboring royal family. She was always thrilled whenever Calem's mother had another request for her. This time, however, she looked agitated. "I'm afraid that, with all of the ladies staying with Lady Garnet, I have a great deal to do. However, I could make your sisters' dresses a priority. However, it will cost extra."

Calem frowned, realizing the dilemma. "Would putting my sisters' dresses first risk any of Lady Garnet's guests not receiving one of your beautiful creations?"

She nodded. "I'm afraid so. Two dozen gowns in two weeks is a tall order, you must understand. I'm not sure I'll be able to finish them all as it is."

Calem searched his mind for an acceptable solution, and after a moment, he struck upon one. "I may have a solution, Madame Jemima. If you would excuse us, I have some business to discuss with Lady Garnet. If all goes according to plan, we shall return shortly." He then turned to his sisters. "Alright, girls, we're going for another walk." A chorus of disappointed sounds followed the statement. "Worry not, for I'm certain we'll be back."

The girls hurried to obey him at that. Collin, who looked relieved to be leaving the fabric-filled shop, was waiting at the door. They departed, and Calem led the way to Lady Garnet's manor. Once they arrived, Calem knocked on the door. Lady Garnet, herself, answered the summons. "Oh, what a surprise!" she said when she saw who had arrived. "Do come in, all of you!"

Calem made quick introductions as they entered the manor house. Then, some of Lady Garnet's guests whisked the girls away to heaven knows where. Collin and Calem, on the other hand, followed Lady Garnet into the drawing room. They each took a seat, but Lady Garnet stayed at the front of hers. Leaning in, she asked, "Now, what brings two handsome princes to my door?"

Calem was about to speak when he remembered that the other prince was his superior. He looked to his older brother, who motioned for him to proceed. Calem turned back to the lady. "Lady Garnet, we have just been to visit Madame Jemima. She told us that she is in charge of making the dresses for all of the ladies here."

Lady Garnet nodded. "Indeed. I wanted them to have the very best for the ball."

"Understandable," Calem replied, "and while I am certain she is more than flattered at your trust in her abilities, she expressed that she is worried she will be unable to finish all of them, especially when I told her that our mother was hoping to secure her services for my sisters."

Lady Garnet let out a sigh. "I suppose it was too much to ask of a single person, no matter how talented she is." She frowned. "What is your reason for coming to me like this, though?"

Calem couldn't completely keep himself from grinning as he voiced his idea. "I know you have been ensuring that all of the ladies currently in your care are receiving a good education." She nodded. "I was wondering if sewing is a skill worth adding to their studies."

Lady Garnet let out a laugh, obviously realizing the direction of his thoughts. "You want them to make their own dresses?" She paused for a moment, pondering. "You know, that is a splendid idea. I think that even two weeks of instruction is enough to get them started. Let me ask my favorites for their opinions." She went to the door and called out, "Gloria! Genevieve! Lia!"

Not a minute later, the three ladies stood in the doorway. Both Collin and Calem stood, remembering their manners after Lady Garnet's jump into action caught them off guard. Miss Lia looked briefly between Collin and Calem before focusing her gaze on the floor. Calem understood. If Collin couldn't see her eyes, he wouldn't be able to read the emotion in them. Calem looked over to find his brother watching her closely anyway. Calem wondered if he had seen anything in that brief moment.

Lady Garnet smiled at the new arrivals and ushered them inside. Rather than sitting, however, she gathered them to stand in a circle. "Ladies, Sir Calem has just suggested something to me that I think would be an excellent idea for all of the ladies to work on."

Miss Genevieve let out a long-suffering sigh. "What have you done this time, Sir Calem?"

Calem grinned mischievously. "I have suggested you make your own gowns for the ball."

Miss Lia's eyes flew to his face as a smile spread across it. She then turned to Lady Garnet with a hopeful expression. "Oh, please! I would love to be able to do that!" Her words warmed his heart. He might not have the chance to marry her, but that didn't mean he couldn't do what was in his power to make her happy. In that moment he decided he could never marry if he couldn't marry her.

Lady Garnet smiled at her. "If I guess right, Lia, you are already an excellent seamstress. I'm certain your gown will be beautiful."

Miss Genevieve, however, looked terrified. "I..." she looked at her hands as if they had suddenly turned into fish fins. She swallowed audibly, then started again. "I've never done anything like that." Calem wondered if the young woman real-ized how significant her statement was. The young lady he had brought out of Farreden would never have admitted to what she perceived as a failing in herself. Gerald had told him about how much Miss Genevieve had changed since their arrival, but this was his first time seeing it for himself.

Lady Garnet patted the distressed young woman's arm. "Which is why I think it would be an excellent idea."

Miss Gloria sighed at the statement. "If that is what you think would be best for us, Lady Garnet."

Lady Garnet nodded. "I do think it would be wise. Sewing is a very useful skill, especially if you wish to attract a man of higher quality." Genevieve looked up at that remark. "Plus, when you go to the ball, you will have with you something you have made with your own hands. I'm sure it will give you a feeling of accomplishment."

Calem watched with surprise as Miss Genevieve's terror was swiftly replaced with determination, another expression he would never have expected from the old Miss Genevieve. "I want to do it." Miss Gloria also looked more interested than she had a moment before.

Lady Garnet clapped her hands gleefully. "Wonderful! I will speak with Madame Jemima immediately." She turned to Miss Lia. "Lia, I want you to come with me, as I may need your persuasive powers." Miss Lia nodded.

"We will accompany you, as well, if you don't mind," Calem said.

Lady Garnet shook her head. "I don't mind in the least."

Calem nodded and headed out of the room. He stopped at the bottom of the stairs and shouted, "Girls!"

Within the next minute, all five of them appeared at the top of the staircase, accompanied by some of Lady Garnet's guests. "Yes, Calem?" Cassandra asked.

"It is time to leave."

While their shoulders slumped, they did as he instructed. As they usually did, they sorted themselves and lined up in age order, Cassandra leading the way. By the time they reached the bottom of the stairs, the oldest three had much more correct posture, though the younger two were still obviously disappointed. However, they cheered up when he told them they were returning to the seamstress's shop.

Once everyone was ready to go, Collin actually led them out the door, though he dropped back once he reached the bottom of the steps. Calem, who was already at the back, sensed his brother wished to speak with him, so he stayed at the rear, letting Lady Garnet and Miss Lia lead their small column.

"I'm tortured, Calem," Collin said. "How can I marry someone when I like another?"

Calem nearly laughed in his brother's face at the irony, but somehow he kept his expression neutral. "Do you *like* Miss Lia, or do you *love* her?"

Collin shrugged and frowned. "I am…uncertain. Do you think it likely to be merely an infatuation?"

Grateful for a question that he could answer completely honestly, Calem replied, "I don't know. You haven't known her for very long, so it is possible it is just a passing fancy. Does she haunt you in your sleep?"

"No," came Collin's quick reply.

"Does she consume your every waking thought?"

"No."

Calem had to swallow past a lump in his throat before voicing his next question. "Are you willing to do whatever it takes to make her happy, even if that means not being with you?"

Instead of answering, Collin raised an questioning eyebrow. "How do you know all of this? Have you felt this way for someone?"

You have no idea. "Yes. Unfortunately, it was when I

believed myself to be betrothed, so I knew nothing could come of it."

Collin grinned. "Well, what are you doing? You have been freed! Go and get her!"

Calem let out a weary sigh. "It's not that simple, brother. She is to marry another, and my duty keeps me here."

Collin frowned and patted his younger brother's shoulder. "I'm so sorry, Calem."

"Thank you, Collin." They walked on in silence for a moment until another thought came to Calem. "Don't forget, the princess may already have feelings for another as well. Would you want to marry her while she loved someone else?"

Collin thought for a moment. "That...is worth taking into account, I suppose. If nothing else, I would talk to King Kelvin about it."

Calem nodded. Perhaps he had planted a seed that would let things work out for the best. He certainly hoped so.

Twenty

Lilia didn't know if Lady Garnet was unaware of the interest the elder Callardan prince had shown toward her, or if the countess was trying to teach her something, but either way, Lilia had never been more uncomfortable in her entire life.

Behind her walked the man she would marry *and* the man she wanted to marry, and they were not the same person. She was grateful the little princesses walked between herself and the brothers, or she might have snapped and said something she ought not. She was fighting the urge to shout at them both as it was.

Fortunately, it wasn't very far to reach the seamstress's shop. Lilia soon found out why Lady Garnet had insisted on Lilia accompanying her. Madame Jemima needed a great deal of convincing, and some negotiating, to allow the work she had been hired to do to be done by the people who had paid her to do it.

"Madame Jemima, I don't understand why you are so set against this," Lady Garnet said. They were half an hour into the conversation and had made little progress. "The girls need to learn how to sew, and what could be more motivating than a royal ball?"

Madame Jemima still didn't look convinced. She turned to Lilia. "What do you think of this idea?"

Lilia gave the woman an eager smile. "I am thinking that I would be more than happy to study under someone who does such marvelous work. Your skills are even heard of in Farreden."

Madame Jemima waved a dismissive hand, but couldn't completely hide her smile. "You flatter me, child."

Lilia grinned, sensing the woman was beginning to cave. "What if you were to do the measurements and cut the fabric of everyone's gowns, and then give the pieces to the girls to sew together? You would be being paid for the fabric, making the pattern, and then instructing us in sewing. Would that satisfy you?"

"I may not know much of the making of clothing, but it does seem like the stitching together of all of those pieces would be the most time consuming part," Prince Calem added. To Lilia, it seemed like he was trying to add something to push his plan forward, even if this part of it was out of his arena.

Madame Jemima let out a smile. "I will admit that trying to finish all of them in time for the ball will likely mean many late nights for me until then." She then turned to where the little princesses were browsing fabric and playing with ribbons. "Would Your Highnesses also be joining us for the lessons?"

All five of the girls grinned and gave the seamstress enthusiastic nods.

Madame Jemima sighed. "I still don't know. There is only one of me and twenty or so girls, not counting the young princesses. How can I make sure they are all doing it properly at the same time?"

"Well," Prince Calem said, "I'm sure that my sisters' nurse and governess, and perhaps my mother's maid, would be able to supervise the younger set."

Lilia grinned again. "And I can be your assistant, Madame Jemima. My father might have been a blacksmith, but my mother made and mended clothes to supplement the income. Also, a few of the other girls grew up in similar circumstances, and likely know what they're doing enough to help out, too." A moment of silence followed as Madame Jemima pondered.

Lilia almost jumped when Prince Collin was the one to break that silence, speaking for perhaps the first time since they'd entered the shop. "What kind of blacksmith needs supplementary income? Especially during a war?" he asked with a raised eyebrow.

Lilia turned to stare down the taller prince until the man started to squirm under her gaze. "A generous one. He did the work because he loved it, not for the money. If someone needed his handiwork, but couldn't afford it, he would take what he thought was fair based on their income. He would repair farm equipment in exchange for a few bushels of wheat once the harvest came in, for example."

Prince Collin's eyes widened. "A generous blacksmith indeed. I am intrigued. Might you have a sample of his work that I could examine?"

Lilia looked to Prince Calem. The royal knight pulled his sword from its scabbard and handed the finely crafted weapon to his elder brother. The crown prince grinned. "My brother is known to be rather...particular when it comes to swords, so his purchasing one from your father means a great deal." He hefted the sword. "The balance is perfect," he said with only the slightest surprise. Then he frowned. "It's a little on the short end, however."

He handed the sword back to his brother, who returned it to its scabbard. "Well, considering that *I* am a little on the short end, I find it a perfect fit," Prince Calem retorted, though he eased the bite from his words by smiling right after. "The man had several others that were of normal length that I believe would suit you perfectly. However, we are not here to discuss swords. We are here to beg this good lady to teach our unruly sisters how to sew."

His sisters immediately protested his choice of words. "We have been very well behaved today," Cherise pouted.

"We have been very polite and quiet while you all have been talking," Cassandra pointed out.

"And we haven't taken any of the fabrics out of their places!" Cecelia added.

"Well, only one," Carissa admitted. "But I put it right back."

"An' we stayed in line on our walks," Camilla put in. "We walked a lot."

"Alright, alright," Prince Calem replied, "I'm sorry, girls, you're right, you haven't been unruly at all today." He smiled at them, and they quickly calmed down. With his sisters appeased, he turned back to the seamstress. "I believe that their good behavior goes to show that they will be quite the eager pupils. After we ask our mother, of course, though I'm sure she will approve. That is, of course, if you agree to teach."

The five young princesses looked at the seamstress with hope-filled faces, and she finally gave in. "Very well, I will work with you all to sew the dresses. To start with, let's measure all of you little princesses."

That afternoon, Madame Jemima went to Lady Garnet's manor to measure all of the girls. Over the next two days, she, with the help of Lilia and Joy, whose adoptive mother was a seamstress in the small town she was from, created the patterns and cut out the pieces from the many shades of fabric that had been chosen.

Once everything was pieced, they wrapped up each bundle and carted them over to Lady Garnet's home. There, the girls waited in varied stages of eagerness and anxiety as their names were called and they were given the bundle of fabric that they would somehow transform into a gown for the ball.

Over the two weeks leading up to the ball, Lady Garnet accepted less than half as many invitations as she had been in order to give the girls sufficient time to work on their dresses. During the first week, Lilia, Joy, and Madame Jemima were in constant demand, as almost all of the other girls learned to sew for the first time. The seamstress was so impressed by the pair that she offered to take either of them as an apprentice if they desired. Prince Calem's suggestion of sending his sisters' caretakers proved inspired, as the three youngest needed help almost constantly.

It wasn't until three days before the ball that Lilia was able to get any time to work on her own dress, and even then it was because she and Joy realized that neither was making any progress without being interrupted within minutes. They began taking hour-long shifts, taking turns working on their own dresses and being on call to help the others. Both of them turned down the invitation to a dinner party two nights before the ball, which gave them both enough of a break from assisting others to get their dresses mostly done.

Even so, Lilia didn't finish hers until the wee hours of the morning on the day of the ball. She was so exhausted that she slept through most of the day, only waking a couple of hours before the ball. Yet even with sleeping that long, she might not have awoken then had not her roommates been preparing for the grand event.

"Ouch!" cried Gloria as Genevieve attempted to help her with her hair. Both were already in their gowns, but Gloria's coiffure obviously needed some work. "Ow!"

Startled, Genevieve pulled the brush away too quickly, making Gloria cry out again. "Oh, I'm so sorry, Gloria! It's no use! I'm useless!"

Lilia let out a chuckle, drawing both of her friends' attention as she slipped out of bed. She went to the dressing table and gently took the brush from Genevieve. She quickly and skillfully smoothed Gloria's hair, then put it up in an elaborate style. Then she made some adjustments to Genevieve's, though Gloria had done a fairly good job already. Both girls sighed. "What would we do without you, Lilia?" Gloria asked.

It was Lilia's turn to sigh. "Well, you're going to have to figure that out quickly, because I won't be here after tonight. I've heard the reports about people who want to kill me, so either I will be dead, or I will be living in the castle, soon to be wed. I'm honestly not sure which of those I would prefer at the moment, since marrying the brother of the man I love is sure to kill me."

As she spoke, she slipped into her ballgown. It was a perfect fit, for she wouldn't have settled for anything less. It didn't quite match the other girls' dresses, as Madame Jemima had allowed her to have a different pattern than everyone else. The design she had chosen was even simpler than the ones for the other girls—which hadn't been all that elaborate either, to minimize the amount of sewing needed. However, Lilia's gown was much more elegant, due to being made almost entirely of luxurious violet silk. The neck and waistlines were simply adorned with silver trim that paired well with the necklace bearing her father's crest.

Once she was ready, she turned and looked at herself in the mirror, but a sudden sigh had her turning her head towards her friends instead. "Oh, Lilia," Gloria said, "you look beautiful."

Lilia grinned. "Thank you. I hope you know that both of you look beautiful as well."

Genevieve rolled her eyes, but smiled. "Thank you, Lia, but I must say, it does you credit that you look better than either of us, even though your dress is more simple in design." She raised a mischievous eyebrow. "I daresay that neither prince will be able to keep their eyes off of you tonight."

Lilia sat down at the dressing table and fixed her hair, making sure to weave the silver trim into it. "Well, I don't care about one, and I can't care about the other, so what difference does it make?" Her fingers trembled as she pinned the last of her hair into place, and she blinked back tears as she inspected her work. She took several deep breaths, but it wasn't enough to hold back the rising surge of panic and despair. Her breathing grew rapid and shallow, and her hands flew to her heart, which felt ready to shatter. "I can't do this!" Tears broke free of her eyes and ran in rivers down her face.

Genevieve knelt next to Lilia and took her hands, clutching them tightly. "Yes, you can," she said forcefully. Lilia looked up in surprise at her friend's tone. "We have a plan, but it will work best if you don't know what it is. However, I'm certain that it will end with you and Calem together. So, chin up! You are a princess!"

Lilia nodded, surprised at how reassured she felt at her friend's words. She took a deep breath, wiped her tears away, and looked between her two friends. "Oh, girls," she said. "I'm so grateful that you are here with me right now. I may have to insist on you moving into the castle with me if this plan of yours works out," she added with a small smile.

Together, Genevieve and Gloria encircled their friend in an embrace. Then Gloria picked up the necklace bearing the king's crest and fastened it around Lilia's neck. Genevieve stepped back and curtsied, and Gloria quickly followed suit. Then Genevieve said, "Princess Kalysta, we await your orders."

Lilia—no, Kalysta—took one last deep breath before standing tall. In that moment, she realized her mother had been teaching her to be a princess all along, knowing one day Kalysta might return to meet her true family. A tear leaked out for her mother, and another for her father, but she wiped away the trails they left and faced her friends. "It is time to let the girls know who I am. They deserve to be the first to know, after all we've been through together."

Together, the three girls headed out of their room, with Kalysta in the lead and Genevieve and Gloria following behind. They met Lady Garnet as they approached the stairs. The countess gasped when she saw them, too startled to hide her surprise. "Your Majesty!" She sank into a deep curtsy immediately. "What brings you to my humble home?"

Kalysta blinked in confusion. "Lady Garnet?"

The countess's eyes widened. "Lia, is that you?" Kalysta could hear the incredulity in the lady's tone.

"Yes, Lady Garnet," she replied. "Did you really think I was the queen?"

Straightening, Lady Garnet nodded. "Yes, you look exactly like Her Majesty dressed like that."

Kalysta managed a smile, despite the butterflies that swam in her midsection. "Now I know what my mother looks like, I suppose," she replied lightly. She took a deep breath to steady herself, then said, "Lady Garnet, I am Princess Kalysta now. Would you be so kind as to announce me to the other girls?"

Lady Garnet nodded and gave a curtsy better suited to their respective stations. "As you wish, Your Highness."

The countess descended the staircase while the trio of girls waited just out of sight. Being out of sight, however, did not mean being out of hearing. "Ladies," the countess began, cutting off the chatter from the crowd below. "You all look beautiful tonight. You will do me proud, I know you will. Before we depart, however, I wish to share with you a secret that I have been keeping these past months. Concern for her safety has made it paramount for none of you to know this before tonight, but she has asked that I make her known to you before we leave for the evening's event."

Excited chatter broke out again even as Kalysta's stomach threatened to drop to her toes.

Once the girls were silent again, Lady Garnet continued. "May I present Her Royal Highness, Princess Kalysta."

Everyone gasped in shock as Kalysta stepped into view. The silence of amazement continued as she descended the staircase. As she reached the bottom, a space cleared before her, and she turned to look at all of the girls. Anna was the first to recover. "Lia!" she cried. "You are the princess?"

Kalysta nodded. "Yes, I am Princess Kalysta. But since we

are all friends, I would like for you to just call me Kalysta, please."

As the shock began to wear off, the girls surrounded her, some expressing their awe, some offering congratulations, and some merely crying joyfully. Joy pushed her way to the front and embraced the princess. "Oh, Kalysta! You deserve this. You are the very best of us, and we are all honored to know you and have you as our friend."

Kalysta blinked in surprise at the watery tone of the usually stoic girl. She looked around, and was surprised to see that every single girl nodded their head in echo of Joy's declaration. Tears filled Kalysta's eyes as joy filled her heart. "Thank you, ladies, but I am the one who is honored to know each of you. Your easy acceptance of my true nature is a credit to each of you and to our wonderful mentor. You are all so wonderful, and I'm so glad we all had the chance to meet each other." She then turned to Lady Garnet. "Thank you, for everything."

As the other girls also voiced their thanks to the countess, Gloria and Genevieve wove their way through the crowd to Kalysta's side. "That being said," Genevieve said impatiently, "we need to get to the carriages so that we are not late."

Genevieve had ever been the voice of reason during the last two months they had been in the capital. Kalysta cast her friend a grateful smile before leading the way outside.

Twenty-One

DESPITE THE FACT THAT THE BALL WAS TO START IN A FEW minutes—indeed, many of the attendees had already arrived— Calem found himself in a last-minute conference with King Kelvin. "You want me to *what?*" Calem was torn. His mind desperately hoped he had misheard the king's request, while his heart hoped for the opposite.

"Dance with her." The king shot the young prince a confused frown. "Is there a problem with that?"

Depends on the perspective, he wanted to say. Instead, he replied, "None, Your Majesty."

The king nodded. "Good. I want to be alerted, before she presents herself, as to which of these girls that will be accompanying Lady Garnet is my daughter. You will give me that signal by dancing with her for her last dance as a commoner. You found her, after all, so you, of all people, deserve that honor."

While Calem wanted nothing more than to seize this opportunity to hold her in his arms, he was also afraid that, if he did so, he would never let her go. "If that is your wish, I will do it," he replied. *Even though it will probably be entirely unnecessary, since you will be able to recognize her on sight.*

The king studied him. Closely. "Is there something you aren't telling me, son?"

The last word nearly made Calem's composure slip as it speared his heart. He longed to be nothing more than the husband of the king's only daughter, to merit being called "son" by this man. Somehow, he managed to keep all of the emotion from his expression, but, never one to lie outright, he said, "Yes, but I have no wish to burden you with it."

The king nodded. "Very well. Now, go. The ladies are sure to arrive at any moment."

Calem gave an appropriate bow before exiting the king's chambers and making his way to the ballroom. The door he entered through clicked shut just as the ladies began to enter through the main doors. Instinctively, he searched for Miss Lia. When he saw her, his mouth dropped open. She was absolutely stunning in her simple, yet elegant, gown.

Calem didn't notice his brother standing beside him until he spoke. "She looks stunning," Collin said, as if reading his brother's mind.

Calem quickly recovered and cleared his throat. "They all do, brother. Which one are you referring to?"

Collin rolled his eyes and scoffed. "Come now, brother. There is no need to hide your fascination from me. No one could fault you for looking at Miss Lia that way tonight. I'm certain you were curious to see what the woman you brought with you looks like in such an elegant gown, if nothing else. If you will look around, every other man here is also staring at her."

Calem did look, and saw that his brother was right. He was

certainly not the only man entranced by the woman's beauty. "She will not be without a partner tonight," he commented.

Collin flicked a nonexistent speck of dirt from his cuff. "Then, by all means, let us go make sure she will save us each a dance."

The brothers travelled together to the group of ladies, passing by most of them to reach Miss Lia's side. When she saw them, she put on a bright smile that all but those who knew her best would see as real. Calem hoped that his brother was not among those who knew her that well.

Collin gave the woman a dramatic bow and placed a kiss on the back of her hand. "Miss Lia, I beg you to please save a dance for me tonight." He was being so overblown that, had it not been Miss Lia he was asking, Calem would have rolled his eyes. Instead, he fought to keep his face from showing any of the anger he felt.

Miss Lia's bright smile remained. "Of course, Your Highness," she said before she curtsied. "I would be honored." She then turned to Calem. "Do you wish for me to save one for you as well, Your Highness?"

Calem saw pain flash in her eyes as she extended the offer, likely the same pain that he felt, but he was grateful that she had made his task a little easier. He gave her a more formal bow. "If you are willing, I will claim the dance at the end of the next hour."

She seemed to understand that there was a reason he was requesting that specific dance, for she nodded immediately. "Of course." She turned her attention back to Collin. "And you, Your Highness?"

He grinned. "I will take the first."

With a wink and a mischievous grin for his brother, Collin

whisked her onto the dance floor. As Calem watched them dance away, Gerald arrived at his side. "Time is running out, Calem."

Calem scowled in reply. "I know, Gerald."

Gerald put a hand on his friend's shoulder. "I swear, I will challenge him on your behalf if you do not. You might win. Your experiences since your last duel are surely very different than his have been. You won't know unless you try."

Calem looked over to find his brother immensely enjoying his partner's company. "Were the peace of two nations not riding on the arrangement, I would do it in a heartbeat, Gerald." He turned to his friend. "What would you do if it were your own brother marrying Gloria?"

Gerald sighed. "I have no idea, because it is not. I don't even have a brother to compare it to. I'm so sorry, Calem. It must be hard to watch the person you grew up with falling for the woman you love. I am thankful that I am not in your shoes, for I feel that I would rather endanger and love than live without love."

"And how would Gloria feel about being the reason behind the deaths of perhaps hundreds, or thousands—heaven only knows—just so that the two of you could be together?"

Gerald frowned. "I hadn't thought of that. You make a fair point." He sighed. "I don't know, Calem. I'm sorry." He glanced longingly in Gloria's direction.

Calem sighed. "Go dance with your lady, Gerald."

Gerald grinned. "Thank you, Calem." He offered one more sympathetic frown and another apology, before leading his lady onto the dance floor.

As soon as Gerald was gone, Miss Genevieve approached

Calem. "Standing around and watching her dance isn't going to do any good for either of you, Sir Calem," she chided.

Calem sighed. "I know."

She folded her arms and began tapping her foot. "Then dance."

Calem managed a chuckle. "Would you care to dance, Miss Genevieve?"

She rolled her eyes before giving him a bright smile. "I would love to!"

Calem found that he was able to relax somewhat when he was able to focus on his own dancing, rather than spending every moment thinking about what would happen later that evening. Miss Genevieve was a pleasant partner, as well. He suspected that, once Miss Lia was no longer the shining star of the ballrooms, Miss Genevieve would be able to secure a match easily, should she wish to.

Once their dance ended, Calem resumed watching the dance floor, but it only took two dances, watching Miss Lia partner with someone new for each one, to realize that he would drive himself mad like this. He had never handled staying still well, and this was even worse. He sought out his mother, taking her out on the floor for the next dance. Little was said between them; she knew he was struggling, and that there was little she could do to ease it.

He didn't dance every dance after that, finding that every other was sufficient to keep him sane. He danced with Miss Genevieve again, and with Miss Gloria—Gerald could not yet claim every dance with her, not until they were wed—and Lady Garnet, as well as a couple of her other guests. Even so, the time seemed to drag on. Yet it somehow felt all too soon that he was leading Miss Lia to the floor. As the music began, he wasn't sure whether to thank or strangle the poor soul that chose a dance that required him to hold the woman he loved so closely in his arms. As their eyes met, however, everything seemed to fade away. Even the burden of their situation lifted for that moment. Nothing else existed. It was only them.

"Miss Lia," he began, but she cut him off.

"I go by Kalysta now."

He could smile at that. "You wear your birthright well."

She looked down and blushed. "It fits me better than I imagined."

He nodded in understanding. "It fills a place you never knew existed."

She looked up, seemingly surprised that he so easily understood how she felt. "Yes, it does."

"Knighthood did the same for me," he acknowledged. "As the younger son, I often felt adrift until I took on that responsibility."

They fell silent for a moment as they moved through a more difficult part of the dance. Once they were back to the easier steps, Kalysta spoke. "You were going to say something before, and I interrupted you. Forgive me."

He smiled. "There is nothing to forgive. I was merely going to tell you how beautiful you look tonight."

She looked away, blushing again. "Thank you." She then shot him a shy grin. "You clean up well, too."

Her words brought out a chuckle from somewhere inside that hadn't yet been shattered. "My mother would never accept anything less than perfect for such an occasion."

She laughed softly, and the sound made his heart race. "She sounds like a good mother."

He nodded. "She is. You are going to love her..." He

suddenly broke off as he remembered who would have the honor of introducing her to his mother.

She seemed to realize the direction of his thoughts, for she suddenly looked up at him with an intense gaze, as if searching for something. "Calem..." Oh, how his heart sang and broke hearing his name on her lips. "Tell me that you love me, right now, and I will refuse to marry your brother."

It took every ounce of self-possession not to give in to temptation and kiss her on the spot. The effort was painful, and he was certain the emotions reflected in his eyes, for he could almost see her heart break as he refused to give her what she wanted. "I love you more than I can possibly say, Kalysta. However, because I love you, I cannot let you break your engagement. You would hate yourself forever if you put the country at war again, I know you would. I cannot allow you to do that."

A tear leaking from the corner of her eye made him wish he could call back his words. "How can I live my life as your sister-in-law and your queen, when you hold my heart?"

He only barely refrained from cupping her cheek. "Well, you are neither yet. Perhaps you never will be. Perhaps a miracle will happen. But for right now, you are the woman I love. Let us have this moment while it is here, for we may never get another." As he spoke, he realized just how much this woman meant to him, and his resolve firmed. He couldn't just hand her over. "I *will* fight for you, my love. I will speak with my brother. I will speak with my mother, my father, *your* father...I will do what I can, but I cannot let you run away." His heart sank as he realized she *couldn't* run away anymore. "It is too late for that, anyway. Your father, the king, knows who you are. I asked you for this dance because it would show him who you are before meeting him." He hung his head in shame, imagining how much she must resent him for laying that trap. "I'm so sorry."

He was surprised when she put a hand on his face and lifted it, bringing his eyes up to look at her again. "Thank you, Calem. Thank you for being strong when I was weak. I needed your strength in that moment."

He searched her eyes and found only sincerity. "I would do anything in my power for you, Kalysta. Unfortunately, this is much bigger than just the two of us."

"I know. And I know that you would."

Her words warmed him, as did her belief in him. But the final chords of the dance made his heart freeze as the magic of the moment shattered, and they returned to reality. They both turned to see that King Kelvin was standing to address the assembled courtiers. "Lords, ladies, distinguished guests," he began, "tonight we are here to welcome my daughter home." Everyone nodded in understanding. Calem gritted his teeth as his brother went to stand behind and to the side of the king, awaiting the identity of his bride. "Now," the king continued, "I beg her to come forward, that I might look upon her face."

Calem took a fortifying breath before leading his beloved to her father. Tears filled the king's eyes as he beheld the daughter he hadn't seen for seventeen years. Collin, on the other hand, beheld the princess as if he had just won a competition, and she was the prize. Calem felt Kalysta's grip tighten, indicating that she, too, had seen Collin's predatory gaze. Calem squeezed her hand to offer what little comfort he could before handing her over to her father. He then stepped back and prayed that the pain he felt was not visible on his face.

The king looked over his daughter before gathering her

into his arms. "My little girl...you've grown into a beautiful young woman. You look just like your mother..." He then held her tighter, and Calem could see the glisten of tears on his face. The assembled courtiers began to clap in praise of the reunion, and several of the women dabbed at their own happy tears.

As most of the crowd watched the scene with happy faces, Gloria and Genevieve approached Calem, taking places on either side of him, and gave him looks of understanding. They placed their hands on his arms to offer comfort, and he folded his arms to place his hands over theirs. He looked down, no longer able to keep back the tears.

The tears were still falling when he looked up again. The king was standing again, now with his daughter at his side. Motioning to her, he announced, "My daughter, Princess Kalysta!"

The crowd cheered.

After a moment, the king held his arms out as a call for attention. Once the crowd settled down, he continued. "As most of you are aware, we would not be standing here like this today had not our neighbors, the wonderful Callardans, helped us to regain the throne. As thanks and to cement our alliance, I am announcing the betrothal of my daughter to Prince Collin, the Crown Prince of Callarda!"

The words speared Calem's heart, and his knees buckled. If not for Gloria and Genevieve bracing him up, he would have fallen to the floor. The words rang in his head, drowning out the applause of the rest of the crowd. After a moment, he was able to recover enough to stand on his own, but the look of despair on Kalysta's face nearly undid him again. Once he was steady, Genevieve released him, put on a determined face, and stepped forward. In a loud voice, she proclaimed, "I object to this union!"

The applause silenced instantly, and all eyes turned to Genevieve. The king quickly recovered, however, and narrowed his eyes. "Why might that be, my dear?" His tone was fierce, and Calem suddenly feared for Genevieve's life. In the silence, he heard the royal guards drawing their swords. "Are you among those who object to an alliance with the Callardans?"

To Calem's relief, Genevieve quickly shook her head. "No, Your Majesty," she replied in a surprisingly calm voice. "I have no objections to the alliance. What I object to is the princess marrying the crown prince!"

The king's eyes widened in shock. "Why?"

"Because Princess Kalysta is in love with Prince Calem!"

Calem felt his brother's gaze shift sharply to him, and he looked up to meet it. He watched as Miss Genevieve's words formed the last and most crucial piece to a puzzle that had formed in his brother's mind. That moment of clarity was followed by an even fiercer gaze. "Why did you not say anything of this before?!" he bellowed.

Calem's fists clenched at his brother's unwarranted anger. "Because I knew who she was the entire time." Where Collin's words were hot and angry, Calem's were sharp and cold. "I knew before even she did. I knew she would marry you before I knew I would not marry Princess Catalina. I couldn't prevent myself from falling in love with her, but I've always known she could never be mine."

"And yet you did not seem to realize the consequences of waiting until now to tell me or the king about this?!" Collin raged.

"Of course I did," Calem replied, his voice even harder than before. "This was not my plan. Yet here we are."

"Enough!" the king said loudly, regaining control of the room. He then looked over the crowd and asked, "Does anyone else object to a union between Prince Collin and my daughter?"

"I do!" one of Lady Garnet's pupils said.

"I do, as well!" Gloria added.

Suddenly, every single girl standing around Lady Garnet voiced their opinions, all in opposition of the union. Calem's eyes widened at the size of the unified voice of Lady Garnet's guests. Although Lady Garnet said nothing, she appeared to agree with the girls around her. Several others in the crowd stepped forward in agreement with the young women, as well. Calem looked to the king as hope rose within him. *Surely he will listen with so many voicing their objections!*

The king studied Calem for a moment, and he instinctively went down on one knee in deference to him. "Well, Prince Calem *has* done a great deal for this country. Indeed, it is due to his diligence that my daughter has returned to us, as well as her eldest brother. I would not be opposed to the union." Calem's hope rose further at the words, but was dashed as the king continued. "But what say you, Prince Collin?" Both the king and Calem looked to find the Crown Prince of Callarda red-faced and fuming.

He met Calem's eyes. "I am not going to just stand by and let you take the woman I want to marry from me, brother!" Collin bellowed, making Calem flinch. He wasn't sure he had ever seen his brother this angry. "This underhanded scheme to force the king to give her to you has insulted and publicly humiliated me, and my honor must be satisfied! Calem, I challenge you to a duel!"

Calem regained his feet, and his cold calmness. "I will say once more that I had no part in planning this, but I don't expect you to listen, so I accept your challenge. We fight here and now, with swords."

Collin cast him a malicious grin. "I accept. Any other rules or conditions?"

Calem was about to say no when Gerald put a hand on his shoulder from behind him. "Don't forget, you aren't alone, my friend."

Calem smiled, feeling the support. He looked around to see Gloria, Genevieve, and several other knights smiling supportively at him. His eyes met Kalysta's, and although anxiety was written in her features, she gave him a small smile as well, which he returned. Looking back at Collin, he asked, "What about seconds?"

His brother scoffed. "You mean in case you don't win?" he taunted. Then he laughed. "I will allow you to have a second, but I don't need one. Who will it be? You know that I can best any man here!"

"I don't know that anyone here would want to stand as your second in this anyway," Calem replied. Knowing that, unless he could wear Collin down sufficiently first, Gerald would stand no chance against his brother, Calem decided not to conscript his friend. "How about a surprise? In the event that I lose, if someone decides to take pity on me and volunteer, you will then fight them, no matter who it is."

Collin smirked. "I love surprises. Very well. I promise to fight whomever decides to take pity on you." The grin turned malicious again. "Let us hope, brother, that your second is able to clean up after you."

Calem nodded. "And when will the duel end?"

Collin grinned confidently. "The duel will end once I draw first your, and then your second's, blood."

Calem nodded again. "Very well. And should we draw yours first?"

Collin sighed as if bored. "Then I will allow you to marry Princess Kalysta."

Calem felt the need to add something more. "And the treaty between our two kingdoms will last at least until all three of us are dead. Agreed?"

"On my honor," Collin replied, sounding calmer and more sincere than he had since Kalysta's presentation. This, Calem felt certain, was why he had felt the need to wait until now to ask for Kalysta's hand. While his brother was generally rational, Calem had been unsure whether he would respect the treaty if he felt robbed by Kalysta marrying Calem instead. He had needed this promise from his brother to keep the kingdoms safe, and now he had it.

"*But,*" Collin continued, "I'm not going to lose, so let's not waste any more breath on the subject."

Within minutes, a servant arrived with a pair of dueling swords, and the king presented them to the two princes. Each of them hefted the blades, getting a feel for them. Both were perfectly balanced, of course—the king would have settled for nothing less, even if they were only intended to be decorative.

The two men stood facing each other, with the king standing in the center to officiate. He must have known something of Collin's skill, for he cast Calem a pitying look. Then he raised his hand and, seeing they were both ready, said, "May the best of you win." Then he dropped his hand and quickly stepped back, signaling the start of the fight.

Collin immediately launched into an assault the likes of

which Calem had never seen before. Calem was surprised by just how fiercely his brother was fighting for Kalysta's hand, as his interest in her before had never seemed so serious. Calem was barely able to keep his brother at bay as Collin's sword slashed quickly through the air with precise, calculated movements.

As Collin began to slow, Calem finally managed a counter attack, forcing his brother to back away. They both took a moment to catch their breaths. "You've gotten better, little brother."

"That tends to happen when one's life is on the line." Calem tried to make the comment sound casual.

"True," Collin conceded. Then he smirked. "However, you seem tired. Have you not been sleeping well? No doubt that woman haunts your dreams and every waking thought."

Calem ground his teeth as his brother flung his own words back in his face, but he refused to show any more emotion than that. He knew his brother was trying to make him angry, knowing that Calem tended to get sloppy when he was angry. So he cooled his temper and kept his body in check, refusing to give in.

When Collin saw that his words weren't going to break his brother, he launched into another round of attacks. Attack, block, counter and be blocked, the next several moments were filled with the sound of blade meeting blade as the two brothers fought for the woman they both wanted.

Once, Calem nearly caught Collin on the arm, but his elder brother backed away just in time, the sword tearing his sleeve but not reaching his skin. Calem waited where he was, and they both took a moment to catch their breath.

"Your defense has gotten better," Collin said. "But why do you not attack?"

"Because I know you, brother," Calem replied. "You fight best when your opponent presses the attack. And as you've just seen, biding my time for my own strike nearly paid off just now."

Collin grinned. "You do remember me, then? Well, what else do you remember about me? Do you remember that I am the older son? That I am next in line for a throne? I will be able to give her an entire kingdom! What can you give her that I can't?"

Calem held his brother's gaze. His voice was cold steel once again. "I will be able to give her the thing she wants most in the world. Something I doubt you can give, and that she doesn't want from you even if you can."

Collin rolled his eyes. "And what is that?"

"Love."

To Calem's surprise, anger flared in Collin's eyes, and he flew into his next attack in a rage. But Calem couldn't rejoice over turning his brother's tactics against him, because Collin's anger gave him strength that Calem had never seen. A moment later, Collin forced his way through Calem's block, and Calem gasped as pain seared through his shoulder. He fell back, away from his brother, and stared in horror at the blood seeping into his shirt. He dropped his sword and looked to Kalysta as pain filled his heart, far greater than the small cut on his arm. *I have failed you, my love.*

The princess met his gaze, and to his surprise, there was no disappointment, no pain, not even a hint of resignation on her face. Instead, it was full of determination, and in an instant, he realized what she planned to do.

He then looked at Collin, who hadn't moved since landing his attack a moment before. He seemed almost surprised at his own reaction, his own anger of moments before. But as Gerald arrived on the scene to press a bundle of cloth against Calem's wound, Collin stood straight, a cocky smile spreading across his face. He turned to face the crowd of courtiers. "Does anyone here wish to take my brother's place and attempt to win the princess's hand for him?"

Calem looked back at Kalysta, still at the king's side and now behind Collin. She gave him a look that pleaded with him to trust her. He took a deep breath before nodding. She stepped forward. "I will take his place."

Collin whipped around as his eyes widened in shock. "You! I can't fight you! You are a woman! And my betrothed!" He glared at her. "This is ridiculous! I refuse!"

Kalysta cast Calem, who had gotten back to his feet, an amused look. "Look, Sir Knight," she said in her rough accent. Calem grinned. "Yer brother's afraid ta fight me. Well, if 'e refuses, don't that mean I win by default?"

Collin glared at her. "You dare call me a coward, woman?!"

She lifted one shoulder in a lazy shrug. Returning to her cultured tones, she replied, "If the shoe fits...and I'd like all to remember that it was your word for yourself, not mine." Calem's jaw dropped as she then pulled a sword from somewhere in the folds of her gown. He recognized it as the one her adoptive father had given her before they departed Farreden. She pointed it at Collin. "You promised that you would fight whomever took your brother's place. No gender was specified, and no exception named. You face me now or yield." Her glare was fierce as she held Collin's gaze.

Collin's glare was equally fierce as he turned to face her

fully. "I *will* have you for my bride, Princess Kalysta." He held up his sword as well and looked to the king, who stood in shock.

The king turned to his daughter. "Kalysta, please, my dear, must I watch you get hurt?" he begged.

Kalysta scoffed and turned to Gerald. "Sir Gerald, you have seen my abilities first hand. Do you think it likely that I will lose?"

The large knight quickly shook his head. "No, Your Highness."

Kalysta turned to her father. "Is that good enough for you?"

The king let out a breath of resignation. "I see that you are determined. Please, be careful."

She nodded. "I am very determined. I am *determined* to have my say in whom I will marry. And I will be careful. I will not allow him to take me from the man I love without a fight."

Calem inhaled sharply at her words, for he had never heard her say them before. "You do love me?"

She looked at him with a soft smile. "With all me heart."

Calem smiled in return. Collin, however, glared at both of them in turn. "Enough of this! Your Majesty, Your Highness, let us begin this."

Calem moved to the side to watch as Collin and Kalysta faced each other across the floor. "No blood, Prince Collin. Only disarming. Should you hurt my daughter, I will not allow you to marry her."

Collin blustered. "Those were not the terms of our agreement!"

The king gave him a hard glare. "First, you never actually agreed on what would happen if you win, you merely assumed that all would proceed as had been planned before. And second, as her father, it is perfectly within my right to decide what happens to her should you draw her blood!"

"If you feel like you'd be at a disadvantage, I'll fight to disarm as well," Kalysta volunteered cheekily.

Collin rolled his eyes. "I can win without drawing your blood regardless. Let's just get this over with, shall we?"

As soon as the duel started, Gloria and Genevieve rushed to Calem's side, each taking an arm, as they had during Kalysta's presentation earlier. He also felt Gerald's presence behind him. He quickly realized they were there to either hold him up, or hold him back. It was a good thing they were there, for a moment later, Collin launched an especially terrifying slash, the same strike that had caught Calem's arm before, making his heart jump to his throat. However, Kalysta merely laughed and danced away. "I thought you would be more of a challenge!" she taunted.

Collin growled an angry war cry and launched at her again. The sound of steel on steel was interrupted only by his rage and her laughter. The moment that Collin relented, stepping back to catch his breath, Kalysta went on the offensive, not even winded from the exchange before. She slashed and slashed again, so quickly that Calem could barely track the blade's movements. Kalysta wore a determined grin, while Collin began to look truly worried for the first time. Kalysta feinted back, at the same time that she unleashed a heavy horizontal slash. She struck Collin's blade just above the hilt, knocking it from his hands to clatter to the ground. He dove after it, but Kalysta kicked it away and held her blade to his throat, guiding him up to his knees with it.

He glared up at her. "Do it. Draw blood."

She glared at him in return. "No. Yield."

His glare became more fierce. "My brother besmirches my honor, and now you expect me to give up my bride *and* my pride?"

She raised an eyebrow. "Which do you value more, I wonder? Be a man and accept your defeat, Prince Collin. There is no shame in honoring the person who bested you. Besides, just as my father didn't want you to draw my blood, I don't want to draw yours unless I have to, so you must yield."

Collin let out a sigh as he let his anger drain away. "I yield," he said as he hung his head.

Worried that Collin was bending down to force her blade to draw his blood anyway, Calem was about to call out, but Kalysta saw and withdrew her sword before he had the chance. Seeming to be resigned after this final defeat, Collin stood and stormed out of the ballroom.

As soon as he disappeared, the crowd burst into cheers, but Calem barely heard them as his heart pounded hard in his ears. He looked to Kalysta. Her sword had disappeared back into her gown, and she was holding her hand out to him as tears of joy ran down her face. As everything finally sank in, he took her hand and pulled her into his arms, pressing his lips to hers. She kissed him back just as fervently, as both of their emotions from the past months were finally able to be relieved.

As they kissed, his heart pounded to the rhythm of a song his soul played for her alone. It was a song of home.

Acknowledgments

First, I'd like to say thank you to my Heavenly Father and Savior. Without them boosting my confidence, this book wouldn't have been published.

Next, I'd like to thank my other half, who helped write this book. Thanks for helping me make my dreams come true. I love you!

Next, I'd like to thank my mother, Chris Wilson, who "forced" (strongly encouraged) me to publish this book. Thanks for all of your love and support. Love ya!

Next, I'd like to thank my early readers Tim Wilson, Briahna Nelson, Nickoli Wilson and Karen Turnblom for reading this story and giving such positive feedback. You help me want to keep writing.

Next, I'd like to thank my writing friends, Mary Locke Jolley, Chantel Burnham, and Nikki Siegel for teaching me how to become a better writer. You all are awesome!

Next, I'd like to thank Jim. He gave me a good pep talk when I needed it. Thank you!

Next, I'd like to thank Laolan for the beautiful cover. It looks amazing!

Last, but not least, I'd like to thank all of you who have read this story. It means the world to me that you decided to take a chance on me.

Kailie has always been an avid reader and and has always enjoyed writing. Her first story, which she wrote in elementary school, was called "How the Cricket Learned to Play". She's been writing off and on since.

Kailie lives in the protection of a mountain with her husband, Chris, and their three children. Her favorite color is purple. Her favorite book is *Pride and Prejudice*.

CHRIS is a reader of many genres. He's also a gamer and dreams of owning his own video game studio. In the meantime, he's helping Kailie accomplish her dream of becoming a published author. His favorite color is yellow. Picking his favorite book is like picking his favorite child, impossible to choose because he likes too many.

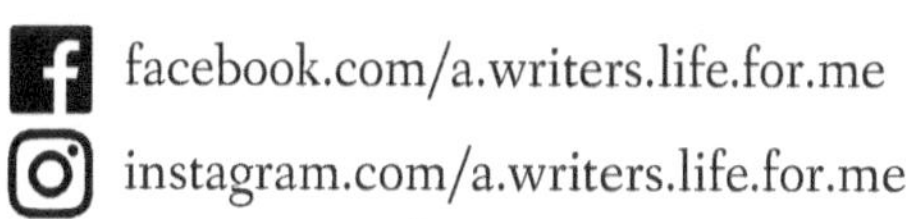

facebook.com/a.writers.life.for.me

instagram.com/a.writers.life.for.me